"He's gone, Noah. Your brother's *gone*. He's left."

"What are you talking about? What do you mean, he's gone?"

"This." Abby fumbled in her skirt pocket and took out a balled-up sheet of lined paper. "This!" she cried.

Noah opened the crumpled paper and scanned the few lines on the page. "I'm so sorry, Abby," he read. "I wish I could have faced up to it, but I just can't marry you...." The letter was signed simply *Jesse*.

Noah swore. His brain was spinning. *Left her!* The stupid, useless son of a bitch had left her. High and dry. Alone. Pregnant. With no one to turn to—except him.

"Come on," he said, leaning down and taking her by the arm. She staggered to her feet. "Come inside and let's talk this over." Noah cleared his throat. "You got any money? Enough to go home?"

"I can't go home again, I just can't," she said, shuddering. "And I quit my job. Who's going to hire a teacher with a baby on the way? No husband? Maybe...maybe I could start over somewhere else...." She buried her head in her hands and her shoulders shook.

He glanced at her. "I have one idea," he said. "You could marry *me*."

Dear Reader,

Every baby ought to be welcomed and loved, but certainly every conception isn't planned—all women know that!

Still, when it happens, expected or unexpected, a woman's life is never the same again.

Usually the expectant mother has the love and support of a good man. When she doesn't, she hopes she can count on the love and support of her family. That's looking on the brightest side. Too often, the single mother is shunned by her community and her family. When she has no man to stand by her, either, where does she turn?

American Abby Steen finds herself in that situation when she moves to Canada, pregnant and alone. Glory rancher Noah Winslow has no plans to marry—ever. But how can he turn his back on a woman in trouble? Especially when it's his brother who's responsible for the whole mess?

I hope you enjoy this new story in my MEN OF GLORY series set in Alberta ranch country. I know you'll recognize some of the townspeople, and the ranch and farm folk, too.

Judith Bowen

P.S. I'd love to hear what you think of Noah and Abby's story. Drop me a line at P.O. Box 2333, Point Roberts, WA 98281-2333

Other MEN OF GLORY titles by Judith Bowen:

739—THE RANCHER'S RUNAWAY BRIDE
791—LIKE FATHER, LIKE DAUGHTER
814—O LITTLE TOWN OF GLORY
835—THE DOCTOR'S DAUGHTER

HIS BROTHER'S BRIDE
Judith
Bowen

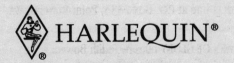

HARLEQUIN®

TORONTO • NEW YORK • LONDON
AMSTERDAM • PARIS • SYDNEY • HAMBURG
STOCKHOLM • ATHENS • TOKYO • MILAN • MADRID
PRAGUE • WARSAW • BUDAPEST • AUCKLAND

ISBN 0-373-70872-6

HIS BROTHER'S BRIDE

Visit us at www.romance.net

Printed in U.S.A.

**For Paula
An Editor in a Hundred**

CHAPTER ONE

Carlisle, Minnesota
November

WHAT IN HEAVEN'S NAME had happened to her friend? She'd gone to the ladies' room nearly fifteen minutes ago.

Abby played with her empty glass and tried to ignore the curls of cigarette smoke that floated lazily in the overheated air. The atmosphere in the bar was thick with sweat and sawdust and booze and hormones belonging to both sexes. Plus the music. She could hardly hear herself think.

She wasn't used to this. The one gin and tonic she'd had was making her feel dizzy. That, and the music. As soon as Marguerite returned from the ladies' she was going to ask if they could leave.

Abby felt thoroughly uncomfortable sitting by herself at a table along the wall. She hoped no one would think she was looking for company. From time to time she glanced around quickly, trying not to meet anyone's eyes. If her father could see her now. If the good folks in Wicoigon, South Dakota, could see her now. Mavis and Perry and the well-meaning Viola Palmerston, the town librarian, the widow who'd had been so helpful to her when Frank died.

Damn. There was a big cowboy at the bar who she swore kept watching her. It gave her the creeps. She didn't dare look any closer. Besides, without her glasses on, what could she see, anyway? That had been an exercise in vanity, leaving her glasses at the motel room, thinking she looked better without them. Who would care?

"Another one, ma'am?" The waiter paused briefly, his tray loaded with beer glasses, pitchers and a stack of flimsy foil ashtrays.

"No, thanks." She shook her head, not sure the waiter could hear her in the din. She was getting out of here. If her so-called friend didn't show in another two minutes—Abby glanced at her watch— she was leaving without her. Trust Marguerite to go off with someone else, or sit down at another table.

Abby would just take a taxi to the motel. Tomorrow was a busy day for Wicoigon Jersey Farm at the stock show, and she could use the sleep. Her father would never forgive her if she blew this fair. He lived and breathed Wicoigon Jerseys, and if he hadn't had a bad fall last week, he'd be here at the agricultural exhibition himself, showing the family company's top young bulls and heifers with Pepper and Will.

But he wasn't. Abby was in charge on her own. Pepper and Will, both eighteen, her niece and nephew, twins, weren't around much except to fulfill their duties of mucking out the stalls and feeding the cattle. They were supposed to be her assistants, but Abby did most of the showing and grooming herself.

Not that she minded. She loved cows. She'd grown up with the gentle doe-eyed Jerseys and they were still her favorite breed, although she hadn't worked on the farm for quite a few years, since before she'd married Frank. The Carlisle exhibition brought cattle of all breeds, both dairy and beef. It was one of the big stock fairs of the year, and Carlisle blue ribbons were valuable additions to any breeder's showroom wall. Wicoigon Jerseys already had nearly a dozen.

Everything had changed. Frank was dead now, nearly two years ago. And then last year…when her baby daughter had been born dead—

Abby released her empty glass from nerveless fingers. She still couldn't bear to think of it. People said things happened for a reason. People said you'd get over it. People said it wasn't as though you'd gotten to *know* the child…. That was the stupidest of all the things people said. She'd so hoped she'd have the baby at least—something of Frank, to keep with her always. She'd longed for that baby, as she'd longed for nothing else on earth. And then? An accident of birth, they said. Couldn't be helped.

And now Abby Steen had no one and nothing.

Frank had been killed in a traffic accident when the rig he was driving smashed into another rig on an interstate in Georgia. Her husband of just over three years had been working extra time to supplement her teaching salary, in the hopes that they'd be able to buy a house of their own, now that they had a family on the way. Abby had been three months pregnant when Frank was killed.

How could such terrible things happen to one person? Her mother had told her that everything happens for a purpose. How could that be true? What horrible purpose was there in two gentle, innocent souls like her husband and her infant daughter dying like that? She'd named the baby, over the objections of her doctor and her parents, who'd said it would only make the pain worse. Mary Francesca, for Frank. How could the pain *be* any worse?

Sometimes Abby didn't think she had anything to live for anymore. She had nothing to hope for. But she stopped that thought as soon as it hatched, as she'd done so often, out of habit. There were her parents, approaching retirement age. They needed her, in their way. And her older sister, Meg. Abby wasn't especially close to her family, but she'd had to lean on them in the past few years. She'd always be grateful that they'd been there for her.

Still, the grief had withered her soul until she sometimes thought she was more like a dried-up sixty-year-old spinster than a young woman. Just twenty-eight. Her friend Marguerite had had to cajole her even to agree to come out this evening. She'd have preferred to stay in the motel and watch something on television and go to bed early.

Which was what she should have done, obviously. Now she had to haul herself out of this den of iniquity, as her mother probably would have called it. She'd had her gin, she'd lost her friend, and now it was time to get out of there and get some sleep.

"Ma'am?"

The rich baritone at her left shoulder had her spinning. She reached up to push aside the blond lock that had snapped across her nose as she turned. "Yes?"

She sounded almost angry. Schoolmarmish. She hadn't meant to. Nor had she been in a classroom for quite a while.

"I'd like to buy you a drink, if I may?" It was the cowboy she'd been sure was examining her from across the dance floor, from his position at the bar. He was big, as she'd thought. Tall and handsome and friendly looking.

Of course, what would *she* know? She hadn't dated since Frank's death. She had very little interest in men, although she dreaded the loneliness that seemed to surround her.

This man had a mustache. A thick, luxuriant brown mustache. Otherwise he was neatly shaved and his hair was freshly barbered. He wore standard-issue Western-type clothing, right down to the string tie and plaid shirt, the brand-new Wranglers and fancy belt buckle. He didn't wear a hat, which she supposed was a departure from the norm.

"Y-yes. I suppose so." Abby realized how ungracious she must sound. She'd noticed his name tag—Jesse Winslow, Winslow Herefords, Glory, Alberta—pinned to his shirt pocket. He must have forgotten to remove it when he left the show barn. So he was at least associated with the stock exhibition.

He introduced himself, reaching up to tip his nonexistent hat. She supposed it was a habit. She felt self-conscious suddenly when he pulled out the chair Marguerite had occupied. The waiter had already taken her friend's empty glass away.

"Mind if I sit here?"

"Er, no." Abby abruptly sat back down in the chair she'd just vacated. Where was Marguerite?

"And you're—?" The cowboy smiled.

For a moment Abby wondered what he was smiling at, then realized she hadn't introduced herself.

"Abby Steen." She reached across the table on impulse and shook his hand. *Be normal. Businesslike.* His hand was large and warm. Callused. The hand of a working man. "I'm, uh, here with a friend. She's just, um, left for a moment—" Abby cast worried eyes in the direction of the ladies' room. Still no Marguerite. Par for the course.

"Are you here with the stock show?"

"Yes. Wicoigon Jerseys. In South Dakota."

"Ah. A farmer." The cowboy smiled again. He had a gorgeous smile, Abby decided despite herself. And he really was a very handsome man. Healthy-looking, virile—she glanced quickly at his hands on the table—and single.

"You could say that. My father's the farmer, actually. I'm just helping him out this year, showing the stock."

"Your dad here?"

"No. He had an accident last week and wasn't able to come. I'm here with a couple of assistants. My niece and nephew."

"I see." The cowboy caught the attention of the waiter and ordered another gin for her and a beer for himself. "A family affair," he finished, with a glance toward her after the waiter left. His eyes were very blue.

"What about you?" Did this qualify as social chitchat?

"I'm here with one helper. My neighbor's boy. My brother and I raise Herefords up in Alberta. Glory. Don't suppose you've ever heard of the place."

Abby smiled and shook her head. "Can't say as I have," she replied, unconsciously imitating the stranger's speech patterns.

"We've just got a few young bulls in the show this year. Normally my brother comes with me and we drive a couple of stock trucks down, but this fall he decided to stay home."

"Oh?"

"Yeah. He's an ornery son of a gun. Not much for shows. He prefers the back-home stuff. Cutting hay and pulling calves. Minding the books. Which is just fine by me." Jesse Winslow smiled again and his eyes crinkled and a pulse bobbled low in Abby's midriff. She realized with horror that she found him attractive—as a man. This hadn't happened, this feeling, since she'd first met Frank at a college track meet years ago. Maybe she'd better leave while she was ahead—

"G and T for the lady?" The waiter put down the glasses with a flourish and Abby watched as Jesse paid for the drinks and gave the waiter a sizable tip. Too late, she realized she should have offered to pay for her own drink. Although he *had* asked....

"Where's your friend?" The cowboy raised his beer glass slightly, then took a leisurely draft.

"Oh, heck." Abby frowned, remembering. "She went to the bathroom and didn't come back. She probably met someone on the way there and took off."

Jesse met her annoyed gaze with a look of surprise. "Some friend. She do that often?"

"That's Marguerite, I'm afraid." Abby tried a shaky laugh, as though she was used to people treating her like that. "I've known her for years, off and on. Her people farm in southern Minnesota somewhere. Shorthorns. I've met her at a lot of the same shows. You know how it is."

"Uh-huh." The cowboy took another drink of his beer and made a quick survey of the room. Abby followed his glance. The band, almost indistinguishable in the corner behind a haze of smoke, had started up an old-fashioned swing tune, and couples were moving onto the sawdust-covered dance floor.

Abby felt comfortable with the handsome stranger, all of a sudden. Maybe it was the second gin. Maybe it was the realization that he'd known exactly what she meant—regulars on the show circuit met people from year to year at the same events. You became friends with someone you saw for only a day or two, two or three times a year. Friendships were struck quickly when there was no time to waste in preliminaries. It was easy to make a mistake that way, but then a few days later, you pulled out of town and left your mistakes behind you. You had a few months, maybe a year to think things over. Generally, by the time you saw the person again, if there'd been any problems, they were all forgotten.

"Dance?" The cowboy was smiling at her and holding out his hand.

Impulsively, Abby took it. Why not? She hadn't danced in ages, and the music was catchy.

The floor was crowded by now, and Jesse Winslow held her close. Abby's head was reeling. She breathed in his masculine scent, so near—leather and sweat and a faint, pleasant manufactured scent of some kind, probably aftershave. His hand on her waist was firm and decisive. He steered her clear of any collisions with the other dancers, a few of whom weren't all that sober. Her hand in his felt very protected, very safe. He was an excellent dancer.

Trouble was, she couldn't think of a thing to say.

Neither could he, it seemed. The silence became heavier and heavier, and Abby's imagination ran wild. One instant she pictured this man, the man she'd met all of twenty minutes ago, naked, all muscle and brawn and hairy broad chest. Then, horrified, she clamped down on her thoughts and the next thing she knew she imagined him kissing her, unsnapping her bra....

Omigoodness. What kind of lonely, sex-starved creature was she?

"Oh, *there* you are, Abigail!" Marguerite yelled, as though it were Abby who'd done the deserting. Marguerite was in the arms of a tall, thin blond man wearing an expensive-looking gray Western-cut suit.

Abby recognized one of the organizers of the stock show. Marguerite obviously had her eye on the main chance....

"I see you've met someone—good! Take your mind off your troubles, hon, just like I told you—" Then, when Marguerite met her again a few seconds later, after the man in the suit had spun her, she continued, "I'll be going to a party with Stan here—" She winked at Abby. "Maybe you could take a cab to the motel? Or drive my car?"

She was being ditched. Abby nodded, embarrassed, and was glad when Jesse steered her discreetly in a different direction.

"Your *friend,* I presume?" he said, gazing down at her.

He was so close. Abby caught her breath. "Yes." She was determined to offer no excuses, either for her choice of friends or for Marguerite's rude behavior.

"You want to drive her car home?"

"No. I'll take a cab." Abby looked up as he held her a little closer. "I don't like to drive when I've been drinking, especially someone else's car."

"Drinking!" Jesse laughed. "How many?"

"That's my second, the one you bought," Abby replied. What was so funny?

"Your second, eh? Well, you aren't exactly drunk, Abby Steen."

"No. But I'm not used to it, either. I feel a little, uh—"

"You okay?" He looked concerned.

"I'm fine. I just feel a little queasy, that's all."

They danced one more number, then returned to their table and Abby finished her drink. Her head was foggy. She was more than ready to go back to the motel. She dug in her purse for change, coming up with everything but a quarter. Jesse Winslow watched her for a few moments, then stood and held her chair.

"Here. Let me take you home. I'm about ready to leave, anyway."

"Heavens, no! I'll take a cab. Can you give me change for a dollar?" She smiled, feeling extraordinarily foolish.

"Forget it." He sounded very firm. "I'll drive you."

Abby closed her purse and got to her feet. Jesse put his arm casually around her shoulders, to guide her through the dancers, now thickly crowding the dance floor. Abby couldn't see Marguerite. Oh well, she'd more or less said goodbye already.

The evening was crisp and cold, and Abby pulled her jacket more tightly around her. She took a deep breath, which cleared the smoke from her lungs. Early November in northern Minnesota could be colder than this. At least, there wasn't any snow on the ground yet.

Jesse led the way to a late-model pickup truck with dual rear wheels, probably the vehicle that had pulled the Winslow stock trailer to Minnesota from Alberta. He handed her into the passenger side, not speaking until he'd climbed into the vehicle and shut the door.

He paused, his hand on the ignition. "Where you staying?"

"The Spruce Valley Inn."

"That's the one right near the exhibition grounds?"

"Yes." The town's motels and hotels were pretty well full this week with the out-of-towners visiting the stock show. Her niece and nephew were staying with some friends they'd met on previous trips to Carlisle with Abby's father, their grandfather. Abby wasn't keen on that situation, as she couldn't keep an eye on them the way she was sure her sister would want her to, but on the other hand, she was able to get the early nights she preferred.

"I'm just down the street. At the Alta Vista."

"Oh." Abby felt like a fool. She was no conversationalist. Why hadn't she taken a cab? They were strangers, although they'd danced and he'd bought her a drink and she supposed he must be interested in her. They had nothing to say to each other, nothing in common except that they both knew the difference between a Black Angus and a Holstein. They weren't even in the same area there—he was beef and she was dairy.

He drove to her motel through the empty streets, not more than a five-minute drive. He didn't say anything. She supposed that was another thing they had in common—neither of them was much for chitchat. Abby looked out the window. The shops were dark, of course, but so were most of the cafés and restaurants. Even the movie theater was deserted. Not even midnight yet, but it seemed the good folks of Carlisle went to bed with the chickens, as her father said. Abby smiled to herself wryly. A live wire like her would fit right into this kind of town.

Abby had often wondered about the kind of town she'd fit into. She'd grown up in Wicoigon. She'd gone to school there, then lived in Grand Falls during her college years. She'd moved back to Wicoigon to teach elementary school. She and Frank had honeymooned in Hawaii, a big splurge that had taken all their meager savings, but that was about as far as she'd traveled. She'd only been out of state a handful of times besides her honeymoon. Twice to a 4-H meet and once to a friend's wedding in Nebraska. The occasional stock fair back when she traveled with her father. Sometimes she recalled the days she'd yearned to see the world, meet other people, go to the places she'd read about in books. All that had changed when she married Frank, and then when both Frank and the baby they'd wanted so much passed out of her life. Everything was different now. She'd gone to earth like an injured fox; she'd turned to her family and the town she'd always known. She had nothing else to turn to. Neither arrangement was perfect, but then life so rarely was.

They were at her motel. She'd have to say *something....*

She had her hand on the door of the truck. "Well, thanks—"

"Wait a minute. You going to be all right?"

"Me?" Abby was slightly bewildered.

"Yeah. You said you weren't used to drinking."

"Oh, I'll be fine," she said, laughing weakly. "I'm not *drunk,* you know."

"I'll walk you to your room. Make sure you get in all right. Stay there." He came around and opened the truck door for her and she scrambled out, in a fairly unladylike manner, she was sure.

He took her arm as they walked toward her door on the lower level, number 101. The sidewalk was frosty, and she was grateful for the support as the leather soles of her shoes slid a little.

"I'm fine now," she said nervously. Did he expect a good-night kiss? What did a person—a woman—do in a situation like this? Abby glanced toward the well-lighted front office of the inn. At least there were plenty of people around.

"Your friend, the one who never came back for you, she said you needed to take your mind off something. Are you in some kind of trouble? Is there anything I can do? Any way I can help?"

This Canadian cowboy, this stranger, seemed genuinely concerned.

Abby stared at him, his eyes looking black under the artificial light of the streetlamp, and to her horror, she felt hot tears running down her cheeks. Something crumpled beneath her breastbone, something she'd clung to like life itself for nearly two years.

"Not unless you can undo the hand of God," she whispered rawly. "Can you? My little girl was born dead. My husband died two years ago, before our baby was born," she rasped, barely recognizing her voice. "That's what Marguerite was talking about when—" Her voice ran out. It just stopped.

Abby swiped at her wet cheeks, suddenly angry that this man had mentioned the one subject that belonged to her alone. She tried to jam the key into the lock.

"Oh, damn. Honey, I'm so sorry—" She felt his hand on her shoulder. He sounded shocked. "I had no idea—I'd never have mentioned it if I had. I thought it was some problem with your stock—"

Abby actually managed a strangled laugh. She jabbed at the lock again—damn this stupid key!— and then Jesse took it from her and unlocked the door himself. The door swung open, the room faintly redolent of air freshener and travelers' shoes and damp carpet. If only it *was* a problem with the damn cows. If only it was something like a missing show halter or a lame foot or a digestive problem one of the heifers was having. Dysentery. Heaves. Hoof-and-mouth. Brucellosis. *Mad cow disease.* She felt hysteria rise within her. The quicker she could get rid of this cowboy, the better.

But he was right behind her. "You sit down, Abby," he said, flicking on the lights and shutting the door. "I'll make you some coffee."

Abby sat heavily on the bed, dropping her handbag to the floor. She wiped her eyes with the backs of her hands. She stared at the unfamiliar sight of the tall, handsome stranger, bustling about her motel room, ripping open the package of complimentary coffee, dumping it into the filter, filling the reservoir with water, turning on the miniature coffee machine, then assembling two mugs by fitting cone-shaped plastic inserts into the plastic receptacles provided. *Disposable. Discardable. Sterile.*

A dam burst in Abby. She sobbed, bolt upright on the bed, her hands in front of her face. She felt the bed sag as Jesse sat down beside her. She felt him put his arm around her, heard the helpless mutterings of manly comfort as he tried to calm her. What a situation for him to be in!

"Please go," she said, pushing him away. "Please leave me alone. There's nothing you can do. It's over, it's past. There's nothing anyone can do—"

"I'll leave. But I want to see you settle down a little first. Drink some coffee. Here, just get it all out, honey." He put both arms forcibly around her and suddenly Abby collapsed into them. It felt good to lean on someone. Finally. She laid her cheek against his shirt and wept. He stroked her hair awkwardly and kept muttering to her.

The relief. The terrible loneliness of weeping by herself... She was not alone now. She was with a strong, handsome stranger. A stranger who, oddly, cared what was happening to her. Of course, anyone would be flummoxed to have a woman collapse on him, the way she had....

"Look, honey. Let me get up and get you a coffee. I think it's ready."

Abby sat upright again, stiff as starch, shocked at how she'd welcomed his arms around her. Briefly. She watched as he poured two cups— "Cream— this whitener stuff? Sugar?"

She nodded. "Cream." She blew her nose loudly on the tissue she'd taken out of her handbag.

He stirred the coffee and brought it to her. He handed her one cup, then sat in an armchair beside the bed and carefully pulled the small bedside table toward her so they could share it. She set her cup down, too.

She tried to smile. "Thank you."

"Hell." He looked ill at ease. He took a sip of his coffee and made a face. "Whew!"

She laughed. "That bad?"

"Pretty bad."

They sat in silence again, as though the emotional storm of the past ten minutes hadn't happened. Abby realized he wasn't comfortable discussing it. She realized that, like so many men, he'd just as soon stick to the present, to the action possible in any situation. The coffee. The news. She thought she'd seen him glance longingly at the silent television in the corner. No way she was turning it on; he wasn't a *guest*. He'd be on his way the instant he finished his coffee. She was fine now. She'd be okay. She didn't know what had come over her.

Anyway. It was done. It was past. She felt a little better now.

Suddenly Jesse put his cup down and stood. "I'd, uh, I'd better be on my way now."

Abby got up, too. She was only a short distance from him. She had to look up to meet his gaze. "I— I want to thank you—" she began.

He stepped forward and put his arms gently around her. He pushed back a strand of hair that stuck damply to the side of her cheek. His eyes didn't meet hers. He seemed to be studying her, as though committing her features to memory. "You're a fine woman, Abby Steen. A fine beautiful woman." His voice was rich and deep.

"Oh—"

"Listen to me. It'll come out all right in the end. Believe me. I know you've heard that kind of thing before, but it's true. You'll, uh—" He met her gaze then and stared at her for a second or two. It seemed like a very long time to Abby's overstretched nerves. "Troubles are bad but uh, you'll—" he began again. He stopped and swallowed.

"Oh, damn," he whispered, then leaned down and brought his mouth to hers and Abby took a long, deep, shaky breath and kissed him back. It felt good, it felt right. It had been so very long since she'd had a man's arms around her, pressing her against him, as though imprinting every curve of her body on his, as though he ached for her as she ached for him. *For someone.*

He kissed her deeply, and she felt the vibrations of what was happening right down to her calves, along her thighs, the inside of her thighs, her breasts…. She clung to him, eager to meet his kisses, to taste all of him.

Then she felt his fingers, strong and expert, on the hook of her bra, through her blouse, pinching, succeeding…*yes,* she exulted silently as she felt her bra loosen and her breasts spring free. *Just as I dreamed, just as I imagined…*

Just as I so desperately need to wipe the pain

away. For a few hours. A night, a day. Maybe forever.

"Don't leave me," she heard herself whisper. "Stay with me. *Please.*"

CHAPTER TWO

Glory, Alberta
March

THE LAYOUT OF THE Lazy SB, home of Winslow
Herefords, was a little unusual. You approached the
ranch by following a long grade that led from the
flat of the prairies, smack against the sky, to the
broad valley of the Horsethief River.

Once at the end of the short graveled lane that led
from the secondary highway, you came upon a fairly
new, white-sided prefab building of modest size,
perhaps twelve hundred square feet. That was where
Jesse Winslow lived. To the south, a little up the
hill from the river, was a trailer, an older model
measuring less than thirty feet. That was where the
Winslows' uncle, Brandis McAffrey, had lived until
he died three years before at the age of eighty-four,
dividing his share of the ranch between his two
nephews. The trailer had been empty since then.

A little higher again, on a gentle knoll, was the
old Winslow family home. It was built of clapboard,
somewhat weathered now, and stood two stories,
square and proud, on the knoll overlooking the ranch
corrals and barns and the Horsethief River in the

middle distance. A fancy-cut veranda, the style of a previous time, wrapped itself around the house, and old-fashioned deep pink roses, long gone wild, small of bloom and long of thorn, climbed up to the roof on two sides. That was where Noah Winslow lived.

The brothers got along fine; they just preferred to live separately. The arrangement suited them. There'd been a third brother, Casey, but he'd died at the age of twelve of a ruptured appendix. Doc Lake had seen to him when Jake Winslow had rushed him to town, after pooh-poohing the severity of the boy's "bellyache," but it was too late. Casey had died four days later of the massive infection that had set in, and the loss of her middle son had hastened Macy Winslow's decline. She'd suffered for many years from a sort of mysterious palsy that incapacitated her. No one knew exactly what it was, but one day, about two months after Casey's death, Macy had gone down for a nap in the afternoon of a bright spring day and had never woken up.

The neighbors had talked. It was a small community, Glory and the surrounding farm and ranch district. People had wondered at the sudden death of a woman in midlife who only trembled a bit, enough that she couldn't hold a teacup steady. There were whispers of suicide—not just because of Macy's losing a son like that but having to live with a man like Jake Winslow. A hard man. Some said a violent man.

But the doctor's certificate had read "unknown natural causes" and that was good enough, as far as the remaining Winslows were concerned. She'd been buried in the churchyard up on the prairie, a church that only she of all the Winslows had ever attended. There was singing at the grave site and purple martins looped overhead as Macy McAffrey Winslow was lowered into the rich brown prairie soil. It was the only time, outside of his wedding, that Jake Winslow had ever been seen at church. Six months later, he'd sold his interest in the ranch to his brother-in-law, Brandis McAffrey, Macy's half brother, and had disappeared. No one knew if he was dead or alive.

Since then Noah and Jesse and their Uncle Brandis—until his death—had been running the Lazy SB. Neither Noah nor Jesse ever talked about the disappearance of their father. Not many people in the area believed he was missed, even by his two boys.

Neither had married. Nor had Uncle Brandis ever married. Noah was close to his mid-thirties and Jesse was twenty-seven. If Casey had lived, he'd be thirty-one.

SPRING HAD COME early to the northern range this year. By late March, the snow had cleared or blown away and most of the newborn calves had a pleasant and peaceful introduction to the world on the Lazy SB. No blizzards. No sudden March northwesters bringing freezing rain. No deep winter snow on the ground to weary the lumbering mothers. Noah and Jesse had ridden the range all month, watching for cows with problems. There'd been a few, but this year they'd lost fewer calves than ever before. Noah was pleased. A dead calf was money lost on a working ranch. Not just the loss of what the calf would have brought, as a feeder or a finished steer, but money lost in feeding the mother for a year without a calf to show for it. Ranch economics were tough and tight.

By the third week in March, Noah figured most of the calving was done. The few cows that hadn't given birth yet were down in the lower field, close to the ranch so that either he or Jesse or Carl Divine, their foreman, could go out and check on them occasionally.

Other ranching and farming tasks were approaching. Seed to get in from Regina for the hay crops he was experimenting with this year. Bulls to examine for health problems and get into condition before turning them out with the cows in July. Roundup to organize, maybe mid-May this year, depending on the weather. Branding to follow, along with inoculating, castrating, dehorning, worming and all the other hundred and one jobs a rancher had to keep up with to look after his cattle properly.

The weather so far was just about perfect. You couldn't ask for a finer spring day. As Noah left Carl in the barn checking veterinary supplies and walked up to the house to get some lunch, he noticed his brother turning into the yard. Jesse didn't stop at his own bungalow, but continued on up Noah's driveway.

Noah waved briefly, then walked into the house to start the coffee machine, which he usually got ready before he left the house in the morning. He opened the refrigerator. Bologna or ham or leftover roast beef? He pulled out the sliced ham and began to gather the makings of the rest of his sandwich. Maybe make extra, in case Jesse hadn't eaten.

Lettuce, pickles, mustard, mayonnaise, cheese slices, a few chunks of raw onion, a tomato slice or two, more pickles—the entire creation topped with a couple of peperoncini peppers and a dab of horse-radish. Now *that* was a sandwich, Noah thought with satisfaction.

Jesse came in without knocking and sat heavily at the kitchen table.

Noah glanced at his brother. "You eat?"

"Not yet."

"Sandwich? Carl's down at the barn."

"Sure." Jesse sighed and Noah spared him another glance before topping the three sandwiches he'd made with a thick slice of Glory Bakery bread. He leaned down on each sandwich gently, just enough to make it all stick together and not topple off before he could wrap one up for Carl and take the other two to the table for him and Jesse. He'd planned to eat down at the barn with his foreman, but now that Jesse was here, he might as well stay up at the house and eat with him.

He set the plate on the table, pushing aside the week's accumulation of magazines and newspapers. His brother hadn't even taken off his hat, which was unusual. He hadn't said another word, either. Noah walked back to the refrigerator and pulled out a couple of cans of beer. He popped the tab on his as he returned to the table.

"Beer?"

"I could use one," Jesse said, reaching for his can and popping the tab, too. "Thanks." He took a long draft and wiped his mustache with the back of his hand. Noah noticed a letter sticking out of the pocket of his brother's shirt. The letter had been opened.

The two men ate their sandwiches in silence for five minutes. Then Noah decided to cut to the chase. "I thought you weren't coming home from town until later this afternoon. That barbed wire the co-op ordered come in early?"

He knew Jesse didn't have the barbed wire, the pickup hadn't ridden as though it had a load in the back. Still, no way was he coming straight out and asking—that wasn't how the men in his world did things. Not men who loved cowboying and the independent life above all, men like him and Jesse. A man was generally his own boss, whether he worked for wages or not. A man worth his grub and his paycheck knew what needed doing without being told.

"Nope." Jesse drained his beer. "Didn't get it yet. I, ah, I had some news in town."

Noah regarded him for a second or two. "News?" He bit into his sandwich.

"Got a letter today." Jesse patted his chest pocket and frowned.

"Girlfriend?"

"This is no joke, Noah." Jesse swore softly under his breath. "No joke at all."

"Well, you'd better tell me then. Save me guessing. I got work to do this afternoon."

His brother heaved another sigh and stood up to retrieve the pickle jar from the fridge. "You recall that exhibition I went to last fall in Minnesota? Me 'n' Barney?" he asked as he stabbed into the jar with a fork.

"Sure do. Got two blue ribbons for those young bulls sired by Mack. Grand champ and reserve." Mack was the pet name Noah had for Macintosh Millicent Merrigoldas Blazes, the top bull on the ranch, the five-year-old Noah would have mortgaged his soul to acquire. He hadn't had to, luckily, and Mack had turned out even better than he'd dreamed. Blood will out, old Brandis used to say. Blood and breeding.

"Well, I met a woman down there." Jesse screwed the lid back on the pickle jar and pushed it to the center of the table.

Noah stared at his brother. He looked unhappy. This wasn't like Jesse. Was he in love? Women were nothing new to him; he had women falling all over him wherever he went.

"And?" Noah took another bite of his sandwich and chased the heat from the peppers with the last of his beer.

Jesse patted his pocket again. "She wrote. Told me, uh—jeez, Noah, I don't know how to put this," Jesse said in a rush. His eyes were hangdog. This was the younger brother Noah had pulled out of quite a few jams over the years. He knew the look well.

"Hell, Jess. How bad could it be? You catch something you weren't figuring on catching? You left her with something she wasn't figuring on getting left with—"

"Yeah. She's having a baby. Mine—"

"What?"

"She's having a kid. She don't want nothing from me. Just figured I should know, that's all."

"What do you mean, she doesn't want anything from you?" He surprised himself with the intensity of his feelings. This was bound to happen. Jesse was a womanizer. Noah was amazed it hadn't happened long ago. Maybe it had. "What did she write for if she didn't want anything?"

"You're a hard son of a bitch, Noah." Jesse stood up. "Some folk are decent, you know." He glared at his brother. "Some people got *feelings*. Some folk figure there's a right and a wrong way to do things."

For a minute Noah thought Jesse was going to leave. But he didn't. He stood at the kitchen window for a few seconds, staring out over the river valley, then sat down again.

"I've thought it over. I'm going to write back and see if she wants to get married."

Noah didn't say a thing. He just studied his younger brother. Then—he wasn't sure why he said it— "Who would she marry?"

"Me, you bastard. *Me!*" Jesse glared at him. "I know how to do right by a woman. You're not the only Winslow knows about honor, damn it."

Ha. Honor. What the *hell* was Jesse talking about? Honor was one thing the Winslows weren't big on, none of 'em. Practical, that was what the Winslows were. Some might say too practical. Noah walked to the fridge and grabbed two more beers. This called for a little celebration.

"What's her name?"

"Abby. Abby Steen."

"Married? Separated? Divorced?" Noah plunked the beer in front of his brother and stood there, popping the tab on his own.

Jesse glared again and Noah saw him bite back a curse. "Widow."

"How old?"

"I don't know. Twenty-two, twenty-three, maybe." Jesse sounded irritable. He grabbed the second beer. "Looks pretty young."

"When's the happy day?"

"The wedding, you mean?"

"Well, I don't mean the kid. I can figure that out, seeing you were in Minnesota for a week in November. You never heard of rubbers?" he added angrily. "What in hell happened?"

Jesse tossed his hat onto the chair beside him and ran a hand through his thick, dark hair.

"Wedding?" Jesse said, answering his first question. "As soon as she can come up here, I guess. That's if she'll marry me—"

"Oh, she'll marry you, all right—"

"What happened? Hell!" Jesse disregarded his interruption and ran his hand through his hair again, and when he spoke he addressed the floor in front of him. None too clean, Noah noted absently. Still, he'd seen it worse.

"I met her in a bar—now, don't you say nothing! I wasn't drinking, not that much anyway. Couple beers. I noticed her sitting by herself. She had a friend with her, turned out the friend had plans to go off with somebody else. So I drove her home."

"So you drove her home, uh-huh," Noah muttered.

"Yeah. When we got there, I asked her if she needed a hand, if she had some kind of trouble, since the friend had mentioned it. I figured it might be to do with her stock, and she just—hell, she just cracked up on me. Started bawling. Told me her husband had been killed not that long ago, and the baby she'd been expectin' had been born dead—"

"And you bought all that."

"Of course I bought it! It was the truth, damn it. Anybody could see that. I told her I'd make her some coffee and I did. We had a cup or two, then—well, then we ended up in bed. It was just, you know—one of those things."

Noah nodded. For guys like Jesse, sure, it was one of those things. Noah couldn't quite imagine himself in that kind of situation.

"We, uh, we spent the rest of the weekend together. The nights anyway. She was lonely. So was I, I guess. I sure in hell didn't think this would happen. We used birth control—"

"Mostly."

"Yeah, mostly," Jesse shot back. "Accidents happen."

"To guys like you."

"What's that supposed to mean? Huh? Guys like

me? Not perfect guys like you, eh?'' Jesse leaped to his feet and for a second or two, Noah thought he was going to take a poke at him. That'd be great, a couple of Winslows duking it out over a woman. Wouldn't be the first time, either.

''Settle down, Jesse,'' Noah said wearily. He frowned. He couldn't waste much more time on this. He had to go down and give Carl a hand and phone in the order to the vet's. What was done was done. ''Okay, so she can come up here, you can get the papers in order, whatever. What about her being American?''

''I already checked in town. She can come up to marry me. Get her papers that way.''

''I suppose she could stay in Brandis's trailer.''

''Why the trailer? She could stay with me.''

''Do I have to spell it out, Jesse? Neighbors are going to talk as it is, her showing up like this out of nowhere. Don't give them any more ammo than they're already going to have once that kid comes. People can count backward, y'know.''

Jesse reached for his hat and jammed it on. He looked like hell. This had been a shock to him, no question. There went his carefree bachelor days, following his happy hormones wherever they led. Noah could see he hadn't had time to take it all in yet. Marriage, a wife, a kid on the way…

''Listen, buddy.'' Noah clapped his brother on the shoulder as he accompanied him to the door. ''Things could be worse. Huh?''

Jesse nodded sheepishly. ''Guess so.''

"Time you settled down, anyway. One of us."
Noah smiled. "Keep the Winslows going, huh?"

Jesse grinned. "Yeah, sure."

"Better you than me, right?"

Jesse shrugged. He didn't say anything.

"She a cowgirl? Know one end of a horse from
the other?"

"Farm family. Teacher by trade."

"Teacher? That's good. What kind of farming?
Sugar beets?" Noah wasn't serious. He was trying
for a lighter note with his brother, although it was
an effort.

"Dairy. Jerseys or Guernseys or some damn
thing."

"That's good. Cows is cows, I guess, even if they
ain't whitefaces, right?"

The two brothers shared a laugh. It was an old
family joke that had originated with Brandis. Jesse
stepped out the door and the screen slapped shut
behind him.

"Jess?" His brother turned to meet Noah's gaze.
"You can count on me. You know that."

"I know that, man. I appreciate it." Jesse's voice
was gruff, reflecting the emotion behind his words.
Jesse had always leaned on his big brother. It was
natural that he'd come to him today. For advice, for
comfort.

"Okay."

Noah watched Jesse walk back to his pickup and
open the door. "Hey!" he called out.

His brother paused, one foot on the running
board. "Yeah?"

"She win anything at the fair?"

"Hell if I know," Jesse said with a wide grin. "I never asked." He climbed in and slammed the door.

You wouldn't, Noah thought, watching him back the truck up to the Y in the road. Still, Jesse was a decent man. Solid, good instincts. Hard worker. Fairly steady. Spent too much money, in Noah's opinion, and there'd been a time he drank too much. That was past. Definitely a good idea for him to settle down. Maybe this widow, coming to Glory with a family already started, was the woman to do it.

No question, things could be worse.

ABBY HUNG HER HEAD over the toilet bowl and wearily mopped her face with a cool, wrung-out washcloth. The doctor had said he suspected twins. She prayed he was wrong, but they ran in the family. She hadn't been sick at all with her first pregnancy and now this—nearly every morning for the past month she'd gotten up sick.

She'd have to tell her parents soon. She wasn't afraid to; after all, she was a grown woman, a widow, who'd suffered more in her twenty-eight years than any woman should be asked to suffer. But they'd be upset. And terribly disappointed. And they'd want to know if she was going to get married again, to the father of the baby. And they'd worry about the neighbors talking. Which they'd definitely do in a small town like Wicoigon.

She was living with her parents and working part-time for her father and part-time as a substitute teacher since the new term had started after Christmas. She'd grown to dread the call in the morning telling her that her services were required in the classroom that day. She taught elementary, grade three mostly. She couldn't forget that her own baby would have been a year old now. Being surrounded by children all day long was like walking on cut glass, Abby had discovered. The constant reminders of the child she'd lost, plus the extra stresses of her pregnancy, physical and emotional, were really getting her down.

It didn't help that she'd begun to find the smell of cows and barns nauseating. Thank heavens she'd convinced her father to let her do his books in preparation for year-end, so she was in his office in the house most of the time. This nausea would pass, and when it did, she'd be finished the accounts and ready to go back and help him with the cattle.

She'd confided in only one person so far, her sister, Meg. Meg had been horrified. Still was. Meg was fourteen years older than Abby, and they'd been more like aunt and niece than sisters. Meg wanted to know right away who the father was, and when Abby told her she'd had a brief liaison with a stranger from Canada during the Carlisle fair, her sister's lovely face had grown stiff with disapproval. Like their parents, Meg was a regular churchgoer. Not that there was anything wrong with that—Abby often wished her own faith would come easier to her—but she really didn't think that her parents or Meg ever thought much beyond the surface.

Shouldn't her sister be thrilled for her, knowing

how little joy she had in her life? Knowing that her only child, Frank's baby, had been snatched from her, born dead? Didn't she realize that Abby welcomed this new life growing inside her womb—that this was heaven's gift to her for all her suffering?

She'd never do anything to jeopardize that life. That was why she'd written to Jesse Winslow. She wanted nothing from him, but she believed he had a right to know. A child had a right to a father and a father had a right to his child. She was going to have this baby and raise it with all the love she had in her heart, and her child was not going to be fatherless. If Jesse was at all inclined, he could see their child whenever he wanted. If he wasn't, well, so be it. She had given him the choice.

And then she'd received the letter from him, asking her to come to Glory and marry him. That was a shocker. They didn't really know each other. He seemed to be a very nice man. Quiet, gentle. She'd found him attractive, yes, for a few days—but could she live with the man? Marry him?

Hardly.

She'd received the letter two weeks ago. Jesse had said he'd wait until he heard from her, as he didn't know her circumstances and he hadn't wanted to call her right out of the blue. But he'd give her some time to think it over. He hoped she'd agree. If so, he'd send her fare right away, and they could get married as soon as she wanted.

Well, she didn't need the fare. Although it was kind of him to offer. She had a few savings. She'd need to work to support her baby and the likeliest prospect was to look for a job teaching full-time. But who was going to hire a pregnant teacher with no seniority? Or a teacher with a brand-new infant— or infants—which would be the case since her due date was August? Even if, according to the law, it wasn't supposed to matter. And then there was the fascinating particular of the new teacher with a brand-new baby but no husband. How would that go over with the hiring committee?

And did she want someone else to raise her child? A caregiver? Put the baby straight into day care? What if the doctor's suspicions were right and she *was* carrying twins?

Abby shuddered at the prospect of the difficulties ahead of her. If her baby had survived, she'd planned to live off Frank's insurance settlement for the first year or two. Day care was inevitable eventually, no matter how much she'd have preferred to be home raising her own child, as she would have done if Frank had lived.

"Yoo-hoo!" It was her mother, downstairs.

"Yes?" Abby called through the closed door. That was another thing; there was so little privacy. It wasn't her parents' fault, but she couldn't help thinking they'd resented losing their own space when their younger daughter had moved back in to save money.

"Breakfast's on! Time's a-wastin', Abigail!"

Time's a-wasting. Yes, wasn't it? Abby thought wearily. She was more than four months gone already. The morning sickness should have passed. She'd be showing soon. She stood, wiped her forehead again, then took several deep breaths. She examined her face in the spotty bathroom mirror over the sink. Long blond hair, average features. Blue eyes. A pleasant smile, people said. Looked like a lot of the Swedish, Dutch, German, Norwegian folks in the district. She looked better when she was pregnant, no matter what she felt. People commented on that. She remembered before, with the baby she always called Mary Frannie in her heart, that she'd felt so happy being pregnant with Frank's child, happy despite the grief of losing Frank. As though having a baby was something she'd always wanted. Although she hadn't really. She'd never thought much about it. It had just happened.

Now, this time, it had just happened again. She must be fecund as a darn bunny rabbit, she thought wryly.

Time's a-wasting. Abby made her way slowly down the stairs.

"—and I told Belle she'd have to step in and do something. Send that girl packing. It's not right to— oh, there you are!" Her mother smiled as she spotted Abby and waved her spatula in greeting. She was busy turning pancakes at the kitchen stove. Her father sat hunched in his chair, as always, listening to the early-morning stock prices on the country station the radio on top of the fridge was tuned to—had been tuned to for thirty years, as far as Abby knew.

"I was just telling your father about the Stovik girl, Abby. Sandra. She's got herself in the family way and her mother's just sick about it. I don't suppose Belle's aware how much people've already been talking. Everybody knows Sandra's been the town bike for years. There's probably not a fit man outside of my Arnie here hasn't taken a ride—''

"Mother!"

"It's true. She's a tramp, Abby. T-R-A-M-P. Tramp. And now she's caught in her own sinning ways. Serves her right. She's expecting, and it's just going to kill Gladys Volstadt when she finds out her first great-grandchild will be a bastard. Well, how else can you put it? Gladys planned to give Sandra the family silver, I know that for a fact, but a common slut won't be getting the Volstadt silver, that's for sure. Gladys wouldn't stand for it.'' Abby's mother turned the pancakes violently.

"She'll just have to take her medicine, maybe even get rid of it, although that's piling sin on sin. Didn't I always tell Belle she had to watch that one, that Sandra, didn't I—''

Abby stood, horrified, as she listened to her mother's litany of condemnation. Suddenly she felt weak. Woozy. She grabbed the doorframe to support herself momentarily—

"Abigail, dear! Something wrong?'' Her mother's voice was sharp. "What's wrong?''

"I'm fine, Mom. I'm just fine.'' Abby walked carefully into the kitchen and sank down on a kitchen chair.

"I—uh, Mom? Dad?''

"Huh?'' Her father looked up, annoyed, from the careful paring of his thumbnail with his jackknife as he listened to the stock prices on the radio. "What's that, Ab?''

"What is it, Abigail, for heaven's sake—''

"I have something I'd like to tell you both. I'll be leaving. I've decided to get married again.''

CHAPTER THREE

IT WOULD HAVE MADE more sense to fly. A thousand miles on a Greyhound bus? Nearly five months pregnant...?

But she'd wanted to see the country. She'd wanted to see the geography change over the course of the two-day trip, from the farming country where she'd been born and raised, through the badlands, into North Dakota, more farming country, mixed forest, wide shallow rivers that fed into the Missouri and the Mississippi and the Great Lakes and then the long, lonely miles to Rugby, North Dakota, which they went through at night. Abby could barely make out the marker in the center of town, but she knew the words on the brass plate: Rugby, N.D., Geographical Center of North America.

From there it was north to the border crossing into Canada at Portal, Manitoba, through the Turtle Mountain country, past Melitta and Brandon and into the gray, windy city of Winnipeg, still leafless in mid-April, its broad streets dusty and littered with grime and debris left behind when the snow melted.

There, in the busy downtown station, she transferred to a Greyhound heading west after a delay of a few hours. She spent the time walking up and down the unfamiliar streets. She sent postcards home to her family, buying the stamps in a drugstore, and bought a paperback novel to read in case she got bored on the long trip west.

Regina. Calgary. Vancouver. The bus was bound for the Pacific Coast. They passed through town after town with unfamiliar names. But except for the occasional rest stop and lunch break, during which Abby got out to stretch her legs, coat drawn close against the chill of the wind, Abby kept her nose pressed to the glass. The paperback novel remained in her bag.

There were so many miles between her old home and her new home. When she allowed herself to think about the life she was entering, she felt her hands grow clammy and her heart pound. Marrying a man she barely knew! She had to be crazy. A man she'd only slept with, and just two nights at that. A man, truth to tell, she wasn't sure she could even pick out of a crowd. At the same time, she was thrilled to her bones. She'd never done anything so impulsive. Not even marrying Frank six months after they'd met.

Jesse had been surprised when she'd called, the evening after she'd spoken to her parents. He'd looked forward to her call, he'd said, and his voice quickly became reassuring. She could tell he hadn't really looked forward to it. But he'd seemed pleased, perhaps even relieved, when she told him she'd decided to take him up on his offer, after all, if he was still willing. She gave him no reasons; he didn't ask for any.

Her mind was made up. After the conversation with her parents, there was no going back. She'd made it clear that she was pleased about her sudden pregnancy and that she was happy to be marrying the father of her baby. She made it sound almost as though that had been her plan all along. When they protested, saying Frank had only been dead two years, Abby had hesitated, struck deeply by the ongoing sadness she carried with her since her young husband's death. It was true; she missed Frank horribly. She'd never slept with another man, just him and Jesse Winslow.

But she lied; she told her parents it was time for her to move on. That Frank was dead, and there was no bringing him back. That time healed all wounds of the heart—wasn't that what they'd told her?—and hers had healed, too. That she wasn't getting any younger and her hopes of marrying again and having children were slight at best if she stayed in Wicoigon. Now, with this chance pregnancy, her decision had more or less been made for her.

She'd handed in her notice to the school board, sold many of the possessions she'd stored at her sister's place, including most of the baby clothes she'd bought for her first baby, which broke her heart. She kept a few tiny sleepers and one special blanket, wanting, somehow, to maintain a connection between her babies, no matter how tenuous. Thank heavens the doctor had thought there was only one baby on the way, after all, at her last visit. He'd told her to see a doctor, though, and have an ultrasound as soon as she got to Canada. Until she had the ultrasound, she wouldn't know for sure.

Then she'd cleaned out her savings accounts and bought her bus ticket. One way.

She'd turned down Jesse's offer to send plane fare. She was a full partner going into this marriage, not some little bit of a thing who needed rescuing from illegitimate pregnancy. She'd meant it when she'd said she was prepared to raise their child alone. That she'd only contacted him because she thought he had a right to know, as any man would.

She still had that option, she supposed, if it didn't work out with Jesse. She had her teacher training. She had some savings. No matter how she tried to replay matters in her head now that she'd left her home behind, she knew she'd burned most of her bridges in Wicoigon when she'd blurted out to her parents that, like the Stovik girl, she, too, was single and expecting. Worse, in the eyes of the town—she was a pregnant widow. And she hadn't hidden the fact that the man who'd fathered her child was a man she barely knew, a fellow exhibitor she'd met at the Carlisle Stock Show. Abby hadn't regretted telling them; they'd know soon enough, anyway, and it wasn't fair leaving her sister with the burden of the entire story.

Her parents had been horrified. She sensed their relief when she said she'd be moving to Canada, thousands of miles away. That had hurt, really hurt. Abby knew it would be a long time before she could go home again.

HER BUS CAME IN to the Calgary depot at seven o'clock. He knew, not because Jesse had told him, but because he'd called to find out himself. The hour and a half from seven to half past eight was the longest Noah had ever sat through. If her bus was on time, if they hadn't stopped anywhere, they should be driving up to the ranch any minute now.

He didn't know why he felt the way he did about Jesse's marriage to this unknown American from South Dakota. He couldn't stop thinking about it. It wasn't that he was worried, or checking up on his brother, exactly, when he'd called the bus station. Jesse had appeared at his door just before he'd left for Calgary, all freshly showered and shaved, wearing a new shirt.

"Wish me luck," he'd said. He looked like a man in love. Almost.

Noah didn't fool himself that Jesse was in love. Jesse was an impulsive, warmhearted, generous man, and no doubt he'd be in love soon enough. Noah cherished no romantic notions about women himself. One was quite a lot like another, as far as he was concerned. If a woman was healthy and clean and moderately pretty, had a sense of humor…well, if you had to, you could probably talk yourself into calling it love.

If Jesse could only bend his mind around being tied down *and* a family man. That was the key. Maybe that was the part Noah was having such a hard time with—it just wasn't like his brother to embrace responsibility quite so enthusiastically.

Of course, he hadn't met this Abby Steen. Maybe

she was the type any man would welcome, pregnant or not. Maybe she was an incredibly sexy, energetic, passionate, unrestrained woman any man would be happy to have in his bed, any time.

Plus, he thought idly, a good cook.

Noah reflected. Did he know anyone like that? Nope. He sighed, and cracked the top on his can of beer, his second. He was sitting on the darkened veranda and just about to go in because the mosquitoes had finally found him when he saw the lights of Jesse's pickup coming slowly down the long grade that led to the ranch. He glanced at his watch. Nearly nine. His collie dog jumped up and barked twice, as she always did when she heard Jesse's truck. Jesse's stray howled in the distance. This was the wild dog his brother had found a year before at the side of the highway, injured, and had befriended and half-tamed. No one else on the ranch could get near it. Champ, Jesse called the animal, although he and Carl never called it anything but Jesse's stray.

That settled it. His brother was back, presumably with the fiancée.

Where did that put Noah? He wasn't sure. He raised his beer and took his feet down from the railing where he'd been resting them, sitting tipped back on the old rocker. His boots made a solid thump on the wooden deck of the veranda. He could hardly saunter on down and introduce himself to the happy pair this evening.

He'd better leave it until Jesse brought her over, maybe tomorrow. Should he do anything in particular for the new couple? Social-wise? Invite a few neighbors? Barbecue? Too early for that; the bugs would kill them. He'd have to get the house cleaned up, which was a drag. Noah was no social animal; the thought of a party, dinner or otherwise, paralyzed him. Maybe he could ask someone else to handle it for him. Who? Donna Beaton? He'd dated her a while back but they'd split amicably months ago. Donna would do it, though, if he asked her. It was the kind of thing Donna was good at.

But he'd sure hate for any notion to get out that he and Donna were an item again. Because they weren't. He'd backed off with Donna when he realized there was no future to their relationship. Not that either of them *wanted* any future together, nor did he want a long-term relationship without marriage. First thing you knew, a fellow could end up with all the obligations and none of the perks. He didn't want to be married, though. Still, at his age— he was pushing thirty-five—it was getting to be a real nuisance wining and dining a lady as a preliminary to getting into her bed once in a while. Then, if the lady was the sensitive type, there was all that trouble extricating yourself from a relationship you knew was a dead end without hurting her feelings.

Damn. Noah sighed again. Maybe Jesse had it figured out, after all. Sow plenty of wild oats, then settle down and start harvesting some of the crop.

He saw the lights go on in his brother's house and heard his dogs barking an enthusiastic welcome. He could mostly hear Stella, the little terrier-heeler cross, his brother's favorite. He glanced over to Brandis's trailer, which they'd gotten ready for

Abby Steen, midway between his house and his brother's. The windows were dark; the fridge was stocked; there were brand-new sheets on the bed. Jesse'd seen to it, at Noah's suggestion. Noah hadn't checked. It was none of his business. He just hoped the fridge held more than Big Rock lager and frozen pizza.

He stood abruptly, draining his beer, and walked into the house. He turned on the hall light, then flicked it off again and climbed the stairs to his bedroom in the dark. Cold and alone, in a bed that probably hadn't been made properly since—when? Since Challa had left? Noah had had a one-time experience with a live-in lover in his mid-twenties. Finally Challa had gotten fed up with his dithering—should they get married, shouldn't they?—and gone home. She was married now to a man from her reserve, a Stoney, and had two kids, last he'd heard. They lived west of Pincher Creek; her man was foreman at one of the big ranches down there. He hoped she was happy.

Oh well, cold and alone or not, he'd do what he usually did—read for a while, maybe, then try and get some sleep. He was meeting a man in town tomorrow, early, around eight o'clock at the Chickadee Café, someone who might do some custom seeding for him next month. He had an interview with the banker, as well, his regular twice-a-year talk. Then there was this business of Jesse and his bride-to-be.

He'd better ask them to dinner, at least. Someone

had to take charge of the social niceties, and he was pretty sure his brother wasn't going to do it.

"SAY, NOAH! Lookee here—"

Noah poured himself another cup of coffee from the counter machine without turning around. He recognized the voice—Wilf van Rijn. One of the dairy farmers just northeast of town. Leisurely, Noah picked up a fresh blueberry muffin from the plate near the coffee machine and nodded to Tina, the waitress behind the counter. She'd put it on his bill.

"Yeah?" He finally turned.

Wilf held up the newspaper he was reading, the *Calgary Herald,* a big grin on his face. He shook the paper. "Right here in the classifieds. A wife for you. City gal."

A couple of the other men glanced up and chuckled. A few slid their eyes toward Noah, who was walking back to the booth he'd chosen. The fellow he was meeting this morning was late. It was already quarter past.

Noah smiled. It was a never-ending joke. Some of the local farmers had decided it was time he got married. Perhaps it was true what they said, that misery liked company. Two of the men's wives were enjoying dalliances around the district—one with a hydro lineman and one with the vet's assistant. It wasn't exactly a secret; it was also none of his business.

"So, what you got there, Wilf?" he asked good-humoredly. He'd considered mentioning Jesse's upcoming nuptials to take the spotlight off himself, but thought better of it. Now was not the time. He hadn't even met the bride-to-be yet. When he'd driven past the trailer this morning, he'd noticed the blinds were shut. That was a good sign. It meant she was sleeping in her own bed—although why the hell he should care about that now, he didn't know. At least it indicated Jesse had taken him seriously when he'd warned about the gossip there'd be, which was some consolation in this whole mess.

"Listen to this—'wanted, long-term partner, nonsmoker'—that'd be you, Noah—" Van Rijn glanced up, grinning, then returned to the newspaper column "—'social drinker, enjoys dancing and going for walks in the country'—" The whole room erupted in a roar of male laughter.

"'Loves Shania Twain and Garth Brooks'—"
Another hoot. Noah smiled.

"'Likes to cuddle on long winter nights.' Oh, *that's* good. 'GWF'—say, what's that mean? 'G-W-F'?" Van Rijn glanced up, a puzzled expression on his broad good-natured face.

"Means she ain't looking for no *man,* Wilf," someone offered. The room erupted in laughter again.

"Well, he-ell," the farmer finished ruefully, folding up the paper and setting it on the table in front of him. "It said 'partner.' Don't say I didn't try, Noah. I'm lookin' out for your marital interests, like always...." He winked at the others and they all smiled and returned to their coffee mugs and plates of fried eggs and potatoes.

As did Noah. "Thanks, Wilf. I appreciate your

interest—say, there's Millard now.'' The man he was meeting was just approaching the outer door.

Five minutes later, he was deep in conversation with Gene Millard, the operator he hoped to hire for some custom seeding next month, and the café banter was forgotten. It wasn't as though that was the first time he'd been through that particular conversation. He got a version of it whenever he showed up in town early for coffee, about the time all the other farmers were having a café breakfast before starting their business in town.

WHEN NOAH GOT HOME, he noticed that Jesse's pickup wasn't in his driveway and there was no sign of activity at his bungalow, beyond the usual barking dogs. The blinds on the trailer were up.

It was after one o'clock. Maybe the lovebirds had gone out for lunch somewhere. Like Noah, Jesse wasn't the world's best cook.

Noah parked in his usual spot beside his house and got out, stretching first and then bending down to fondle Pat's ears. Pat, his collie dog, was getting on, nearly twelve now, but still one of the best dogs for cattle know-how he'd ever owned. He walked up the steps to his kitchen door. The house wasn't locked. He rarely locked it, unless no one else was at the ranch and he was going away for a few days. Carl was around somewhere, and wherever Jesse was, he'd be back soon.

The house was dim with no lights on and rather chilly, even at midday. He'd turned off the furnace at the beginning of the month, but he was beginning to think he'd been a little hasty. April had started off sunny and unseasonably warm, but that hadn't lasted. The past few days had been windy, and wind sure chilled a place fast. He made a mental note to relight the furnace pilot when he came in for supper that evening. Speaking of supper…Noah walked over to the refrigerator and pulled a pound of ground beef out of the freezer compartment and tossed it into the sink to thaw.

These were the bits and pieces of his life, he thought gloomily as he began to climb the stairs to his bedroom to change into working clothes. They'd always been good enough before—why was he obsessing about them now? Because Jesse had landed himself a bride? Because he wasn't going to be the main person in his brother's life anymore? It was crazy; he and Jesse weren't any closer, now that they were both grown, than any other pair of brothers. They'd been close as kids, but then farm and ranch kids usually were. There was work to do together and fun together in isolated circumstances. When Casey'd been alive…

And Macy, their mother.

Noah shook his head. No sense dwelling on the past. Macy'd never been in good health, and if she was alive today she'd be close to seventy. As for his father, no one knew what had happened to Jake. Most days, Noah was glad he was gone. Some days, he wished he at least knew if he was dead or alive.

Noah quickly changed into jeans and a well-washed flannel shirt, the sleeves of which he rolled up halfway to his elbows. He took his battered Stetson off the rack in the kitchen as he went out. It was lunchtime but he wasn't hungry.

Pat didn't get up, merely slapped her full-feathered tail slowly against the worn porch boards. Noah adjusted his hat against the sunshine. He'd go out to the machine shed and see how Carl was doing with the alternator part that had come in for the Massey Ferguson yesterday. Then there was that new colt he wanted to check on. He'd bred his favorite mare to one of Jeremiah Blake's stallions over at the Diamond 8 last summer, and the foal was a beauty. He'd had a rheumy running eye, though, the past week, for which the vet had sold him ointment to administer twice a day. The eye seemed to be clearing up just fine.

Noah headed toward the barn, followed by a couple of the ranch dogs that generally hung around by the bunkhouse. Right now Carl was the only one in residence there, but at roundup and branding times and during the haying season, the bunkhouse would be full. He'd need a part-time cook then, too. Always something to do or think about on a ranch.

Noah rounded the corner by the barn, intent on his tasks for the afternoon. He stopped dead when one of the dogs froze, alert, one paw raised.

The east side of the paddock was mostly in shade from the big feed silos thirty feet farther to the east. Shafts of April sunlight stabbed through, between the silos. In one of those shafts of sunlight was a woman, leaning on the fence, holding out her hand to the curious foal, making small, soothing noises that Noah could barely hear. The dog must have heard her before he did.

His heart hammered. Damn it! This must be Jesse's woman. Where in hell was his brother?

He stood still a few more seconds, rapidly taking in the medium height, the slim build, faded jeans, baggy T-shirt, sneakers, the long pale hair hanging loosely down her back. She was turned away from him and Noah didn't think she was aware of his presence.

He cleared his throat and the dog bounded forward, released from his watch instincts. He saw the woman's hands tighten on the top rail of the paddock, and the foal, snorting, raced back to his dam, his broom of a tail standing straight up. Noah's mare whickered to him, but didn't emerge from the shade of a big cottonwood where she stood swatting flies.

Then the woman turned. She had a calm, pretty face—nothing fantastically beautiful—wide blue eyes and looked very, very young.

He stepped forward, clearing his throat again. "I'm, uh, Noah Winslow, Jesse's brother." He extended his hand automatically. She looked at it for a split second, then offered hers. Her hand was small and soft and, like his, tanned. A sensible hand, the nails trimmed short and unpolished. He dropped it like a hot potato. "You must be Abby."

"Yes," she said softly, her eyes meeting his and causing something to twist hard in his gut. He fought to hold her gaze, forcing himself to look at her face when his first instinct had been to glance at her belly. To see the swell there that was his brother's child. The reason she was here in the first place.

"Yes, I'm Abby," she repeated quietly. "Abby Steen."

CHAPTER FOUR

"WHERE'S JESSE?" he demanded.

The man standing before her looked angry. Jesse had said his brother was difficult. The word he'd used was *tough*. This man was older than Jesse, and perhaps an inch taller. He was a big man, but where Jesse was broad and deep-chested, this man was lean and tough looking as nails. Right now he looked like he could chew the zinc coating off a few.

"He's gone to town," Abby said, twisting her hands behind her. She wasn't afraid of him but she'd seen the way he'd fought to keep his eyes from her waist, and it had embarrassed her. Not enough to shelter her belly, though. She was proud of her pregnancy; she wanted this baby. Husband or no husband.

"He's in town?" Noah Winslow glanced behind her, toward the paddock. "And he left you here?"

"Yes." She didn't feel she needed to add any reasons, or justify Jesse's behavior. He'd done nothing wrong.

Abby could hear the soft pad-pad of the mare approaching across the grass. With the foal, she hoped. She loved horses and as a child growing up had often wished she could have one. Her father regarded a horse as a poor investment. She'd been involved with 4-H, as many farm children were, but she'd always bought and raised a Jersey heifer, one of her father's animals. Her father had put the money she paid for the calf into a fund for her and her sister's further education. Then, when she and her sister sold their animals, they were expected to add to the fund.

Noah shot her an odd questioning look, then stepped closer to the fence, with what she realized was a rare flash of tenderness on his grim face. For the foal. Perhaps he reserved all his feeling for animals. He held his hand out to the mare and scratched between her ears. He looked briefly toward Abby. "What did he go to town for?"

It was a simple, direct question. As though he'd half expected to find her here. As though he already knew who she was, where she fit in. That she belonged to Jesse. She supposed Jesse had told him. But did he know how scared she was? Did he know how many second thoughts she'd had since Jesse had picked her up at the bus station the night before?

"He said he wanted to get the marriage license and make a few arrangements," she said, explaining after all. She took a deep breath, for calm. "We've decided we should get married as soon as possible."

Then he looked at her waist. Abby had the distinct feeling he'd wanted to all along and couldn't stop himself now. His eyes immediately returned to the mare, but she hadn't missed the tightened jaw, either. "Makes sense," was his noncommittal comment.

He reached out and tried to touch the foal, which jumped back at the last moment and went to stand at his mama's flank. "I thought maybe he'd have taken care of that by now. The license, I mean."

She met his level questioning glance. His eyes were a greenish-hazel color, not blue like Jesse's. "He said he was waiting until I got here. That I might have some papers he'd need."

"Uh-huh."

Noah stepped onto the lower rail of the fence and threw his left leg over the top rail. Then he was inside, approaching the foal with a low, soothing tone, his hand out. The foal stood nervously, ready to run. Expertly, with slow, steady movements, Noah wrapped his arm around the foal's neck and held him firmly. He bent and drew the lower eyelid down with one thumb, while the foal struggled futilely in his grip.

"Is something wrong with him? With his eye?" Abby moved closer to the fence, curious, her hands in her jeans' pockets.

Noah didn't look up. "He's had a bad eye for a few days. Seems to be cleared up now." He stroked the foal's white blaze and then scratched between his ears briefly before releasing him. With a high-pitched squeal, the foal wheeled and galloped awkwardly to the far side of the paddock. The mare merely turned her head and gave her offspring a mild wondering glance.

Abby smiled. "She doesn't seem too concerned."

"No." Noah glanced her way and for a second or two, she thought he'd smile, too. At her. Then he returned his attention to the mare. "She's a good old girl. One of the best." He patted her neck affectionately and the mare tossed her head up and down vigorously, almost as though she were answering him.

"What's her name?"

"Peg."

"Peg?" Abby thought that was a very ordinary name for a horse. "What kind of horse is she?"

Noah threw her a surprised look. "Quarter horse," he said, his tone leaving no doubt that he considered her a complete idiot.

He came toward the rails of the corral. "When did my brother say he was coming back?"

"He didn't say. Soon, I think."

"I see." He studied her briefly. Abby had the impression he didn't miss much. "You settle in all right?" he asked.

"In the trailer? Yes, thank you." She stepped back and watched as he climbed back over the rail. "I'm delighted. I didn't know I'd have my own little place."

He frowned. Perhaps he didn't care for small talk. *Surly brute.* "You have lunch yet?"

"Well, there's some frozen stuff in the fridge I planned to take out—"

"Come on up to the house," he interrupted. "I'll give you a sandwich or something." He paused, hesitated, frowned again. Then he fell into step beside her. Abby heard the clang of metal on metal from behind the barn; someone must be working on some machinery back there. In a way—she didn't know why—she was relieved to know there was another person on the place.

"Thank you, but I wouldn't want to bother you. I'm sure you have plenty to do—"

"No bother. I've got stuff to do, yes, but I can't let you miss lunch because Jesse's gone off to town and hasn't got back yet—"

Abby was going to protest again, then realized that, like many men, he probably thought she was in a fragile condition because of her pregnancy and couldn't possibly miss a meal. The truth was, she *was* hungry. And when she'd looked inside the trailer's fridge and seen only a quart of milk, a six-pack of beer, some margarine, a loaf of the most hideous white sliced bread and vinyl-packaged orangish cheese slices, as well as a freezer full of pizza cartons, she'd lost her appetite, despite her hunger. All she'd had for breakfast was a glass of milk. Since she'd gotten rid of her morning sickness in late March, she hadn't suffered from any loss of appetite. Until today.

"All right." She took a deep breath and glanced up at her future brother-in-law. He was only trying to be hospitable, in his straightforward way, she supposed. She had to do her best to make this new life work out, and one of the jobs she'd have would be to get along with all of Jesse's relations. Including this brother.

"All right, I'll have some lunch, if you're sure it's not too much trouble. Jesse should be back by then." She didn't add that she'd been alarmed when Jesse had come down to the trailer to tell her he was going to town to do some business. Somehow she'd thought their reunion would be a bit more romantic. That maybe he'd even take her to town, introduce her around. Still, his excuse to leave her behind— that she needed to catch up on her rest—made sense, too.

Noah nodded briefly and led her toward the shabbily painted white house on the hill—the house Jesse had told her belonged to his parents before him and was now his older brother's. The house was surrounded by thickets of unkempt grass and unpruned rose creepers. The family home. From the look of the place, you certainly couldn't accuse the Winslows of being house-proud.

ABBY DIDN'T THINK she'd ever seen such a shambles in her life.

The house wasn't, well, *dirty*—although she was pretty sure it hadn't seen more than a broom in quite some time—but it was a general mess. There were newspapers piled high on a rocking chair. There were magazines and jars of peanut butter and honey and sugar and jam and industrial-size cardboard containers of salt and pepper on the table. There had to be at least five or six calendars stacked behind the current one on the wall, all hanging from a six-inch nail. When the nail was full, did he remove the earliest calendars and discard them? Probably not.

The sink was full of rinsed-but-not-washed dishes, and Abby noticed that Noah retrieved clean plates and cutlery from the dishwasher. He was obviously of the philosophy that you took clean dishes out of the dishwasher until it was empty, then you loaded it back up with the soiled ones. This could take time. And for a single man, it probably meant several days with dishes stacked in the sink.

The concept of replacing clean dishes in a cupboard and keeping the dirty ones in the dishwasher, not the sink, was clearly a foreign one. Abby could relate—her father was like that. Not that her mother ever left her father alone long enough to have the dishes stack up to any degree.

There was an elderly dog asleep under the table. It didn't move when they came in, and Abby hoped it wasn't dead. The microwave looked well used, and two burners of the stove were covered with a metal tray holding first-aid materials—bandages, Mercurochrome, Vaseline, burn ointment, tweezers, disinfectant. She supposed that was because it was handy. It also indicated he didn't cook much, or not with the range, anyway.

"Sandwich?" Noah waved her toward the table and stood with the refrigerator door open. She could see that it was well stocked.

"S-sure. A sandwich would be fine." She sat down on a hard wooden chair.

"Grilled cheese? Hot Reuben? Ham, mustard and pickle?"

"Uh." *Hot Reuben?* "Whatever you're having."

"Okay. Reuben, it is." He glanced at her and again, Abby glimpsed the humor that lay beneath the man's craggy exterior. He was probably joking. She was game.

Abby watched as he took rye bread from a cupboard—at least it wasn't sliced white—and liberally spread four slices with butter and mustard. Then he piled on cheese slices—Cheddar, not Swiss or Muenster, but that was okay—and pastrami, topping the whole with some sauerkraut he spooned out of a jar he'd taken from the fridge. He only looked over at her once. "You can dump the junk that's on the table onto one of the chairs, if you want," he invited cordially.

She did; meanwhile he took the sandwiches to the microwave and nuked them for a minute or so, then retrieved two glasses from the dishwasher. "Milk, juice or beer?" he asked, holding up the glasses.

"Milk for me," she replied. She found this whole process fascinating. He appeared to be very comfortable in his own kitchen, as though he'd traced the path from refrigerator to table to microwave so many times he could make a sandwich and get a beer in his sleep.

Noah brought two plates and another plate with the sandwiches on them. The bread was steaming—not exactly grilled, but definitely hot. Then he went back to the refrigerator and got out a jug of milk and a can of beer, which he held in one hand, the two glasses in the other.

Abby poured herself a glass of milk, while Noah settled himself on the chair opposite her.

"Eat," he said, gesturing at her sandwich when she hesitated. Well, that was plain enough. No niceties here. He picked up his own sandwich and paused, looking her straight in the eye.

"So, you intend to marry my brother, do you?"

"Er—" Abby quickly put down her sandwich, which she'd been about to sample. "I didn't come all this way *not* to marry him, did I?" She was annoyed at the direct question. More than annoyed. Really, it was none of this man's business what she wanted.

"That doesn't answer my question," he replied, taking a bite of his sandwich.

She chewed daintily, ignoring him, then swallowed and sipped at her milk. "No," she agreed. "I don't suppose it does."

He stared at her, then popped the tab on his beer can. "I guess that *is* my brother's child you're carrying?"

"Has anyone ever told you that you are an extremely rude man?" Abby snapped angrily, forgetting her manners. "In the first place, I had no intention of marrying your brother or anyone, whether I was pregnant or not. I am perfectly capable of having this child and raising it by myself."

"I have no doubt of that," he murmured, not meeting her eye. He examined his sandwich critically, then took another bite.

Abby was so mad she could've spit. She wished Jesse would get back. She certainly was beginning to get an idea of what he meant by "difficult." For two cents she'd just walk out, but she wasn't going to give Noah Winslow the satisfaction.

"So," she said, after counting silently to ten, "what do you grow on this ranch?" A change of subject was in order.

"Grow?" He looked at her, astonished. "We

raise cattle. Herefords. We also raise hay and some feed grain. We don't *grow* anything. This isn't a farm, you know.''

''No, Jesse did tell me that much.'' She managed to mangle and swallow another bite of sandwich. The milk was cold and good, and the sandwich, she had to admit, wasn't half-bad. ''I'm from a farm, you see. We had Jerseys.''

''Uh-huh. What made you change your mind? If you don't mind me asking,'' he said.

''Change my mind? What—about the farm?'' She was thoroughly confused.

''No. About raising your baby yourself.''

Abby stared at him and he stared right back. ''As a matter of fact, I do mind you asking but I'm going to tell you anyway, as we're going to be related soon and I see no sense in not doing my best to get along with you, rude man or not.'' She paused, collected every ounce of teacher-trained serenity and went on. ''Now, what *exactly* do you mean, 'changed my mind'?''

''Why'd you decide to marry my brother, after all? Considering you figured you'd raise this kid yourself.'' His gaze was level and cold as steel.

''Because your brother *asked* me to marry him,'' she replied calmly, even loftily. ''And I said I would. That's why.'' Thank heavens! Thank heavens *that* was the truth.

''You must have expected he'd ask—''

''I had no idea he'd ask me to marry him. It never crossed my mind. My only thought was that he had a right to know about the baby. You can believe me or not, I don't care. Has anyone ever told you how incredibly, detestably rude you are, not to mention nosy?''

''Once or twice. You hardly know him. I don't mean in the Biblical sense—''

''I know him well enough to know he's a kind, gentle, generous man!'' she cried. ''I know him well enough to know he'll make a good husband and a wonderful father.''

''Ha!'' Noah drained his beer. ''I'm afraid I know him a lot better than you do, and I can only say I hope you're right.''

''What's that supposed to mean?'' Abby was lost. First it seemed he didn't want her to marry his brother; then it seemed he did.

''Just what I said. I hope you're right. Woman in your condition doesn't have a whole lot of time to check things out.''

Abby and Noah finished their meal in silence. Abby poured herself another half glass of milk, just to show that she wasn't rattled in the slightest, drained it, then stood. ''Thank you for lunch. It was very kind of you to offer,'' she said, smiling sunnily, hoping the irony wasn't lost on him. She was sure it wasn't.

He stood, too. The dog under the table got up and waddled out, woofing softly. Then they heard a pickup drive up and screech to a halt outside. The dog barked twice. Footsteps took the porch steps several at a time.

Jesse!

''Noah? You here? Where's Abby?'' Jesse called

through the open screen door. "She's not in the trailer. You seen her around?"

Abby looked triumphantly at her prospective brother-in-law across the table. *See? He's a kind, generous man who cares a great deal for me, just as I said....*

"Come on in, Jess. She's right here." Noah stepped away from the table and walked to the door just as Jesse pushed it open and walked in. His gaze went swiftly from his brother to her. She smiled.

"Noah gave me some lunch," she said simply. "Wasn't that neighborly?"

Jesse beamed. "Hey, that's great! Well, I got everything done in town—" He took a deep breath and turned to his brother. "Got the license and everything. We're gonna get married on Friday."

It was Thursday now. "Tomorrow?" she asked softly, unable to stop herself from a quick, indrawn breath. This was all happening so quickly....

"No, next week. Magistrate was all booked up until then. That okay, Ab?" Jesse looked worried for a moment.

"That's fine." She moved over to stand close to Jesse. Noah's expression was skeptical. She took Jesse's hand in hers, wishing he didn't look quite so surprised when she did. "That'll give me time to get ready. Buy a dress. Do some shopping. Write a few letters home."

"You finished here? You ready to go back to my place?" Jesse asked.

"Uh-huh." She glanced at Noah and then hated herself for the blush she felt rising to her cheeks.

She knew Jesse only meant that she should come to his place to discuss their plans, maybe have coffee or something. She was a little taken aback by how distant he'd been, physically. He'd done no more than hug her when she got off the bus and hadn't touched her since.

But that wasn't what Noah was thinking... *knowing him in the Biblical sense,* as he'd said. He thought they were going to Jesse's for some leisurely afternoon sex. She felt more acutely aware of everything she said and did around Noah than she did around Jesse, the man she planned to marry. The man who'd made love to her and who'd fathered the child she carried.

Everything was mixed up; everything was wrong.

"You going to the Dexters' anniversary on Saturday?" Noah asked his brother. "Mona will be expecting you."

Jesse smiled at her. "Sure am. Gonna introduce Abby to all the folks."

"The Dexters?" Abby asked. "Who are they?"

"Oh, just some neighbors, Ab," he replied, glancing at his brother. "Old Man and Old Lady Dexter been married fifty years and some of the family got up a surprise party for 'em. At the community hall. We're invited. Noah, too."

"I see." Abby smiled in return. "I'm looking forward to it. Shall we go now, Jesse?"

"Yeah. Let's go." Holding her fiancé's hand, Abby left the kitchen, feeling completely silly about everything that had taken place there. She couldn't help imagining she felt the heat of Noah's gaze on them all the way to Jesse's pickup, but she'd be damned if she'd look back to see if she was right.

And she didn't. She'd finished looking back when she left South Dakota.

CHAPTER FIVE

THE DEXTERS' ANNIVERSARY celebration began with a tea for the older folks on Saturday afternoon, followed by a buffet dinner and dancing at the Glory and District Community Hall.

Noah had decided they'd show up about five, introduce Abby around and then get the hell out of there before the dancing. Normally, he might have considered staying for the whole event, but now that his brother's bride-to-be had arrived from out of nowhere, he figured the best plan was to get in and get out. Avoid the overcurious. The tough part was going to be introducing her as Jesse's surprise ladylove to all their neighbors and friends. No one would be expecting what could only be described as a shotgun wedding from either of the Winslows.

Jesse and Abby were riding with him, as Jesse owned only his pickup, while Noah had both his pickup and a six-year-old four-door Chevrolet sedan, as well. Low-end, nothing fancy, but it served its purpose, which was mainly long highway trips and the occasional date. Taking a woman out to a decent restaurant in a work truck was a teenager's trick, in his opinion.

By half past four he was ready, wearing dress

pants and boots, a crew-necked white knit T-shirt—
Noah couldn't abide ties—and a Western-cut jacket.
He wore a wide-brimmed hat, as usual, only this was
his going-out model, a fine tan-colored beaver-felt
Stetson. He had to adjust the seat on the Chevy,
since Carl had driven it last, then put it into gear
and eased slowly down the hill. He was picking up
the lovebirds at Jesse's house.

He parked in the driveway, and when no one appeared right away, leaned gently on the horn. He
glanced in the rearview mirror. Pat was walking
slowly to her favorite spot behind one of the feed
sheds and, as he watched, she turned three times and
settled down, gazing sadly toward him. That old
poser, he thought. He often took the dog with him
in his pickup, but never in the car.

Where the heck were they? Frowning, Noah got
out and walked toward the back door. Just as he
raised his hand to push the bell, the inside door
opened and Abby appeared behind the screen. She
seemed a little out of breath.

"You two ready?" Noah demanded.

"I—I'm not sure. Jesse isn't feeling well," she
began, hurriedly stepping back as he pulled open the
screen door and walked in.

She had on a mint-green sundress, high-waisted—
to disguise the slight mound of her pregnancy?—
short-sleeved, round-necked. Pearl earrings. She carried a white cardigan sweater over one arm. Her hair
was loose, pale and shining. The dress looked terrific
on her. Very feminine. He'd only seen her in jeans

and a T-shirt until now. "What do you mean, not feeling well?"

"He's got pains. Bad ones. In his back or something. He says he thinks he'd better stay home—"

"No damn way! Where is he?" Noah strode past her. "Jesse, where are you? You'd better get your ass out here right now—"

"Noah!"

"Sorry. I—where in hell is he?" he asked irritably.

"In the living room."

Noah pushed open the glass-sectioned door that led from the small kitchen into the living-dining room of the bungalow. Jesse was perched on the sofa. His hair was awry and he didn't look good. He was wearing jeans and an old work shirt.

"What's wrong with you?"

"I don't feel so hot, Noah," he muttered. He was sweating; Noah could see the beads of sweat standing out on his forehead.

"What—you need a doctor? Should I call someone?"

"No," Jesse said quickly. "No, I'm not that bad. I'll be okay. Just got a few pains in my back and side. I—I think it's from loading that seed order yesterday at the co-op." The day before, Jesse and Abby had gone to Glory. Maybe that was where she'd bought the dress she was wearing. Or maybe she'd brought it all the way from South Dakota.

"Well, damn! This is just *great*—" Noah wheeled.

Abby stood there, clutching her sweater, her eyes huge. "Do you think he *is* okay?" she whispered.

"Oh, he's okay. At least he'll be okay in a day or two," Noah replied. This was a hell of a note. It made him mad. He half believed that Jesse wasn't as bad off as he let on. But damned if he was going to stand here and argue with him in front of this woman.

"You go on ahead, without me," Jesse got out weakly, glancing guiltily up at him.

"Take Abby, you mean?" Noah frowned.

"Sure. Take her along. No sense her sitting out on all the fun just because I'm not up to it."

"Abby?"

She stared at him for a few seconds. "W-will that be all right?"

"Hell, yes. The Dexters won't care. How am I going to introduce her, Jess? As your bride-to-be?" Noah wasn't entirely serious.

"I guess so." Jesse grinned sheepishly. "If that's agreeable to you, Abby."

"Oh, sure. It's fine with me. I just wish you were feeling all right. I hate to leave you like this."

"You go ahead," Jesse repeated, waving at both of them, looking somewhat martyred to Noah's skeptical eye. "Leave me alone here. I'll be fine if I just stay flat on my back for a few hours."

You just do that, Noah thought, stifling a savage oath as he stalked to the car, followed by Abby, who'd run back at the last minute to fetch her purse. *You just lie there and catch a little afternoon wrestling on TV while I ferry your lady to the Dexters and introduce her around as your fiancée. You think there'll be a biddy there who won't notice she's five months gone? It'll be all over the district by the end of the evening. That's if the municipal clerks aren't talking already. Then the surprise wedding coming up next Friday? Hell's bells. Just icing on the cake.*

I'm not going to do it, Noah thought, as he turned out of the ranch lane onto the highway. *Damned if I'm going to be roped into running interference for him.* Not this time. Jesse's a big boy. Big enough to get her pregnant; big enough to handle the ramifications himself.

"Look here, Abby," he said, when they were nearly at the community hall. He realized he'd been rude in not talking the whole way there, but he'd been afraid that if he opened his mouth he might end up having to apologize for what he'd say about his brother. "I'm just going to introduce you as a friend of the family—that okay by you?"

She looked bewildered. "I—I suppose so. Why? Is there some problem?"

"Well, to tell you the truth, I don't like the way I've been set up here—"

"Set up? What, you don't think Jesse's sick?" She sounded alarmed. He reminded himself to take it easy. Here she was, a stranger, pregnant, about to marry a man she barely knew. A man who'd never, in his hearing, used a word of endearment beyond a shortening of her given name. And now he was about to cast doubt on the character of that man— his brother, no less.

"Oh, he's not feeling too great, no question.

Probably strained something. He's had, uh, a back injury before.'' That was sort of a lie. Jesse had pulled a few muscles in his shoulder playing old guys' hockey last winter, but he'd been fine since, as far as Noah was aware. "I'm just not all that comfortable explaining your relationship to my brother and all—do you get my meaning?''

"I do.'' She blushed furiously, but she held his gaze. He had to hand it to her; she had spunk.

"So, if it's all the same to you, I'm just going to let folks think what they want to think, okay? As far as I'm concerned, you're a friend. Friend of the family, that's it,'' he finished firmly. He thought back to their first interchange, at the kitchen table in his house and glanced quickly at her.

She'd already thought of the same thing, he could see, and her eyes were dancing. *"Friend?''*

"We-ell,'' he drawled, allowing himself a smile. "Maybe we won't go quite that far, eh? An acquaintance?''

"That's better.'' She smiled, too, as he returned his attention to the road. So she had a sense of humor about everything that had happened. He was a little ashamed of how he'd grilled her the day he'd met her down by the barn.

He felt a whole lot better now. Damned if his own brother was going to get the jump on him. Jesse could say what he wanted to when he sprang his marriage on the town next week.

It was none of Noah's business, that was for sure.

ABBY FELT she'd never been so looked over in her life. This was what a 4-H heifer must feel, being led

around the show ring! Was it because she was new
to the area? Clearly very pregnant? Or because she'd
shown up more or less on Noah's arm? She suspected the latter. Not exactly his arm—she didn't
think he'd go so far as to offer *that*—but she got the
distinct impression that showing up with Noah
Winslow at all was some kind of notable Glory
event. Either he had a reputation as a loner, which
she could well imagine considering his personality.
Or he was reputed to be quite a womanizer, and she
was the latest living, pregnant proof of that. She
actually got quite a lot of enjoyment out of his dis-
comfiture.

Not that he was rude in any way. In fact, his manners were impeccable. He introduced her to their
hostess, Mona Dexter Wolinsky, as a "friend of the
family, up from South Dakota," which pretty well
took care of everything. She noted a few of the
women glancing casually at her left hand, no doubt
to see if there was a wedding ring on it to go with
the bulge under her dress. She never mentioned that
she was going to marry Noah's brother, nor did he.

Until she'd left Wicoigon, Abby had been happy
that she'd shown little evidence of her pregnancy.
Since then, she'd expanded almost daily. Her jeans
were already too tight at the waist and she'd been
wearing them unbuttoned with a T-shirt overtop
since she'd arrived. Luckily she'd seen this dress in
a shop window in Glory the day before, when she'd
been to town with Jesse, and it had fit perfectly.

While not a maternity dress, it would do for another month or so. She'd need maternity clothes soon.

They'd arrived at the Dexters' anniversary party about five o'clock and, at first, Noah had introduced her to several groups of people at breakneck speed. Abby had never thought of herself as an outgoing person, and she dreaded this kind of situation, especially in her circumstances. It was clear to her that Noah would rather have talked tractors and weather with some of the other ranchers and farmers gathered in little knots at the edge of the dance floor, but he stayed at her side, although the rate of his introductions slowed somewhat. He was probably as nervous about this as she was. She appreciated the fact that he stayed with her. These ordeals were like running some kind of social gauntlet, where you might be alive at the end, but you'd definitely be bruised and bleeding.

Yet this was to be her community. She had to make as favorable an impression as she could. For her sake and for Jesse's. And for the sake of their unborn child, who would grow up here, if everything worked out. That thought gave her strength and she put on her brightest smile and most cheerful expression. It helped that she had a farming background herself. She had something in common with the wives and daughters of farmers and ranchers attending the Dexters' anniversary. She could talk dairy and potluck suppers, at least.

The elder Dexters lived in town now, but were retired grain farmers, from southeast of Glory, almost directly east of the Winslow ranch on the

Horsethief River. Their sons, Norris and Randall, had taken over the family farm, she learned, and were there along with their wives and children. There must have been a hundred people gathered at the old community hall, which echoed with laughter and conversation, and the sounds of the amateur band—fiddle, guitar and accordion—tuning up for the dancing later on.

Abby collected a cup of juice and a slice of banana bread from the long buffet table set up along one end of the room, loaded with refreshments and a variety of sweets. As she'd seen so many times before in rural gatherings, many of the women who arrived carried a plastic-covered square tray or a pie with its meringue protected by a disposable shower cap. She felt even more of an outsider, arriving empty-handed, although some of the other women hadn't brought goodies, either.

"You okay?" Noah asked her once, bending toward her in a press of younger folk, newly-marrieds who'd all gone to the same high school.

"I'm fine," she whispered back, very aware of his being so close to her in the crowd, his hand on her arm. He was an attractive man, she had to admit. Not in the open, smiling manner of his brother. But dressed up, in his white T-shirt and jacket, Noah stood out, tall, even handsome in a dark, lean way. She observed more than one lingering glance from women in the crowd. Noah seemed not to notice any of the attention, but Abby could definitely understand why the women's gazes lingered.

Then she felt shocked at her own perceptions. She

was going to marry this man's brother in less than a week! The last thing she needed was to feel any kind of unseemly attraction toward her future brother-in-law. Good grief! The sad fact was, Abby realized, she was starved for male attention and affection, and that must be why she was having these less-than-appropriate responses to a man like Noah.

Except for the hug when she'd arrived, Jesse still hadn't touched her. No kisses, no hugs, no endearments at all. It was as though she were his sister, arriving pregnant and penniless for a short visit. He was taking care of her, but he wasn't acting in the least like a husband-to-be. She hoped it was temporary. Pregnant or not, burning her bridges back in Wicoigon or not, how could she marry a man who couldn't bear to touch her? Things would have to change, and soon, before she'd irrevocably committed herself by marrying him. She had less than a week to find out.

Noah turned to her. "Abby, there's someone here I'd like you to meet. Kate?" He turned to an attractive, sandy-haired woman with keen eyes.

"Oh, hello, Noah! How are you?" The woman clasped Noah's hand in both of hers briefly, her smile warm.

"Kate, this is Abby Steen. She's a friend from South Dakota who's, uh, visiting. Abby, Dr. Kate Pleasance."

The two women shook hands. Noah moved toward one of the men, in response to something he'd said, and Abby smiled at the doctor, eager to make her acquaintance.

"I'm delighted to meet you, Abby. I see you're, uh—'' she gently nudged Abby's waist and winked in a very friendly manner "—in the family way. How far along?''

Somehow Abby knew it was pure professional interest, not nosiness. She felt relieved. Her doctor back in Wicoigon had urged her to see a doctor in Canada as soon as possible. "Just over five months.''

"Any movement yet?''

"No.'' Abby frowned. It worried her a little that she hadn't felt anything yet. She was quite sure there'd been plenty of movement by now when she'd been carrying her other baby.

"First pregnancy?''

"No. I—I had a baby born dead a year and a half ago.''

"Oh, dear. I'm sorry to hear that.'' Kate Pleasance squeezed her arm gently. "How long are you here, Abby? Would you like to come and see me next week?''

Abby could have kissed her. "Yes, I would,'' she confided. The two women exchanged smiles. Abby liked this sandy-haired young woman. "I've been a little worried. And I'll be here in Alberta for, uh, quite a while actually.''

Kate put her hand on Abby's shoulder. "Nothing to worry about, I'm sure. We'll have a look, listen to things, take some measurements. Next Tuesday? Around noon?''

"Great. I'll be there.'' Abby watched her move

off, smiling and greeting other people, as Noah returned to her side.

"How did you like Kate? She's a doctor, you know."

"I know," Abby said, nodding. "You mentioned it when you introduced us." She appreciated his subtlety, which she wouldn't have expected.

"Yeah, well. Listen, you feel like staying, or you want to get out of here?"

She felt better after speaking with Kate Pleasance. It was an enormous weight off her to have met a medical professional she instinctively liked so soon after arriving in Canada. She'd dreaded the job of finding one. "I wouldn't mind staying for a bit—if you don't mind?"

Noah stared at her for a few seconds. "I thought you'd want to get out of here as soon as you could," he said flatly. "Considering."

"Not really. I'm enjoying this—considering," she added with a smile. It wasn't completely true, but she felt a strong inclination to push Noah. Not to agree with everything he said, to show him she had a mind and a will of her own. She didn't think his opinion of her was all that favorable, so far. She was almost of the belief that he felt she'd entrapped his brother somehow, not that he'd ever come right out and accused her of it.

Let him think she was having a good time this afternoon, regardless of whether *he* was or not. Then she had another thought— "Oh, gosh—you mean Jesse? Maybe we should go. Maybe he needs some help."

"Forget that," Noah snapped, looking over her head toward the buffet table, which had now been set with hot and cold dishes, buns and butter, coleslaw and lettuce salads, pickles—the works. He frowned.

"Let's get some plates," he muttered. He grabbed her hand and led her through the crowd to the line that had formed at the food table. He released her hand as soon as they got there, but Abby couldn't help wondering why he'd done it at all. Probably just didn't want her getting stepped on in the crush, she thought. He'd want her returned to his brother in as good a condition as she'd left him. That was Noah Winslow. Responsible.

They had supper and even stayed for a few dances. Not that Abby danced with Noah, not even once. But despite his looks of annoyance, she danced two dances with a very nice young man who'd spoken to her several times that afternoon. Ben Longquist. And she danced once with an older man who said he worked at an insurance company in town. She couldn't remember his name. And she even danced one dance with an old cowboy from the west side of Glory, who had to be seventy-five if he was a day, although his age hadn't affected his two-step. If she had it right, his name was Henry Hilton. He'd arrived with a small, soft-spoken woman who looked as though she was of South Pacific extraction, the Philippines or Fiji. Abby had noticed she didn't dance at all, simply sat at the side, smiling serenely, her hands folded neatly in her lap, her head bobbing gently to the music.

All in all, Abby had a very good time. Considering. Considering what she'd expected when they left the ranch.

Noah said nothing all the way back, about half an hour, and when they stopped at Jesse's house, she thanked him for taking her and asked if he wanted to come in and check on his brother.

"No. You call me if you need anything," he said brusquely.

Abby got out of the car, bending down to retrieve her purse. "Well, thanks again, Noah. I appreciate the chance to meet your neighbors. Yours and Jesse's."

Noah nodded, rather impatiently, she thought, and she shut the door firmly. He didn't even wait until she'd gone in before putting the car in gear and stepping on the accelerator.

When she went inside, she found Jesse lying on the sofa where they'd left him. A frozen pizza carton on the coffee table and two empty beer cans indicated he hadn't starved while they were gone. The television was on, with a hockey game in progress.

"How are you feeling, Jesse?" she asked softly, sitting down beside him.

He inched over, a little closer to the back of the sofa. So she'd have more room, or so he wouldn't have to touch her?

He flexed his shoulders, as though testing himself. "I'm a lot better. Never mind about me. How was the party?"

"Oh, okay." She smiled at him. "It would've been a lot more fun if you'd been there."

"Oh?" His eyes were suddenly guilty, and Abby recalled what Noah had said about his brother's back problems maybe not being as severe as he'd wanted them to think. "Why's that?"

"Well, just so we could've made things a bit clearer, you know. That's all—"

"What do you mean, 'clearer'?"

Abby looked into his eyes. He seemed very ill at ease. Maybe he was still in a lot of pain. "Noah didn't want to introduce me as your fiancée. He just said I was visiting from the States. He didn't go into any details."

Jesse stared at her for a moment. Abby could have sworn he was relieved. Yet at the same time, she had the impression he wasn't happy with Noah.

"Jesse?" Abby said hesitantly. She would have given anything to be able to take his hand in hers. To have him reach for her, put his arms around her. Hold her.

"Uh-huh?"

"Are you really sure about this?" she asked. He looked tortured. She wished she knew if it was because of his back or because of what he thought she was going to say.

"You mean getting married?" He gave a hoarse laugh. "'Course I am, Abby. I said I wanted to marry you, didn't I? I asked you, didn't I?"

"You did." She smiled and stretched out a hand and he grabbed it and pulled her closer to him.

Awkwardly he kissed her. It didn't do anything for her, and she was sure it didn't do anything for him. It was a fumbling kiss, the kiss of a teenager, not sure of himself at all. Not the assured, confident lover she'd had in Carlisle for those two short nights.

"Oh, Jesse," she said, stroking his cheek and gazing deeply into his eyes. "I was so worried you'd changed your mind about all of this—"

"Have you changed yours?" he interrupted bluntly.

Her eyes searched his. "No. No, I haven't," she repeated. "I was worried you had, though."

He laughed again, a raw sound that barely resembled laughter. "Don't worry about me, Ab. I want to get married. That's my baby you're carrying. I want to be a decent father, a decent husband. You don't need to worry about me."

Abby sat straighter. Now wasn't the time to push for more physical intimacy. Jesse was obviously hurting, and it must be his back. Like most men she knew, he didn't want to admit to the pain.

"I met a doctor today—"

"Oh?" His eyes had wandered to the television, but they shot back to her now. "Who's that?"

"Someone named Kate Pleasance. Do you know her?"

"Yeah, I know her," he said.

"She seems very nice. I'm going to see her on Tuesday."

"What for? Something wrong?" He sounded alarmed.

"No, nothing wrong, Jesse," she said, a little surprised at his reaction. "It's the baby. I need to get things checked out regularly, you know. The doctor back in South Dakota thought it might be twins at—''

"Twins!"

Jesse sat straight up and stared at her in shock.

"Oh, I'm sure it's not twins, Jesse." She felt hurt, damaged by his reaction somehow. "But would it be so terrible if it was? I have twins in my family, you know. My sister's kids are twins."

"Hell." Jesse ran his hand through his dark hair and managed a grin. "I suppose not. Two's no different than one, I guess. Just surprised me when you said that."

"Well, the doctor back home decided it probably wasn't. But I need to see someone as soon as I can. I should be feeling some movement at this point, and so far I haven't."

Jesse was obviously uncomfortable. He reached for her hand, and patted it roughly. "Don't talk about it, Ab. Please don't. It gives me the creeps. I'm sorry, but I'm just not good with that—that doctor stuff. Innards and all. I can't hardly stand being around when calves get born. That's Noah's department."

Abby smiled. "All right. I won't say any more until I've seen the doctor on Tuesday. Now—how about some hot tea or coffee?"

"Tea? Sure. A cup of tea sounds fine." Jesse smiled at her again and she felt her fears subside. He was scared, just as she was, but he was a good man. Somehow they'd see this through. She'd be kind and gentle with him, as he was with her. She'd try and keep most of the physical stuff about the baby to herself. *Innards and all.* It wasn't the way it had been with Frank and her; Frank had been as eager as she was about each new development.

And then Frank hadn't lived to see the baby they'd both wanted so much. And then, her baby had been stillborn.

Abby shivered. A goose walking on her grave, the Wicoigon grannies had said. She stood. "I'll put on the kettle."

She paused at the doorway to the kitchen, and when she glanced back, Jesse was already watching the television again. "Yesss!" he shouted as the crowd noise swelled on the small screen and she heard the announcer's excited babble. A goal had been scored. She felt cold and slipped on her sweater before she ran the water for tea. There was a small sound of something scratching at the door. It couldn't be Stella—Jesse's small dog was with him in the living room.

She opened the door. It was the half-wild dog Jesse had rescued. He'd told her about it when she'd first arrived. Champ. He'd told how shy it was. She hadn't even caught a glimpse of it until now. The dog gazed into her eyes for one startled second, then was gone like a shadow around the corner of the building. Poor thing.

She closed the door and went back to the stove.

Just as she turned on the burner under the teakettle the phone rang.

CHAPTER SIX

NOAH SAT IN HIS CAR for a full five minutes after he came to a stop in his driveway. He saw Pat waiting for him on the porch, her tail wagging slowly.

He wasn't proud of himself. Should he have danced with Abby? He was ticked off with her for wanting to dance at all. In her condition? Damn it, it wasn't right. His brother should have been there looking after her, making sure everything was okay. Dancing with that kid, Ben Longquist, and then that old fool, Henry Hilton. You'd think Henry would have his hands full with that Filipina nanny of Cal Blake's he'd been squiring for three or four years now.

But Letty Esperanza didn't dance. And Abby did.

He recalled the way she'd looked on the dance floor. You could barely tell she was expecting. If you didn't know, you probably wouldn't guess. She'd been happy, her face flushed, her eyes bright. Her hair had swung like liquid silver in the lamplight. He'd actually seen her laughing at some of Henry's jokes, which was saying something. Even Bruce Twist, the insurance salesman, had taken a turn with her.

He was glad she'd agreed to leave after that.

There was going to be enough gossip in the district come next Friday. His brother didn't need any more talk, not about his fiancée cutting up on the dance floor with the district bachelors.

Well, then, why in hell hadn't Jesse come along! Bad back or no. Damn it. Noah got out of the car. Oh, well. He'd done what he could. At least people had had a look at her now. The rest was up to the two of them.

He walked into the house, Pat following, and flicked on a few lights.

He didn't feel good. He felt restless. He felt frustrated. He felt on edge. Things hadn't gone the way he liked them to go, uneventful and easy, not since that woman had arrived. She seemed nice enough— what had Jesse ever done to deserve a nice woman? Even if he *had* gotten her pregnant?

Maybe he should have gone to Jesse's house and taken a look at his brother. Maybe he should have given him the benefit of the doubt. In the back of his mind, Noah always thought of Casey almost dying right here in this house because their father had taunted the boy for a sissy when he'd complained of a sore stomach. When the old man had finally taken it seriously, when his mother had screamed and pleaded with him to take their son to the hospital, it had been too late. In the end, Casey had died of a ruptured appendix. There was nothing old Doc Lake could do.

Sighing, Noah reached for the wall phone and punched in his brother's number.

"Abby? How is he?"

He listened for a few minutes to her report on Jesse's condition. He could tell she didn't think he was doing too badly. If he'd gotten up and fixed himself a frozen pizza and retrieved a couple of beers from the fridge, he couldn't be too sick, Noah snorted to himself. The day Jesse couldn't reach the beer fridge, he was in trouble.

"Okay. Well, listen. I wanted to tell you this on the way back, but I forgot. You go ahead and use my car for anything you need, okay? I've got the pickup and you might as well have a car if you need to go into town or something. I'm heading to Calgary early tomorrow, but I'll leave the keys on the steps of the trailer."

She was grateful. Apparently she'd already arranged an appointment with Kate Pleasance for Tuesday. That was good. Noah hung up the phone and walked to the sink and drew a big glass of cold water. He drank it standing at the counter.

Damn it. He hadn't felt the need of a woman for a long time. Going on a couple of months now. Why in hell did he feel like he did now?

He walked to the pantry and poured out some kibble for Pat and replenished her water dish. Carl took care of the rest of the dogs down at the bunkhouse, from feed Noah provided.

He stared at the black phone on the wall for a long time. He was hornier than a you-know-what-kinda fox in a forest fire, he might as well admit it. Finally he strode to the phone, swearing under his breath.

"Rachel? You expecting company this evening?

Okay, I'll be over, about half past nine.'' Noah smiled as he hung up. Thank God for women like Rachel. Simple, uncomplicated, honest. No games. A woman in a million.

NOAH DECIDED to spend the night at the Bow Valley Inn when the Calgary dinner meeting with a couple of his buyers turned boisterous and boozy and went well into the evening. Not that Noah drank too much. He never did. He couldn't remember the last time he'd been drunk. He'd seen too much of it as a boy, with his father, to ever want to get tangled up with that particular devil.

He liked his beer and he drank wine from time to time, usually on dates, and occasionally he had a glass or two of the hard stuff. Rye whiskey, generally. But he knew his limit and stuck to it.

Still, a good night's sleep in a clean, nondescript hotel room, with a big television at the end of the bed and all the cable you wanted, seemed like a good idea. He hadn't slept much the night before.

His get-together with Rachel hadn't gone the way he'd thought it would. He'd figured a quick roll in the hay was what he needed, but it turned out he was wrong. He ended up sitting in her barn office with her while she sat behind her big scarred wooden desk and did her farm accounts. They just talked. Rachel ran a pig business, selling high-quality breeding sows and boars to other hog farmers. She was five years older, a Jewish woman whose Ukrainian Catholic husband had left her with a barnful of pigs and passel of kids to raise by herself, the last two children still at home. Noah and Rachel had known each other for eight or nine years and been occasional lovers for the past half dozen. This time, he discovered he had no inclination to take his pants off and Rachel never even mentioned it.

She was a good friend, that was all. She was a good friend—in more ways than one—to several men in the district, who regularly stopped in to keep her ''company.'' The men were well aware that they shared Rachel's generosity, but it had never, ever come up for discussion among them. They respected her too much. No one even knew if she and the Ukrainian were legally divorced.

And, truth was, in the past two years or so, his visits to Rachel had fallen right off. He just wasn't interested in plain, uncomplicated sex the way he once was. The way she was. Maybe the idea of Jesse's suddenly getting married and becoming a father had affected him. But when he thought of a half-hour quickie with Rachel on the sofa in her barn office where they always met—she had two teenagers in the house and a barnful of expensive stock she liked to keep her eye on—all he could think of was a mint-green dress, swirling blond hair and a sunny smile. Cornflower eyes. *Jesse's woman.*

Damnation. He could only hope it would be different once they were married. If not, maybe it was time for the brothers to split and go their own ways. It wasn't the first time he'd had the notion, although he and Jesse had never seriously discussed it since Brandis's death. The old man had left his share of the ranch to Noah, which left Jesse with a quarter, half of his mother's share.

He had a meeting as soon as the bank opened in the morning, and then he was going to head home, right after lunch.

He got back to the Lazy SB about two o'clock. He noticed that the pickup and horse trailer Jesse had parked by his house that morning were gone. Maybe Abby was with him. Jesse often moved his own cutting horses and mares from ranch to ranch, lending or renting them out if a rancher was short, or having one of his mares covered by a neighbor's stallion. Noah never inquired and Jesse never told him his personal affairs. They shared a business and they were brothers, but they weren't in each other's pockets, like some families. Things worked out better that way, in their view.

The car was parked by the trailer. He was glad Abby had decided to use it, after all. Maybe she'd driven it to the doc's office this morning.

He got out of his pickup, bent to fondle Pat's ears, then went upstairs to change into work clothes. He planned to ride some fence this afternoon, maybe check on the new calves. Carl was still working on the machinery, readying it for spring planting.

He'd just pulled on his jeans and grabbed a shirt when he heard a commotion downstairs. Pat barked excitedly. Someone was yelling—

"*Noah!* Oh, Noah! Are you home?" It was Abby.

Noah raced down the stairs, carrying his shirt. What the hell—

"Oh, Noah, I'm so glad you're here—" Abby

collapsed against the outside of his screen door. "I don't know—" She buried her face in her hands, her forehead bulging weirdly against the screen, her image fuzzy through the wire. "Oh, what should I *do?* I don't know what to do now," she moaned.

"Abby! What the hell's going on?" Then he remembered she'd been to see Kate....

"Here." He pushed at the screen door, forcing her away, then stepped out. He grabbed her shoulders and shook her slightly. "What's the matter? Is it something to do with the baby? Something's wrong with the baby—what? *Answer me!*"

"No, it's not the baby—it's Jesse!"

Jesse? "What about Jesse? His back?" Damn, he wanted to shake her silly. She'd put one hand on her belly at his mention of the baby. Thank God everything was all right there. "What about him?"

She took a deep breath and stared at him, tears welling up and spilling over to run down her pale cheeks. "He's gone, Noah. *Gone.* He's left. He's not coming back—"

"Damn it, woman!" Noah released her and angrily pulled on his shirt, his eyes searching hers as he rapidly buttoned it. "What are you *talking* about? What do you mean 'he's gone'?"

"This." She fumbled in her skirt pocket—he only really noticed then that she was dressed for town—and took out a balled-up sheet of lined paper. She gave it to him. *"This!"* she cried. Pat whined anxiously and tried to lick her hand.

Noah opened the crumpled paper and scanned the few lines on the page.

I'm so sorry, Abby. I wish I could have stayed and faced up to it, but I just can't. I can't marry you. I'll never bother you, I promise, no matter what. I'll send some money when I get settled, for you and the baby, care of your folks.

The letter was signed simply, Jesse. Noah swore and then he turned around and swore again at the empty doorway. His brain was spinning. *Left her!* The stupid, useless sonuvabitch had left her. High and dry. Alone. Pregnant. Up here in Canada, nowhere to go, no one to turn to—except him. Had Jesse counted on that? Had Jesse counted on him providing her with money, with whatever it took to get her back to South Dakota, back to her former life?

Suddenly he was furious—with her. "Didn't I *tell* you he wasn't the man you thought he was? He's a damn fool and a coward, that's what he is! Didn't I tell you I knew him a lot better than you did?"

"Noah!" she wailed. "How can you say that now? Now that he's taken off? I can't believe you could say such a stupid thing!" She actually stamped her foot she was suddenly so angry. At *him!* "What if he *hadn't* taken off—then what? Would that change it? Would he be the man I thought he was then?"

Pat came over and tried to lick her hand again. "Oh, heck, I can't explain anything." She sank down onto the porch and wrapped her arms around the collie's neck and buried her face in the dog's furry ruff, sobbing.

Noah felt like a heel. A monster. What a creep. *That's all she needs, you whaling her out. None of this is her fault, none. Except for sleeping with the jerk in the first place.*

"Come on," he said, leaning down and taking her by the arm. She staggered to her feet. "Come inside and let's talk this over."

She followed him into the kitchen. He sat her down on a kitchen chair and went to the fridge. Iced tea. Regular tea would be better—his mother had always sworn by a cup of tea in any crisis—but there was no time for that. He poured her a glass of the iced version and set it in front of her.

"Drink that."

"I don't want it." She sniffed and ground the heels of her hands into her eyes. "Do you have a Kleenex?"

He handed her a roll of paper towels. Then he ran the faucet and filled the kettle and put it on the stove, after setting the tray of first-aid materials on top of the fridge. They might need that tea yet before this was all sorted out.

He sat down opposite her at the table and observed her silently for a few minutes, while she got hold of herself. She looked pretty, despite the puffy red eyes. She had on a denim skirt and a T-shirt. Gold hoop earrings. She must have gotten dressed up to go into town. *Town.* He wanted to know how it had gone with the doctor, but this wasn't the time to ask.

"You have any notion he planned this?" Noah

had his own suspicions, but he was keeping them to himself.

"No." She wiped her eyes with a crumpled paper towel. "I brought it up when we got back from the anniversary on Saturday. You know, getting married. I was worried he'd changed his mind and I asked him if he had and he said he hadn't, that he wanted to be a good husband and a good father."

Noah set his jaw grimly. "You two, uh—you know, make love since you got here?"

She looked dismayed. "No. He—he never even touched me. That's why I thought maybe he'd had a change of heart," she whispered, obviously embarrassed. Her cheeks were very pink. "He seemed very—well, distant." She glanced up at him, as if *he* had any answers.

He didn't. "Distant" didn't really sound like his brother. "When do you think he took off? When you went to the doctor?"

"I guess so. I left here about half past eleven and he was down at the house. He carried some boxes out to the trailer behind his truck this morning, but he told me he was just clearing out some old junk so we'd have more room once we were married."

"Bastard!" Noah ignored her shocked expression. "Liar! He was probably moving out whatever he wanted to take with him. I bet if we go down there, we'll see he's taken his clothes, his saddle, his boots, his stereo—"

"I had a quick look around when I went in. The house wasn't locked. I think you're right. I think some of that stuff was gone." She was calmer now.

She stared down at her lap, twisting the piece of paper towel.

Noah cleared his throat. "You got money?"

"A little." She shrugged. "Enough."

"Enough to go home?"

She didn't reply at first, and Noah cursed himself silently when he saw the tears roll down her cheeks again. "I can't go home again, I just can't," she said. He had to strain to hear her words. "I told everyone I was getting married in Canada. They all know I'm pregnant and a widow and you have no idea how that news went over with my parents or my parents' friends." She shuddered. "It was horrible—*horrible!* How can I go back and say I'm not getting married, after all?"

She tried hard to stifle her tears, with very little effect. She mopped at her eyes. "I quit my job. I don't think I could get it back—who's going to hire a teacher who's expecting in August? A widow with a baby on the way? No husband? Maybe—maybe I could start over somewhere else—" She buried her head in her hands again and her shoulders shook.

She looked frail. She looked hopeless and helpless. All Noah's deepest instincts told him that this was not how things should be. A pregnant woman was sacred. A pregnant woman needed protection. A pregnant woman was a gift to the community. She brought life into the world, regardless of the circumstances.

The kettle had started to boil. Noah got up and took it off the stove and poured some hot water into a teapot. He swirled the water around and dumped it in the sink, then stuck two teabags in the pot. He poured more boiling water over the bags and put the lid on. Then he reached up into the cupboard and got down two mugs. He carried the teapot and the mugs to the table.

"You take milk or sugar?"

She shook her head. "I don't care for hot tea."

Noah took his own mug to the fridge and slopped in some milk. He dropped in two sugar cubes from the box on the counter. Then he returned to the table.

"It's just called tea, Abby. Okay? Up here, in this country, we drink *tea*," he said irritably. "*Iced* tea is the other stuff." He absently fastened the lower two buttons on his shirt. Then, after the tea had steeped for a few minutes, he poured himself a mugful of the steaming brew on top of the sugared milk.

He glanced at her. She was gazing out the window on the far side of the kitchen. She looked drawn and very tired. Lost. "I have one idea," he said.

"About this?" She waved a hand weakly toward Jesse's bungalow.

"About this." He blew on his tea and sipped carefully. It was damn hot.

"What's your idea?"

"You could marry me."

"*You!*"

"Yeah, me." He looked at her. She was aghast. Jeez, this wasn't very flattering. "Why not?"

"Why *not?*" she echoed. She spread her hands wide and glanced wildly up at the ceiling for help. "Because—because you have nothing to do with this! Because this isn't your concern. Because I don't even know you—''

"You didn't know Jesse all that well,'' he interrupted dryly.

"Yes, but...that was different. We'd met. We'd—we'd—'' She stopped. He knew what she'd been thinking. They'd made love. They had a baby in common.

"Sure,'' he said. "You're right. It's not the same. Forget I mentioned it.'' He sipped at his tea, which had cooled a little now. "You got any other bright ideas?''

"I—I can't believe you're serious!'' Abby stared at him. "That you said this! *Marry* you?''

"Serious as can be. It makes a lot of sense. You're up here now and you can't go back home, you say. I can see why not. Then there's the fact that I'm not married. You're not married. You've been here a week already. Nobody really knows why. People are talking, though, that's for sure. No one knows you planned to get hitched with Jesse on Friday. Unless some clerk's been talking, which I doubt. I mean, hell, maybe people think *I'm* the one responsible for getting you pregnant!'' The thought hadn't really occurred to him. Until now. The urge to laugh died as suddenly as it had arisen.

"But—''

"Don't get me wrong, I'm not trying to talk you into anything, but you could do a lot worse. I'm healthy, I'm normal as far as these things go—'' He ventured a quick glance at her shocked face. "I'm pretty well set, no money problems to speak of. I don't have—well, I don't have real high expectations of any kind about a woman or about marriage.'' That was true enough; until ten minutes ago he'd never even thought of marrying. At all.

"But you don't even *like* me!" she said on a rising note, with an exasperated motion of her hands.

"That's true. I didn't like you much at first. I figured you'd set my brother up or something. I had no idea what he was getting himself into and I wasn't sure he did, either. I felt I had to look out for him." Noah paused and gave Abby a deliberate smile. "So? My opinion has changed. I don't mind you all that much anymore. You've got grit. I like that in a woman."

"You're crazy, Noah Winslow. Do you realize that?"

"Probably. Anyway, this is just temporary talk. To solve the current problem. We could get hitched, you have that baby in the summer. Who knows, maybe Jesse will change his mind and come back, maybe he won't. Either way, you can do what you like once the baby's born and you're healthy and everything's all right. I don't care. Move back to South Dakota when you feel you're up to it, if that's your preference." He waved one hand. "Divorce is easy enough. Marry Jesse if you two have made up by then. Don't marry anybody. Doesn't matter to me."

"What if I want to stay married? To you," she blurted out, looking as surprised that she'd said it as he was to hear it.

"Me?" That hadn't occurred to him.

"Yes, you. I'm not sure I like the idea of getting married and unmarried and then maybe marrying someone else. I mean, for what?"

He considered. "There's always that possibility, I suppose. But, to be honest, I don't think things would work out with me. I'm not the husband and father type. We could keep an open mind about it, though, keep our options open. I suppose things could change. Sure, why not?" he finished quickly. "It's an option."

She observed him silently for a full minute or so. "You really are *serious,*" she said finally, still looking astonished.

"That's right. I really am."

CHAPTER SEVEN

THE NEXT MORNING, Noah knocked at the trailer door before Abby had finished breakfast. It was a gorgeous spring morning, absolutely quiet except for the occasional cry of some prairie bird, a goldfinch or a warbler, perhaps, swooping high in the clear air. Yesterday, with all its upset and surprise, might not have happened.

Except it had. She had only to glance in the direction of Jesse's house to have that horrible feeling of being abandoned come right back again.

Now Noah was marrying her. Her head was spinning....

"Good morning!" She might as well be positive. She hadn't yet come to grips with the change in her circumstances; that would take more than one night of fitful sleep. But she'd decided there was only one way to go on and that was straight ahead. On the other hand, she didn't want him to think she'd expected or planned this outcome, marrying him instead of his brother. Well, how could she possibly have known Jesse would take off? Then she had to laugh at her own notions—the evidence clearly showed that she'd marry anyone who asked!

"'Mornin'." Noah nodded briefly. "I stopped by

to tell you Donna will pick you up just before eleven. That okay?''

"Fine." Abby still wasn't sure what she thought of this—one of Noah's old flames taking her shopping for wedding clothes. He'd called Donna Beaton yesterday afternoon, before Abby had left his house, to see if she'd oblige. It had been his idea, one hundred percent. Abby would've been happy wearing the dress she'd worn to the Dexters' anniversary party. She was surprised, frankly, that Noah would either notice or care what she wore to her own wedding. What did it matter?

"I'll be gone most of the day," he said, lifting his hat, raking back his hair, then settling it again. "Looks like decent weather." He cast an experienced eye at the horizon. "I've got to check out some of the dugouts on the other side of the river today, make sure the cattle are getting enough clean water."

Abby watched him get back in his pickup. So that was that. Business as usual. Pat woofed from her position in the passenger seat and wagged her tail. Abby smiled and waved at the dog. And at Noah.

He waved briefly and put the pickup in reverse, backing out onto the graveled roadway that connected his house and Jesse's. Then he and the dog were gone.

Abby took a couple of deep breaths of the clear clean air. She felt the tiny flutter of movement deep in her belly and put both hands against her sides. She felt relatively good, considering what had happened yesterday. She was healthy; the baby—or babies—was healthy. Thank heavens for that. She had a doctor now, someone she liked. A home, of sorts. She was marrying a rather strange and formidable man on Friday, but, oddly enough, he was a man she trusted completely. Right now, unbelievable as it was, acquiring a husband and a home and some security was more important than who that husband was. She couldn't go back to Wicoigon, and Dr. Pleasance suspected she was carrying two babies, after all. They'd be born in a few short months. Right now, she desperately needed someone to lean on. Noah was that someone.

For a woman in her…unusual circumstances, life was about as good as it could be.

Donna was the soul of discretion. She was a pretty, dark-haired woman in her mid- to late-thirties. She told Abby that she had a son and daughter, both in high school, and ran a small business, a gift shop, in the town of Glory. Today, Wednesday, was a half day for her. She had a girl in the shop who'd close up at noon.

"I'm looking forward to this, to tell you the truth," she said cheerfully as they drove toward Calgary. According to Donna, Calgary had far more to offer than Glory or High River. "Not often I get to shop for clothes for someone else. Jen just hates it if I buy her anything. You know teenagers."

Abby smiled. She thought of her niece, Pepper. She'd heard her sister, Meg, bemoan the fact that she couldn't buy anything for her twins anymore. They had their own definite ideas of what was cool and what was not.

Abby wasn't sure about Donna's relationship with Noah, and she didn't ask. She wasn't entirely sure she wanted to know. She knew they'd dated in the past, but that was apparently ancient history. Thank heavens, Donna knew about her pregnancy—also thanks to Noah, she presumed.

"When's the baby due?" Donna asked casually as they approached the outskirts of the city of Calgary. Donna had mentioned trying South Centre first, a mall that apparently had a lot of ladies' clothing shops. It didn't matter to Abby where they shopped.

"August." Abby smiled proudly and clasped her hands over her swollen waist. "It might be twins. I'll know for sure next week after the ultrasound."

"Twins!" Donna whistled, her eyes wide. "Wow, that'll be a big change in your lives. Noah will love it. He likes kids, but I guess you know that."

"I didn't know," Abby began, genuinely surprised. Then she stopped, not wanting Donna to guess how very little she did know about her prospective husband.

"Oh, he's definitely the homebody of the two brothers, that's for sure. Jesse was always here and there, and Noah was back home, looking after the cattle. The calves. The horses. Whatever." Donna smiled. "I get the impression Noah's always liked the idea of being a daddy, but he was never too interested in getting married. Guess he changed his mind when he met you, huh? I knew he was away for a while last fall, but I didn't know he was down visiting you. I'm thrilled to hear about it, you know. You and Noah and this family that's coming along soon. Noah's been the sly one, all right!''

That was the understatement of the year, Abby thought, dismayed. Visiting *her?* Noah had obviously let Donna think he and Abby had had a long-standing relationship and that he'd fathered the baby or babies she carried. They hadn't talked about it, except for the supposition he'd thrown out yesterday that maybe folks around Glory would just naturally assume she was Noah's intended. She had no idea what to say about all that and hoped Donna wouldn't inquire further.

Definitely time to change the subject. Luckily, they were turning into the parking lot of a big mall just then.

The two women spent a pleasurable couple of hours trying on clothes. Abby got into the spirit of the occasion, although she hadn't been keen on it at the beginning. Donna was irrepressible, always full of ideas. She made Abby try on a purple velvet gown and platform high heels. They both laughed and laughed. Abby realized she wasn't just acquiring a wedding wardrobe; she was acquiring a friend, as well.

Had Noah known she'd need someone besides him in her new life in Glory? A woman? If he had— and she doubted any man could be quite so insightful or subtle about it—he'd done the right thing suggesting this day trip with Donna Beaton.

She ended up with a gauzy sleeveless cotton dress, cream-colored and high-waisted. Donna made her buy some shoes to match, strappy white sandals, although she had a pair of plain pumps at home that would have done perfectly well.

Home. The trailer. The ranch.

"You need a hat to go with that," Donna decided, when they got back to her car with their packages. "I know just the place, downtown."

"A hat!" Abby put both hands to her head. "No way I'm wearing a hat."

"Oh, yes, you are," Donna said mildly. "It's a wedding, isn't it? You've got to have a hat."

Abby humored her, with no intention of buying a hat when they actually got downtown. She came out of Madame Horrick's boutique in the Eau Claire area an hour later, clutching a hatbox containing a pale broad-brimmed Panama hat with a dreamy satin ribbon that matched her dress perfectly. Donna, who'd admitted she was mad for hats, came out with a purchase, too.

The two women had a late lunch at Desiree's on Tenth, stopped at the Hudson's Bay Company department store for baby supplies—again, at Donna's insistence—and headed home in the late afternoon. Happy, hopeful and thoroughly exhausted. A girls' day out. For a few hours Abby had forgotten what a mess her life was. The day had been so...so refreshingly *ordinary*.

THAT WAS HOW, at ten o'clock Friday morning, Abby Steen found herself marrying Noah Winslow, instead of his brother. Noah, practical as ever, had simply gone to Glory the day after he'd come up with his amazing proposal and gotten a new marriage license with his name and birth date on it, and Abby's, and they used the appointment Jesse had already made at the Glory courthouse. Only a clerk or two would ever know that she'd originally planned to marry another Winslow.

Just as they turned onto Main Street, Noah pulled in beside a florist's shop and got out, telling her he'd just be a moment. He reappeared in a few minutes with a gorgeous wedding bouquet of tiny roses and irises and miniature calla lilies, in shades of cream and pink and yellow. Abby gasped, stunned at the thoughtfulness of the gesture, and then had a fleeting thought that perhaps Donna was behind this, too.

"Thank you," she said and took the arrangement from him, burying her nose for a moment in the cool, delicate fragrance.

"A bride needs flowers," Noah said gruffly. She stole a glance at him. He seemed determined to do everything the way he felt it should be done.

He continued to the courthouse, where they were being married in ten minutes. Abby felt her heart pounding in her chest. Her babies were restless, too. Was she doing the right thing, marrying this man?

Too late to change her mind now.

When they'd parked, he turned to her and tilted her chin toward him—for a moment she thought he might kiss her. Then, with a serious expression, he straightened her hat ever so slightly. "You're a beautiful bride, Abby. I'm a lucky man. No matter how this started out. I never planned on getting married, I'll admit. But that's all in the past. What's done is done. I'm glad I'm marrying you, I want you to know that, before we go through with it."

She felt tears spring to her eyes. "E-even with my tummy out to here?" she said in a quavery voice, desperate to keep back the tears.

He placed one hand briefly on her waist. "I think it's fine. I've always thought a pregnant female is the most beautiful creature on this earth." Which stunned her. Until she realized he could as easily have been talking about mares or cows. Or hippos.

There was no one in attendance. No relatives. No friends. Donna had said she'd like to be there, but Abby had insisted she stay away, promising to wear the hat and dress for her another time. A couple of part-time clerks on coffee breaks witnessed the necessary documents uniting the serious-looking rancher and the very pregnant stranger.

When the judge invited Noah to kiss his bride, he did. He pulled her roughly into his arms and gave her a masterful kiss—powerful, deep, thorough. Not satisfying at all. Frightening, in fact. Abby was thrown into a panic. What about this side of things? The physical side. They hadn't discussed anything but the mechanics of getting through the marriage ceremony. They hadn't discussed being husband and wife, and what that meant. Presumably, considering the peculiar circumstances, there wouldn't *be* a physical side to the marriage. After all, this was a marriage of convenience, by the clearest possible definition. Wasn't it?

Noah seemed oblivious. He took Abby for lunch to Molly McClung's Delicatessen, a small deli-cum-

restaurant on the town square. There was nothing
upscale about it. They had cream of asparagus soup
with barley and a vegetarian lasagna that was the
lunch special. Followed by apple pie for Noah and
ice cream for Abby. Several people who knew Noah
came in during the hour or so they were there, and
Noah nonchalantly introduced her as his wife, Abby
Winslow. He ignored their surprise. Or enjoyed it.
Abby couldn't tell.

At least it didn't interfere with his appetite. He
ordered a second piece of pie and then they left.
Abby felt ill. Too much had happened, too fast. She
was married to a man she didn't know. She'd come
here to marry his brother—also a man she barely
knew.

What was the matter with her?

And her new doctor had informed her she was
quite sure it was twins, after all. Kate had booked
her for an ultrasound the following week.

She hadn't told Noah yet.

EVERYTHING SEEMED pretty straightforward. Noah
was surprised, though, at how little his new wife
said on the way home from town after the wedding.
He thought she'd be full of questions, about this and
that. What did she expect, a honeymoon?

Surely not. Although she looked gorgeous enough
in that wedding dress to go for the whole nine
yards—wedding, dance, honeymoon.

When they stopped at her trailer, she gazed at him
anxiously for a few seconds, then got out. He got
out, too, and stood beside the car as she walked

toward the steps of the trailer. He had to take it easy.
Not rush her into anything. He had a feeling he'd
pushed things a little already by kissing her the way
he had after the ceremony. He didn't want to scare
her. *What did he want?*

"Can you pack up all right by yourself?"

"Pack up?"

"Your clothes and stuff," he said, frowning.
"You're moving up to the house with me, right?
Now that we're married?"

"We never talked about that."

"We're talking about it now. I think you should.
We *are* married, and we'd better look like we're
married."

"I suppose so." She glanced doubtfully at him,
then turned back to the trailer. It was a shabby affair,
old and weathered. He was going to disconnect the
plumbing and electricity and pull the trailer out back
behind the bunkhouse, as soon as he figured out
what to do with Jesse's prefab. He wasn't going to
rent it. He was finished with having people live on
the place. People besides cowhands, anyhow. From
now on, Winslow Herefords and the Lazy SB Ranch
were his operation. His and, now that he was married, Abby's.

But you couldn't leave a house empty for too long
or it'd start to deteriorate. The question was, would
Jesse be coming back? And the next question was,
if he did, would Noah allow him to stay here?

He didn't know the answers yet. But he did know
he had to get settled in the house with his new wife

and get back to his regular activities. And the sooner the better. He had work to do.

"An hour or so?" He shaded his eyes against the early-afternoon sun. If he was lucky, he'd have a few hours with Big Blue, the quarter horse-cross he was training. He still had some fence to ride and the horse would be frisky. He'd give him a good gallop while getting some work done. No sense putting off until tomorrow what you can do today, Brandis had always said. Or, as Jesse used to kid him, was it the other way around? "I'll come down then and pick up your stuff."

He climbed back in the car and drove toward the house. When he got there, he happened to glance in his rearview mirror. Abby was still standing outside the trailer in her wedding finery, staring at the car.

Strange woman.

What the hell was wrong with her?

Noah didn't have a lot of useful experience with the fair sex. And as for marriage, none. Mind you, this wasn't a normal sort of marriage, the way it had come about. Anyway, all he had to do was get along with her for a few months. And if she wanted to stay, as she'd suggested? He didn't think that possibility had a snowball's chance in hell, but he'd keep an open mind. Anything could happen when the baby was born.

His niece or nephew. According to the law, his son or daughter.

Noah recalled the soft pressure of Abby's mouth when he'd kissed her. He had to admit he'd been itching to do that for quite a while. The humor of having to marry her to get the opportunity didn't escape him. He smiled as he climbed the stairs to his room to change.

She was kissable, all right. Whether he would've given her a second look in other circumstances—well, who could say?

Noah stood in the doorway and studied his bleak, sparsely furnished room. Maybe he'd better give her this one, since it had a bathroom across the hall. There was a smaller room farther down, at the corner of the house, Casey and Jesse's old bedroom when they'd been kids. He could move his stuff into that. There was an iron double bed in there, with a dresser and a lamp and a chair, if memory served him.

He walked down the hall and pushed open the door. He was right. An upholstered chair. A closet. Even a student desk with an old-fashioned goose-necked lamp on it that must've been left from when the boys were small. Everything was thick with dust. Noah entered the room, leaving a ghostly track in the dust on the wooden floor. Damn, when was the last time he'd even been in here? He'd have to get the house cleaned, he supposed. At least vacuum it. He supposed he could handle that himself. He sighed. He couldn't remember the last time somebody had slept in this room. Jesse or Casey? Challa had shared his bed.

He opened the window wide, with its full view of the Rocky Mountains in the distance, and let the spring breeze in, blowing the dusty curtains back. A good cleaning and some fresh air. Maybe dab some paint here and there. Abby could have done worse for herself, he was sure.

Best bring his stuff over to the corner bedroom, before he got her things. And put new sheets on the bed. That was the least he could do.

Noah changed his clothes and then vacuumed the spare bedroom, cursing that he hadn't thought of this earlier and hired someone. He stripped the sheets from the bed in his room, stashed them in the laundry downstairs and piled a new set he'd found, not even opened, on the mattress. Just for the hell of it, he gave his old bedroom a run-over with the vacuum and tossed out a bunch of magazines that had accumulated on his chest of drawers. He gave the bathroom across the hall a swish or two. He cleared out everything he owned and carried it to the room he'd chosen. They'd have to share the bathroom on this floor. The whole job took him just over an hour.

Then, with a glance across the river to see how the weather was holding, he left the house and drove the short distance to the trailer. She came out right away and stood on the steps. She hadn't changed her clothes, although she'd taken off the hat. It didn't look as though she'd done anything at all.

"You ready?"

"I'm staying here until tomorrow, Noah," she said firmly. She folded her arms across her chest. He noted that the swell of her pregnancy had begun to form a little shelf just below. "I've got a few letters to write home to my folks and things to do and—well, I'm going to stay right here until after breakfast tomorrow. I need to do some thinking."

Noah paused and stared at her. He was surprised. But, on the other hand, he wasn't. Nothing much surprised him anymore. "Okay. Fine." He settled his hat on his head. "I've got a few things to do this afternoon myself. I guess you can get your own supper?"

"Yes."

"Fine," he said again. "I'll stop in tomorrow after breakfast." He turned to leave, to get back into his pickup. "There's a room ready for you upstairs. I've fixed up a room for myself down the hall. You don't have to worry about me making myself disagreeable." *Or agreeable.* He cracked a smile and thought he saw her shoulders slump a little. Had she been worried he would?

Hell.

"See you tomorrow, then," she said, and waved.

He waved back.

Funniest damn pair of newlyweds Glory and district had ever produced. Good thing nobody would notice, except maybe Carl Divine, his foreman, and dollars to doughnuts Carl wouldn't notice a thing, either. Carl generally kept to himself down at the bunkhouse.

Well, at least his foreman was going to be pleased about the trailer. Noah would hand it over to him. Cheaper to heat for one fellow. Carl could have his privacy, smoke the cigars he liked so well, sing along with that squeeze-box of his whenever he wanted, and they'd just open up the bunkhouse when they hired a crew. Branding, haying, spring and fall roundup.

Noah parked the pickup and walked down to the barn to fetch a rope to throw on Big Blue. Blue had a little Thoroughbred blood in him. Nothing like a good hard ride across the spring grass on the hills to settle a man's blood. And his thoughts.

NEXT MORNING, Abby gazed around in dismay as she walked through Noah's house. The living room was about as cluttered and depressing as the kitchen and the upstairs. The window blinds were down—old-fashioned dust-gathering venetians that looked like they were rarely raised—and even the pictures on the walls were dim with neglect. Ancient, holey knitted afghans and crocheted throws covered every bit of furniture. It gave her the creeps. Old magazines were stacked in piles. On one end table was a shoe-polishing kit, with brushes and cloths. On another stood, oddly, a ceramic mug filled with new, freshly sharpened pencils.

Abby wandered over to the older-model cabinet TV in the corner, its top littered with pictures that had obviously stood there for years. A grim-looking man who looked remarkably like Noah, and a pretty woman, a wedding picture. Maybe his parents? A curling trophy—Glory Bonspiel, 1984. A photograph of a horse, grazing in a field, with mountains in the distance. Several cow trophies, brass on mahogany, festooned with cobwebs. A framed snapshot of three boys, freckled, grinning. They must be Jesse, Noah and a friend. Or was there another brother? She inspected the photo closely and then set it down and wiped her hands on her shirt.

How long had Noah lived here? Had he ever bought anything new? Thrown anything out? Had he ever had the place cleaned properly? Had he ever changed anything from the way his parents had left it?

And what had happened to his parents, anyway? Jesse had said that their mother was dead, but there'd been no mention of a father.

She shuddered and climbed the stairs again, to the room she'd been assigned. Noah had brought her things up to the house, as he'd said he would, after breakfast and then he'd left her, saying he had stuff to do and he'd try and be back around suppertime. He gave her the keys to the car and told her it was hers to use whenever she wanted. He also laid a wad of twenty-dollar bills on the kitchen table and told her to buy what she needed. After he'd left, she'd counted them. Four hundred and sixty dollars.

She was relieved that he was leaving her alone for the day. She found his presence very unsettling. She had no idea what was in his head, none at all. At times he seemed so serious. Other times, she'd have sworn he was laughing at her. Then there were the odd glimpses that showed her he was a man with a man's feelings. *For her.*

She didn't know what to think anymore. But she reminded herself that she had a lot to do before her baby—babies—were born, and afterward. She was trying to train herself to think of two babies now, not one. She couldn't stand about mooning over a man she barely knew. Even if he *was* her brand-new husband of all of twenty-four hours.

Dr. Pleasance had said that it wasn't uncommon for a second baby to be overlooked in the early months. But now both babies had grown and a second heartbeat was quite distinct. The ultrasound scheduled for Monday would settle things. On the one hand, Abby was delighted. On the other, wouldn't twins make it that much harder to start a new life for herself if she did return to South Dakota in the next year or so?

Two babies, she thought. Just like Meg. Boys? Girls? One of each? Would her parents be pleased with two new grandchildren, once they'd recovered from the shock of her sudden decision to leave and get married in Alberta? She hadn't told them of the change in her plans. She hadn't mentioned that she'd married the babies' uncle, not their father, after all. Why complicate things? They were tangled enough as it was.

She had absolutely no faith that Jesse would return, or that he'd want to be a father to her babies sometime down the road if he ever had the nerve to come back. But she could hardly rule it out. In fact, given time, the possibility wasn't that remote. He was Noah's brother and business partner; these were his babies she was carrying. He could very well have a change of heart and want to be part of their lives. She hadn't thought of how she'd deal with that, if it happened.

Deep down, she didn't really want him to come back. He'd deserted her. Left her. He'd wounded her deeply by abandoning her the way he had, leaving only a note. Noah was right; it was the action of a coward. Yet she could understand the pressure he must have felt. If she'd had any idea how ambivalent he felt toward her and marriage and fatherhood, she'd never have left South Dakota. She would've worked things out for herself and her babies, somehow.

For now, Jesse Winslow was out of the picture. Noah Winslow was the man she needed to focus on. She had no more expectation than he did that their marriage would amount to anything, despite her statement to Noah that she had no interest in getting married, then divorced. Looking at it rationally, this quickie marriage had just been a convenience—for her, mainly. She had no idea why he'd really married her. Perhaps to save face in the community, since he'd already been seen with her and she was clearly in the family way, as the doctor had so quaintly put it. And now that he *had* married her, he wasn't going to confess to his friends and neighbors that his brother was responsible for her pregnancy, was he? Still, she couldn't quite see Noah Winslow caring a heck of a lot what other people thought of him.

Hands on her hips, Abby surveyed the bedroom she'd be sleeping in. She couldn't stand the walls, a sort of dirty tan. Oyster? Mouse? She couldn't bear the thought of using Noah's blankets and pillows—*any* sheets and blankets, for that matter. She was used to a feather duvet, the most common bedcover in the Scandinavian and German communities of South Dakota.

Thank goodness at least the sheets were new. She

glanced again at the empty blue-glass cough-mixture bottle with the pussy willows stuck in it, which Noah had left on the dresser as a sort of silent welcome. It was a deeply sweet gesture. Wholly unexpected. It made her think that perhaps the wedding bouquet had been his idea after all, not Donna's.

Abby checked her watch. Not quite eleven. She had plenty of time to fix up this room before she had to sleep in it. She went downstairs and picked up the money on the table and stuffed it in her handbag, along with the car keys. Then she carried down all the blankets that had been on Noah's bed and started the first load going in the washing machine, which looked fairly new. In fact, the stove, washing machine and dryer, refrigerator and microwave all looked new.

Once the washing machine was humming, Abby inspected the contents of the refrigerator. There were pickles and mayonnaise and beer and sliced meats, bacon, eggs, a crisper full of straightforward vegetables like carrots and celery, quite a few kinds of cheese and salsa and two or three hot sauces, plus a bottle of a dark, evil-looking sauce called HP. The freezer contained frozen meat, fruit juices, Sara Lee cakes—mostly chocolate—and frozen fries.

Singing softly, aware that she was actually enjoying herself, Abby took out the makings for a stew. It was like playing house—only this was a real house, and it was hers now. She put the meat in the microwave to thaw while she went through Noah's cupboards. *Her* cupboards, she reminded herself. She was definitely going to do something with this kitchen. Make her mark. Clean it up, reorganize it. Get rid of the clutter. Move some furniture around. Sew new curtains.

In the back of a lower cupboard, she found a heavy cast-iron enameled casserole that looked like it hadn't had much use and browned the meat in it, then added vegetables and whatever seasonings she could find. A can of beer and a gravy mix went into the sauce. She got the casserole bubbling gently on the rear burner, then turned it off and put the lid on. She'd finish the stew when she came home. She found a package of buns in the freezer and set them on the counter to thaw.

Then she went out the kitchen door, grabbing up her jacket as she left. Surely the town of Glory would be able to supply the necessaries—paint, a feather duvet for her bed, new towels, cleaning supplies, muffin tins, a new broom, floor wax....

CHAPTER EIGHT

NOAH CAME BACK to the ranch a little earlier than he would have normally, because he wanted to see how Abby had managed that first day. He'd left Carl to fix the last stretch of fence in the bulls' pasture by himself. His foreman hadn't been surprised when Noah had told him, when they stopped for a break during the afternoon, that he was married now.

"That young lady who's been staying at the place for a week or two?" Carl asked, inspecting the sandwich he'd pulled out of his lunch bucket.

"Yes. Abby Steen, er, Winslow now, I guess," Noah had answered, a little embarrassed by the whole business.

"Nice-lookin' woman." Carl nodded amiably and Noah had thought that was the end of the conversation. Then his foreman added, with a guileless sideways glance, "Expectin', ain't she?"

"Yes. We're, uh, we're expecting a baby in August. I'm—" Noah had taken a deep breath and stretched his arms and shoulders. He'd managed a smile. "I'm gonna be a father, Carl. How about that?"

His foreman had shot him a look with more understanding and insight than Noah had expected.

"Good fer you, boss. Good fer you." It seemed that Carl Divine approved. Noah couldn't believe how relieved he felt. First time was hardest, even though it was only Carl he was telling. Second time would be that much easier.

But after munching on his sandwich for a while, Carl looked his way again. "This have anything to do with Jesse pullin' out, boss?"

"What do you mean?" Noah asked carefully. Carl's query was unusually direct, for him.

"Well, women troubles, y'know. That's all. Wouldn't be the first time a woman's come between brothers," Carl said philosophically, gazing toward the horizon. Carl Divine was a man of few words, so Noah knew the subject had been sitting heavy on his foreman's chest. He'd been waiting for Noah to bring it up. Of course Carl would wonder—Jesse taking off the way he had. Out of the blue. Still, maybe he'd said something to Carl. Confessed. They'd always been close.

"Naw. Nothing like that," Noah said, then added, "Jess say anything to you before he left?"

He couldn't leave this to chance. It was too important. He broke the rural westerner's cardinal rule by coming out with a direct question. But then his foreman's query had been pretty direct, and Noah had to know.

Carl fixed him with his pale blue eyes. He cracked a smile, a series of leathery creases on his sun-hardened face. "Nuthin' he shouldn't have, boss. Nuthin' at all."

Noah breathed a sigh of relief. He knew what Carl

was saying: whatever had been said—if anything—
was strictly between him and Jesse. No one, not
even Noah, would ever hear a breath of it.

Noah had to know, because there was no way in
hell he was letting on that Abby's baby wasn't his.
Not to Carl, not to anyone. He'd have to be sure she
understood. The kid was getting his name, he was
legally married to the kid's mother, and for all anyone around here knew, he'd had a relationship for
quite a while with a woman south of the border. It
could be true; he left the place from time to time.
Noah Winslow wasn't in the habit of informing anyone as to his private business.

The lie was for Abby's sake more than his. No
damn way he wanted the community burning up the
phone lines with the news that one Winslow had
screwed her and the other had married her. Plus the
fact that Jesse had left so abruptly. The situation was
too open to speculation, all the way around.

If Jesse came back, and if he and Abby wanted
to get together again, Noah would deal with it then.
If Abby wanted to go straight back to South Dakota
the minute the baby was born, fine, she'd go back
as a respectable woman, with her legal husband's
offspring. No sense making things more complicated
than they already were.

Noah had ridden over to the bull pasture on Blue,
a good twenty-five-minute ride, meeting Carl, who'd
driven the pickup with the fencing supplies. The
horse needed the workout, and Noah enjoyed riding.
It was one of the real advantages of country life, in
his view. He wondered, vaguely, if Abby rode.

Back at the barn, he quickly threw off the gelding's saddle and bridle, then turned the horse loose in the small corral with Peg and her foal. He tossed some oats into the feeder while the gelding grunted and rolled in the grass. Grinning, he watched the foal sneak up and try to steal some oats from the feeder. Blue lurched to his feet and snorted. He made a beeline for the feeder, ears laid back and teeth bared, and the little fellow hightailed it back to his mama, squealing all the way.

Noah walked toward the house, chuckling to himself. Then he looked at the house and stopped short.

Damnation! What the hell was going on?

The windows on the second floor were all wide open. He saw the carpet from his bedroom bunched up under one window, on the grass, and a lampshade on top of it. By the other window, below the room he was using, he saw another carpet pitched out and a roller blind.

He came around the side of the house and saw all the blankets he'd had on his bed pegged to the clothesline, gently swaying in the light breeze. There was music coming out the window of the kitchen, also wide open. The radio was tuned to a rock and roll station.

Noah climbed up the porch steps and pushed open the kitchen door. He wouldn't have recognized the place. The table was set for two, with a tablecloth he'd never seen before. The plates matched. The counters were clear and wiped clean. Where was all his stuff?

The stainless-steel sink was sparkling. Something

smelled delicious. Noah started to tiptoe in, with his boots on, then had a guilty thought. The floor was even clean. He took his boots off at the door and walked in in his socks. Man, that smelled good!

He opened the oven door cautiously. The aroma was coming from whatever was in the oven.

"Abby!" he called. Was she home? He reached up to the top of the refrigerator to turn down the volume on the radio.

He started up the stairs. "Hey, Abby, you home?"

"I'm up here." Sounded like she was in his bedroom.

"Uh, can I come in?" He paused at the half-open door, just in case.

"Sure, come on in. I'm just thinking of getting started here. Maybe I'll leave it until after supper." Her voice was muffled behind the door.

He walked through. "May I ask what the hell is going on?"

"Where?" How could she look so innocent?

He waved wildly. "In my house. What have you been doing—tossing stuff out the windows?" He glanced around the room. It was bare, except for the bed and dresser and chest of drawers. And the pussy willows he'd set on the dresser in a weird, impulsive moment, which he now regretted. He wished she'd tossed them out, too.

"As a matter of fact I have," she replied, her eyes narrowing. "I threw out things that should have been thrown out years ago."

"Like what, my rug?"

"Your ratty rug, yes. And your ratty blinds. And your ratty lampshade with the piece broken so it doesn't fit, anyway—"

Noah stared at her. She looked mighty appealing in her jeans and her old loose T-shirt and her hair all tied up in a bandanna. One of his bandannas, he noted. Her face was flushed pink and smudged with dust.

She stared right back, her blue eyes shimmering. All of a sudden, he felt like a jerk. Why did she have this effect on him? He was always jumping to conclusions with her. Whoa. He reminded himself that this wasn't just his house anymore. She lived here, too.

"You left money. You said I should get some things. I paid for the bedclothes—" She made a gesture toward the bed, which had a big package on it, covered in plastic. "I bought my own duvet. I used your money for the broom and cleaning stuff and paint and—"

"Paint!"

"Yes, paint." She moved toward the door and partially closed it. Behind the door were several gallons of paint, one with a streak of dark reddish-pink down one side, as though she'd already inspected the color.

"Paint—what for?"

"This." She took the whole room in with one graceful gesture. "Look at it!"

"What's wrong with—with *this*?" He swung his hand around, in a gesture that mimicked hers.

"Everything. Anyway, it's my room now and I'm

painting it. Tomorrow.'' She frowned up at him mutinously.

''Not in your condition, you're not.''

''Sez who?''

''Sez me.'' He looked her over, from head to toe, his gaze pausing at her belly. ''I'll paint. You've got a baby to take care of. What if you fell off the damn ladder? Nobody around, what then?''

She took a deep breath and held it. Then she blew it out forcefully. Finally, she nodded. ''Okay. If you really want to.''

''I don't *want* to, Abby Steen Winslow, but I intend to,'' he said grimly, and she smiled a little. She looked about nineteen, although he now knew from the information they'd supplied the province that she was twenty-eight. He found himself reaching out to tuck a blond lock behind her ear, then thought better of it and stuffed his hand in his pocket.

''Noah?''

''Yes?''

''Sorry this is all so unexpected. I would've told you if you'd been around today. I guess you're back for supper now?''

He'd try his best to get along. He'd been on his own too long, even he knew that. He held the door for Abby, giving the bare room a last look before shutting off the light. Coral pink—for his *bedroom?* She moved out into the hall ahead of him. ''Yeah,'' he said. ''Let's eat. We'll talk this over later.''

''STEW.'' SHE PULLED the casserole dish out of the oven and set it down heavily on the range top.

"Could you bring it to the table for me, please?"

Noah stepped forward, relieved that she'd asked. "Sure smells good." It was a pretty lame remark but she brightened immediately and he was glad he'd thought to comment.

The way things were going around here, it seemed as though she intended to do everything by herself. Without even asking him. It wasn't right. She'd done the work of six men in this house already from the looks of it. She was pregnant, for cripes' sake! He'd have to call Nan Longquist or Louisa Robeson and see if one of them knew anyone he could hire to clean the place up properly. No way was he letting his wife do this kind of work, whether she liked doing it or not. Not going on six months pregnant.

His wife. Tablecloth, stew, a bedroom resembling the inside of a conch shell...

"Are you really planning to paint that bedroom pink?"

"Watermelon, not pink."

Watermelon was pink in his books. It was going to take some getting used to, that was for sure. He was almost afraid to venture into the living room.

They had supper to get through first.

Noah couldn't think of a thing to say. He was used to eating alone, either in front of the television in the living room or reading a newspaper or magazine at the kitchen table. He wasn't used to a full set of cutlery, a glass at his place—certainly not a tablecoth, wherever she'd managed to dig that up. He'd even been known to stand at the stove, eating straight out of the frying pan while he leafed through a *Reader's Digest* or a stock magazine.

He was a bachelor and he had a bachelor's ways. He was used to living alone, thinking his own thoughts, talking to Pat if he felt like it, listening to his choice of radio station or none at all. He was used to following his own timetable. Eating when he was hungry, for instance, never mind mealtimes.

He stole a glance at the woman sitting on the other side of the table. She seemed preoccupied. He wondered if she felt as nervous about this whole thing as he did. The bright overhead light in the kitchen winked off the brand-new wedding ring she wore. Just a plain gold band, fourteen karat. It was that kind of marriage.

"So, what did the doc say when you saw her Tuesday?" Noah finally began. That had to be safe enough. The baby.

She frowned and colored and hurriedly swallowed the bite of stew she'd taken. She patted her mouth with her napkin—that was another thing, napkins!— and returned it to her lap. She picked up her water glass and took a sip. Noah regarded her closely. What the hell was the matter with her? "Anything wrong?"

"Er, everything's fine. Blood pressure's all right, weight gain, all the stuff they check," she murmured and picked up her fork again. He had the distinct impression she was purposely not looking at him.

He was about to say something else when Pat got to her feet and walked slowly across the kitchen. Noah heard the old dog break wind. Ordinarily, this would have been a nonevent in the Winslow kitchen, but this time, horrified, he got up and shooed the dog outside, much to Pat's surprise.

"Sorry about that," he muttered as he sat back down.

She giggled. "Never mind. You should see cows, when you're milking them," Abby replied. "Used to make my dad so mad." Her eyes danced. She was clearly aware of his embarrassment over his dog's digestion.

"Oh?" He helped himself to more stew. Better drop the subject. "By the way, this stew is terrific."

"Is it?" She colored again. It must be that fair skin, that went so well with that pale silvery hair. She definitely blushed easily. "Nothing special, you know, just what I could find in your cupboards."

"It's great. I never bother with anything that complicated. I'm big on sandwiches, beans, barbecued steaks, bacon, fried eggs, that sort of cooking."

"But there was stewing beef in the freezer."

"Yeah, for chili. I make a pot of chili with beef chunks and plenty of peppers once in a while. The hotter the better."

She regarded him gravely, as though he'd just told her something really important. She finished what was on her plate without saying anything else.

Noah cleared his throat. "It's just that I wanted you to know I can appreciate a woman's cooking," he went on, aware of his words lumbering awkwardly into the silent kitchen. "I don't get that much of it."

She nodded, still grave. "Uh-huh."

There was a long pause, of several minutes' duration. Noah wished now that the radio was still on. At least that would provide a distraction.

He put down his fork and leaned back. "Want some coffee? I can make a fair to decent cup."

She hesitated. "Well, I guess so." She glanced at her wristwatch. "It's still early. Sometimes coffee keeps me awake." She rested her hands, both of them, across her belly. It was a purely practical gesture, but it emphasized the growing swell.

"Tea?"

"No, coffee's fine." She nodded, then looked up at him, her eyes dark with emotion. "Noah?"

"Yes?" He paused, turning back to her as he reached the cupboard where he kept the coffee.

"About the baby." She twisted the hem of her T-shirt.

He frowned. "What about the baby?"

"Well, Dr. Pleasance says it looks like there might be two—"

"*Two?*"

"Twins."

"*Twins!*" He swore, then regretted his outburst when he saw her blanch. "Damn it, I'm sorry, Abby. I was just surprised, that's all."

She nodded nervously. "There's twins in my family, you see. So I wasn't really that surprised. My sister has twins and I have two aunts who are twins...."

Twins. It was a shocker. But even more of a shocker was acknowledging his first semirational thought: *one for Jesse and one for me.* That made no sense at all.

"Well, sure. I guess it runs in families." He tried for nonchalance. After all, it was no big deal. Twins were born every day of the week. "You tell Jesse this?"

"Not really," she said, looking down at the hem of her shirt. "I didn't know then. Not for sure—I still don't know totally for sure, not until they do an ultrasound," she rushed on. "Dr. Pleasance is sending me for one on Monday at the hospital in Glory."

"But you did mention the possibility to him?" Things were falling slowly and painfully into place for Noah. He felt the simmering anger he harbored toward his brother rising dangerously close to the surface. *The low-down coward.* To distract himself, he made the coffee, measuring carefully.

"I mentioned the possibility on Saturday, after you brought me back from the anniversary get-together. I mentioned that I *might* be carrying twins, that the doctor back in Wicoigon wasn't sure...."

He had to ask, even though he knew the answer. "How'd he take it?"

"Jesse?"

Well, who else? "Yeah, Jesse. How'd he take it?"

"He was—" Abby paused and took a deep breath, raising her eyes to his. She dropped the bit of hem she'd been twisting. "Well, he was pretty shocked. I guess that would be the best way to put it."

Noah snorted. "He would be."

"Do you—do you think that's a fair thing to say?"

"Well, hell. He ran, didn't he? Cut loose and left you high and dry?" Noah was really angry now. "Deserted you—and his own kid? Are you *still* defending him?"

"Any man would be shocked, don't you think? I mean, even you were just now, when I told you...." Abby's eyes were full of pain. This meant so much to her, obviously, and so little to him in the end. He half remembered Abby's tale of woe, how she'd lost her husband and her only child—frankly, he didn't want to know any details. Not now. Maybe not ever.

"Okay. I was surprised. Shocked might be, well, a little strong." He handed her a mug of coffee and pushed the cream and sugar toward her. "I got over it. See?" He threw both arms out, sarcastically. "It's okay. I'm over it. So you're having twins? That's great. Double the fun. When?"

She smiled a little hesitantly. "The ninth of August."

"Great." Noah got up and flicked on the radio. He doctored his coffee with double sugar and cream, noting that she used cream only.

He stood with his coffee. "Look, I, uh, hope you don't mind, but I've got some book work I need to catch up on. I have an office there in the back bedroom on the main floor. I'm sure you've noticed it." He waved through the kitchen toward the hall that led to the rest of the house. "I hate to be a party pooper, but this has been a busy week for me and I've let things slide a little."

"Oh, don't mind me." Abby stood, too. The bulge beneath her shirt was clearly visible these days, no matter how baggy the clothes she wore. "I'll just clear up here and—"

"Do you mind doing that tonight? We could share the work, dishes and stuff. Even steven."

"No, I don't mind. I prefer to do it myself. I like keeping busy."

"No painting, though," he warned.

She smiled. "No painting."

"Well, take your time, finish your coffee. TV's in the living room. If you want me to do anything, let me know. Otherwise, I'll probably see you in the morning. I'm going to hit the sack early." And probably lie awake half the night wondering what kind of fool Noah Winslow had turned out to be—cuckolded by his own brother before the wedding. Picking up the pieces, as usual.

"Okay."

He carried his mug steadily, careful not to slop. He was still furious. With Jesse. He noticed that she hadn't moved from the table. He saw his brother's smiling face before him as he walked down the hall. He wanted to smash it. Wipe that smile off his handsome face. He remembered Jesse reproaching *him* for thinking he was the only Winslow who knew how to do the right thing by a woman. *Understands duty, honor, huh?*

Well, what did you do, Jesse-boy? When things got hot? You ran, you bastard. That's what you did. Your so-called bride is my wife now. You've made your decision. Now you better live by it.

Just as I've made mine and I intend to live by it.

ABBY DISCOVERED that, in Canada, ultrasounds were regularly performed on pregnant women at eighteen weeks. She was already nearly three weeks past due, by Canadian standards. The ultrasound was the definitive tool in establishing multiple pregnancies, among other things.

"Well?" Abby couldn't wait. She raised her head and looked tentatively at the technician—she'd introduced herself as Sally—who was pushing a smooth metal probe lubricated with some kind of special jelly over her swollen abdomen and intently examining a video screen alive with gray and black and white areas. It didn't mean a thing to Abby.

"You've got two babies here, sure enough," Sally said cheerfully. "Right on the mark for twenty-one weeks, although one's smaller than the other. That's normal, hon. Your doctor should be pleased—is that Kate?"

"Yes, Dr. Pleasance," Abby replied, leaning her head back on the too-firm pillow. She was stunned. It was one thing to suspect she was carrying twins, another to have it confirmed.

"Your husband here? In the waiting room?"

"No." Noah had shown no interest in coming with her, after she'd said she could drive herself. She was just as happy he'd stayed home.

"Lotsa fellas like to come along. You know, take a look themselves," Sally said with a quick smile. She kept her eyes on the screen, running the smooth steel probe over Abby's abdomen again and again, pausing occasionally. Every once in a while, the screen would freeze for a few seconds.

Why? So Sally could take a better look? Was there a problem? Abby forced herself to calm down. It was typical to imagine the worst. And hadn't Sally just said everything was fine?

"Well, not *my* husband," she said firmly. This wasn't the usual sort of happy-couple visit to the ultrasound lab. But under no circumstances did she want this woman to know the details of her marriage.

"You want to know the sex?" the attendant casually asked, eyes still fixed on the screen. "Or sexes, as the case may be?"

"No!" Abby practically yelled, then instantly apologized. "I'm sorry—it's just that I'm kind of superstitious about that. I'd rather wait and be surprised. I don't want to know."

"That's okay," the technician said cheerfully, removing her probe and wiping Abby's abdomen with a tissue. "Lots of people don't. I have no idea why. I always think it's easier to decorate if you know. I mean, what the heck?"

"Decorate?" Abby felt muzzy. She was still half-stunned by the reality of having two babies, not one. *Two.*

"You know, pink or blue?" The technician put away her equipment.

"Oh." Abby hadn't even thought that far. How about green? Or yellow? Or harvest-moon orange?

"You can get dressed now, Mrs. Winslow. I'll let the doc look at this and then send this info over to

Kate right away.'' With a parting smile, Sally left the room.

She still wasn't used to being called Mrs. Winslow, either. She supposed she'd better get used to it. Her babies were going to be little Winslows, too.

Babies.

All the way home, she thought about how she was going to tell Noah. Of course, the worst was over; she'd already mentioned the possibility to him on Saturday at supper. She'd barely seen him Sunday. He'd spent the morning down at the barn, and then had driven off. He didn't tell her where. She wasn't sure how she felt about that. On the one hand, he didn't have to tell her everything about his day, or his plans. On the other hand, it would be nice to know if she could expect him at meals, or where he was if she needed to contact him in an emergency. After all, she *was* pregnant.

As a married couple they still had a lot of things to sort out.

When she first saw the big van parked at Jesse's house, she thought he'd come back. Changed his mind. Her heart pounding painfully, she was aware that her first reaction was overwhelming disappointment. Why? she quickly asked herself. Was it because she'd married his brother, and now there was no going back? No, she was glad she was married to Noah. She'd always been somewhat uncomfortable with Jesse, like having to face a stranger in the morning after you'd gone to bed with him. Which was essentially the way it really *had* been with Jesse.

Noah made her feel safe, even though he kept her

pretty much off balance emotionally. But she had a deep, rock-solid feeling that he'd look out for her and the babies, that he'd never do anything to hurt them, that he'd stand by her no matter what happened. It was a feeling she desperately needed. In the middle of this pregnancy, the last thing she wanted was more upset. Which meant, she didn't need Jesse coming back into her life. Not just now.

The van had Art's Moving and Storage, Glory, Alberta stenciled on the side, and as she drove slowly by, she could see that a stout bald man and two young helpers were removing furniture from the house.

Noah was there, and he waved at her as she drove past. A few minutes later, she saw him coming toward his house—*their* house.

"So?" Noah took his hat off as he walked up the porch steps, his eyes on hers. "What's the verdict?"

"Twins."

"Hey." He actually smiled. "Twins. Double trouble. That's great."

"You really mean it, Noah?" she asked softly.

"Sure, I do," he said. He shrugged, then smiled again. "Sorry I gave you a different impression the other day. It's a lot of extra work for you, but hey— might be fun."

Abby tried hard to contain her pleasure. "What's going on down at Jesse's place?"

Noah replaced his hat. He turned, with her, to look down toward his brother's house. "I got a fellow in from Glory to buy up whatever he wants out of the house. Guy with a secondhand furniture business.''

"You did?'' She felt confused. "I guess you really don't think Jesse will be back—''

"He won't be back,'' Noah interrupted grimly. "Not on this place. He's finished here. I'm depositing the proceeds from the sale of his stuff in an account at the credit union for him. Same with his horses, if I find a buyer.''

Abby was silent for a few minutes, thinking about that. It was for the best. How could she possibly face Jesse on a daily basis if he came back here? Married to his brother now? And what about the babies? It was too awful to contemplate and, truthfully, she hadn't thought too much about it. Noah had.

"Are you going to rent out the place unfurnished?'' She still wasn't clear on what Noah had in mind.

"No. I've got a buyer for the house, too. Fellow down by Strachan who needs a place for his new ranch manager.''

"He's going to, what—take it away?'' Abby was trying to grasp the concept.

"Yep. That old trailer's going to be moved, too. Out behind the bunkhouse. Carl's going to live there.''

"I haven't met Carl yet,'' Abby mused.

"I'll take you down there right now.'' He grabbed her hand. It seemed a natural gesture. "Carl's in the barn. He'll be expecting to meet you, too. I told him I was married.''

Abby cast a quizzical glance at Noah. What kind of weirdo was this Carl? Worked for Noah and had been around the place like a shadow since she'd arrived, yet she hadn't ever seen him....

"Okay. Shall I change first?"

Noah looked her over briefly, then met her gaze. Something in his eyes made her cheeks burn. She blushed too easily; she always had.

"You're fine just the way you are. Come on down and meet my foreman."

"Does he—" Abby paused, desperately searching for the right words. "Does he know I'm pregnant?" she asked.

Noah tugged her hand gently. "Come on. Yes, he knows. I told him. He thinks you're carrying my child."

Abby's eyes swung guiltily to his—she hadn't thought this through. "He does?"

"Yes," Noah replied in a low, even voice. "And I have no intention of him finding out any different. Or anyone else, for that matter. That's what I want people to think. Do you understand? I married you. You're my wife and as far as anyone has to know, you're having my baby. Babies, I mean."

Abby nodded and followed him down the steps. She'd been warned. She understood Noah's meaning fully.

Her husband intended to be a father to her children.

CHAPTER NINE

CARL DIVINE LOOMED out of the dimness of the barn. He'd been working on one of the stalls and had a hammer in his hand.

He immediately took off his cap, revealing sparse tufts of reddish hair, cut short and badly, then shifted the wad of whatever he had in his cheek—probably chewing tobacco—from the left to the right. He smiled shyly and his pale blue eyes lit up like stars.

"Carl, I want you to meet my wife, Abby. Abby, this is the best man you'll ever run into for gentling a mustang or playing a jig, Mister Carlos Leonard Divine," Noah said with a grin. Abby was pleased to see the relaxed expression on her husband's face. He always seemed so grim to her. But maybe he was different with people he knew well, people like his foreman, whom he was clearly teasing.

"How do you do, Carl—may I call you Carl?" she said formally, extending her hand.

"Well, he—cripes, missus. You call me Carl, everybody else does." He took Abby's hand as though it were gilded and made of Venetian glass and released it almost at the same time. "Hellfi—I mean, cripes, boss. Even my ma never called me Carlos!" He sounded disgusted.

Noah laughed. Abby was amazed. She'd never heard her husband laugh before. This wasn't a laugh that was hard and harsh, but the rich, pleasant sound of someone truly amused.

"Well, this is Abby and she's my wife, and as I told you, Carl, we're expecting some little Winslows in August. The doc just informed Abby she's carrying twins."

"Twins!" Carl spit—Abby was sure he thought he'd done it discreetly—and shifted his cheek's burden to the other side. "Man alive! Well, ain't that good news, missus. Two little gaffers. We could use the extra hands 'round here, that's fer sure."

He smiled and she felt her heart go out to this strange, solitary man, who hadn't prejudged her for arriving at the Lazy SB out of the blue, pregnant, and then marrying his boss inside of a week. Now, seeing him with his strange carrot-colored hair, his tall, lanky, severely thin build, his huge hands—sticking out of sleeves that were too short—his suspenders holding up work pants he'd never fill out in a month of Sundays…she had to admit that she liked Noah's foreman on the spot.

"Ma'am." Carl nodded and replaced his cap. Abby realized that the social niceties were over and she'd been dismissed.

Noah smiled at her and winked. "How about we go take a look at that foal again?"

"Sure." Abby followed her husband out of the barn, leaving the foreman to the cavernous gloom that suited him so well.

"What did you think?" Noah asked as they made

their way toward the small corral at the side of the barn.

"I like him," Abby replied simply. "I like him very much."

Noah favored her with a smile. "He's a good man, Abby. You can count on him. A loner, not many close friends, but a heart of gold. Carl wouldn't hurt a fly."

"How long has he worked here?"

"Years. He started here when I was still in high school."

"Where's he from?"

"No idea. Back East somewhere, I believe. He just showed up one day, said he'd been traveling for a while, here and there, and was tired of that and my father hired him. He's been on the Lazy SB ever since. Good man with a horse and rope."

His father. Noah had never mentioned anything about his family. Now didn't seem the time to inquire, though.

The foal trotted toward them, the mare walking more slowly behind. Noah produced a lump of sugar from his shirt pocket. The youngster nuzzled it, squealed and raced back to his mother. Peg took the sugar cube gently and crunched it, her benign gaze moving from Noah to Abby.

"You ride, Abby?"

"No," she said with real regret. "I've always wanted to ride, but I never had the chance."

He glanced at her middle. "Yeah, well. Maybe after the babies come...."

"Yes. That would be very nice." She smiled up at him. "I'd like to learn."

"By the way," he said, clearing his throat and looking across the field into the afternoon sun, "I've hired a crew to come out and paint the place. They should be able to start Friday."

"Thank you," she said. She'd been wondering about the painting. Maybe she'd have his crew paint the kitchen and living rooms, too. Get the whole place spiffed up, if Noah had no objections. Was this the "nesting" instinct that was supposed to go along with advanced pregnancy? She was nearly to the end of her second trimester.

She thought about his reference to "after." He'd spoken as though there was a future for them here. As though he assumed they'd still *be* here—the two of them—after the babies came.

What was in Noah's mind? She hadn't had an opportunity to talk seriously with him about...any of this. There'd been so much to do since she'd arrived, so many changes. Maybe in the next few weeks they could talk about the "after." She hadn't dared think that far ahead.

The future remained an unknown; she had her hands full right now just dealing with the present.

THREE NIGHTS LATER, Abby woke suddenly from a deep sleep. She lay there for a few minutes, getting her bearings. Her heart was pounding, but otherwise she felt fine. Maybe she'd had a mad, crazy dream she couldn't remember. Maybe she'd eaten something at supper that hadn't agreed with her. Now that the babies were getting larger, she occasionally found she got heartburn after meals or if she snacked too close to bedtime.

But that wasn't what had awakened her. She heard Pat bark, a fair distance away. What was that old dog doing outside? Usually she slept in Noah's room or in the kitchen, under the table.

She listened. Farther, much farther, was an answering howl from a dog or coyote. Was that Jesse's stray? Abby pushed back the covers and walked barefoot to the window. To the east she saw the flicker of a light. A bonfire, it looked like, behind the trees. Down near Jesse's house. It was too dark to see the actual house, but the barking dog was definitely in the same vicinity. Who could have set a fire? And where was Noah?

Abby slipped into her bathrobe and went down the hall. The door to Noah's room was standing open.

"Noah?" There was no answer.

Feeling brave, she switched on the light inside his door. He wasn't there. His bed hadn't been slept in. She'd left her watch in the bedroom and had no idea what time it was. She saw the dim light of the clock on his bedside radio and crept closer. Nearly half-past one.

Where was Noah?

Abby turned on the hall light and went downstairs, removing her woollen jacket from behind the kitchen door. She threw off the bathrobe and shrugged her jacket on over her nightgown, and pushed her feet into her canvas sneakers, which waited by the door.

Nervously surveying the darkness outside, she left the house. Noah must be down at Jesse's place, with Pat. But why would he have lit a fire?

Abby's apprehension turned into real fear when she realized what her husband was doing. She stood near a tree at the back of Jesse's yard and watched as Noah, shirt open and streaming with sweat, brought out odds and ends, chairs and boxes from Jesse's empty house and heaved them onto the fire. She watched as he took an ax to two chairs and in three or four violent strokes reduced them to kindling, which he tossed onto the fire, sending showers of sparks, up, up, up into the midnight sky. Pat kept him company, walking back and forth from the house to the fire. Magazines, lampshades, empty boxes, old boots…

Abby couldn't believe her eyes. What was he *doing?* He's getting rid of every stick belonging to his brother, that's what.

But why? In the middle of the night like this? What demon had kept him from his bed, brought him out after midnight to do a job he could so easily have done during the day? Or hired someone else to do?

She shivered. It was cold, cold and dark, with a moon covered by clouds. She hadn't heard the stray howl since she'd come outside. The thought of that dog, hungry and fearful somewhere, was so sad, so pitiful.

She watched Noah work for maybe another

twenty minutes. She didn't know what to do, whether to sneak back up to the house and pretend she'd never seen this or to step forward.

She must have made a sound, or perhaps the wind had blown her scent to Pat, because suddenly the old dog stood, stiff-legged by the fire, and barked loudly in her direction. Noah paused, looking the same way. Surely he couldn't see her....

"Carl? That you, Carl?" Noah called.

Abby stood still for one more agonized moment, then stepped forward. "No, it's me. Abby!"

Noah swore. "What the hell are *you* doing out here?" He sounded angry. He strode toward her, Pat following eagerly, tail wagging. Noah was breathing hard as he reached her. He lifted one arm to wipe the sweat from his forehead with his sleeve.

"I—I could ask the same. I woke up. I saw the fire. I wondered what was going on—"

"That's the stupidest damned thing I ever heard." Noah swore again and she stepped back. If anything, he sounded angrier now. "Why'd you get up? Why didn't you stay in bed?"

"Well, what *are* you doing?" Abby returned, gesturing toward the fire.

"I'm clearing out the rest of Jesse's junk," he said tersely. "What does it look like I'm doing?"

"In the middle of the night?"

"I couldn't sleep. I thought I might as well get it over with. I'm nearly finished the job. You go on back to the house."

"But—why?"

"Damn it, woman! You don't get it, do you?"

"No, I guess I don't!"

"Okay, listen, while I spell it out for you. My brother, who's never been able to keep his pants on, gets you pregnant one weekend. Okay? Then, when he's got the chance to do the right thing for once in his life, he buggers off. Leaves big brother to pick up the pieces. Just the way he's always done. Hell!" Noah dug one hand through his hair in an impatient gesture and swore again. "I'm finished with him, do you understand? *Finished!*"

Abby stood there, horrified. "And you're furious with him, your own brother? You hate him." Then, voicing her deepest fear, she whispered, "And *me?*"

"Hell, no! Not you. Damn it. You're the only good thing that's come out of this, you and the babies—" Noah fastened his eyes on her. They glittered in the firelight. With anger? Or with…something else?

"Listen, Abby." He reached out and swung her into his arms. His voice was hoarse. His arms closed hard around her. "I can't really explain it. I feel so…so frustrated. I'm mad, yes, mad as hell at Jesse. But you're right, he's my brother. He's the only one I've got left—in my family." Noah laughed bitterly. "Of the Winslows, anyway. Not that any of us were ever worth much. But now I've got you, right? A wife. And kids on the way? Babies? I sure never saw that coming, did I? Ha!"

He paused and Abby shrank in his arms. He frightened her. All this talk of hating his brother. Burning the last of his brother's possessions in the middle of the night. The crazy talk of being alone, with no family left. She heard that thin howl again in the distance and shivered. Noah held her closer.

"What do you mean, Noah—the only one left?" She put her hands tentatively on his chest. She didn't trust this situation. She didn't want his arms around her, either.

"We had a brother, me 'n' Jesse. Died when he was twelve. Casey." So there *had* been a third brother, in that picture. "Our ma died shortly after, and then my dad took off. We've never seen him or heard from him since. Then it was just me and Jesse and my uncle Brandis, my ma's stepbrother, until Brandis died, a few years ago. He was old. Now—"

Noah stopped, and Abby felt her heart squeeze with emotion for him. This must be so hard to talk about. She was his wife, yes, but still a stranger in almost every way. "Now Jesse takes off," he said in a rough whisper. "He's gone, too."

"I'm here." Abby wasn't sure exactly what she meant by that. Just some comfort? One human being to another?

"Yeah, you're here," Noah said and tightened his arms around her. "Believe it or not, I'm glad of that." She could smell the acrid smoke of the fire on his shirt, on his skin. "Ha!" He laughed hoarsely, as though short of breath. "Yeah, I've got it made, haven't I? A wife I can't touch, a wife I can't make love to—pregnant with my brother's babies!"

He swore and then, with a groan, lowered his mouth to Abby's and kissed her. A hard, savage, demanding kiss. Abby gasped in surprise, but as he held her tighter, she began to respond. A huge thrill went through her, from her heart to her knees. Her arms crept up until she held him against her, held his head against her mouth, offering even as he took, eager...

With a moan, Noah wrenched his mouth from hers, breathing hard. "Damn it, Abby. I didn't mean that. I mean, I *did* mean that. Hell, I've wanted to kiss you for a long time. *I have.* But I know this isn't right, this isn't why you married me—"

"Shh..." Abby's heart was beating fast. *Oh, Noah, don't apologize.*

Suddenly she felt her babies stirring, and she wanted to focus all her attention and energy on that sensation. The tiniest of butterflies fluttering under her heart...

"Oh!" She broke away from his embrace.

"What is it, Abby? What's the matter?" he asked hoarsely.

"The babies, Noah," she whispered. "The babies *kicked* me. Hard! They're really—really *in* there."

Noah's gaze dropped to her belly. He raised one hand as though to touch her, then dropped it. "You must be freezing," he said dully, his voice raw. "You've only got your nightgown on."

Had he just noticed that? Abby couldn't stop smiling. "Oh! There it is again—do you want to feel?" *Oh, please, let him want to.* She took his hand in hers and placed it on her belly where she'd felt the kick. Just then her baby—one of them, maybe both—kicked again. In the distance, the stray howled again. Noah's hand molded her abdomen tenderly, automatically.

"I felt that, Abby. I really did. It's…it's amazing." He cleared his throat and reached up to tuck a lock of her hair behind her ear. He stepped back, cleared his throat again. "Listen, you go home. I'll be up as soon as this fire dies down a little."

"You want some coffee or something?" Noah's kiss, the fire blazing against the black sky, the healthy, strong kick of her baby… She felt strangely excited—and strangely content. The least she could do was fix him a hot drink or something.

"Never mind that," he said grimly, moving away from her. "Just go back to bed. Go!"

Abby stared at him for a few more seconds, then turned and made her way to the house. Pat came back with her. The old dog settled herself under the kitchen table with a couple of grunts and Abby headed upstairs.

Somehow, she felt better having the old dog in the house, especially since she had no idea when Noah would be back. She tried to warm herself under her down quilt. Her husband had kissed her…he'd kissed her as a lover would, or a man in love. He wanted her. Maybe there was a future for them. Maybe they could make something of this crazy, mixed-up marriage, after all. He was a good man. A man worth fighting for.

The reverence when he'd touched her, when he'd felt the life she carried…

She thought of her poor lost baby girl. The baby she and Frank had wanted so much. Perfectly formed, but dead. She remembered her horror when the doctors had told her. How she'd screamed and screamed until the nurse had poked a needle in her arm and then...thick, blissful silence. Until she awoke.

And Frank, killed at twenty-six. Strong and fit one moment, broken, *gone,* the next. Both dead, and now new life growing inside her. Two babies. She felt hot tears dampen her pillow. Happiness. It was true; a person really could weep with happiness. Sorrow and happiness at the same time.

HE NEVER SHOULD HAVE grabbed her like that. Never should have kissed her. It wasn't right. She'd married him in a panic, and as for him—he wasn't entirely sure *why* he'd offered. Maybe because he didn't want the good folk of Glory to think any worse of the Winslows than they already did. Maybe to hide the fact that his brother had disappeared—blown out of town with his little Stella dog beside him and no goodbyes. Noah didn't know where he might have landed. Nor did he care. He just hoped Jesse stayed away.

He wished Jesse had taken the other dog with him, too. It made him shudder to hear that animal howl at night. And no one could get near him since Jesse left. Carl had tried. If Carl couldn't get near him, no one could. His foreman had put food out, too, and told him that once in a while the food was gone in the morning. Whether it was eaten by coyotes or by Jesse's stray, no one knew.

So far, none of his neighbors or acquaintances had

brought up the subject of Jesse's disappearance. Once he had the house moved and the trailer pulled away—which he'd do this week—they'd notice that things had changed around the Lazy SB, all right. They might think he and Jesse'd split over the American woman. His new wife. The way Carl had suggested. And they had—only it wasn't quite the story folks would suppose.

He had the trailer to get moved. Amos Petersen was coming over to haul the house away at the end of the week.

There was roundup and spring branding to organize. He was figuring on the end of May for that, about two more weeks or so. Adam Garrick had his gather planned for the May long weekend, and Noah normally would have helped out. Now, with his new wife being pregnant, he'd begged off.

Maybe early June for the Lazy SB. There were hands to hire, and neighbors to talk it over with— they generally pitched in with each other's roundups and brandings, regular annual events that felt more like parties, sometimes, than hard work. Cal Blake would likely show up, and his brother Jeremiah would no doubt send over a few hands from the Diamond 8. Ben Longquist was a regular at the brandings, even though he was a farmer's son and had been at college now for a couple of years. Ben was finished with school for the summer and itching to get his hands dirty again. He was a good worker and, in fact, Noah had thought of offering him a job through until next fall. And there was Ben's younger brother, Trevor, coming up, nearly fifteen he'd be now. He was a darn good little roper—Carl had shown him a few tricks last summer.

They'd need an experienced cook for the crew. And maybe someone to give Abby a hand in the house. She couldn't cook for a branding crew, not with the babies coming so soon. Noah had noticed since their marriage a couple of weeks ago, how much she'd grown around the middle. He supposed that was the twins, because she was as slim and graceful as she'd always been everywhere else. Pregnancy suited her; she had a glow and a bloom that he'd often noticed on expectant women.

He had to admit he had the hots for her, pure and simple. Was it her, or just any woman? he wondered. Some nights he lay awake in his bed, thinking about her sleeping in his room down the hall. The room that had been his until Abby came along. Now she slept in his bed. Except that he wasn't in there with her.

Not only was she his wife pretty well in name only, she was hugely pregnant. And not with his baby. Everything was much too complicated. Mixed up. Maybe it was time for another visit to Rachel. But now? With him a married man? Impossible, even if he'd wanted to, which he didn't.

He was double damned both ways, no question about it.

CHAPTER TEN

FOR A WOMAN who'd been brought up on a farm, Abby Winslow hadn't realized how lonely living in the country could be.

Noah had neighbors, certainly, but the nearest was more than a mile away on the main road. There was some traffic, mostly recreational, on the ranch road leading to the wooden bridge that crossed the river. Fishermen with their Jeeps and quads out for the weekend. Dirt bikers, whom Carl hated with a passion, and a few picnickers and hikers.

Noah apparently didn't mind members of the public crossing his land, although he was cautious about campers and overnighters. He or Carl usually checked with most people who crossed the river; there was also a big sign that warned the road was on private land and no fires or overnight camping were permitted. Other large signs warned of no hunting at any season of the year, and stipulated that gates must be left closed at all times.

So far, Noah said, they hadn't had much trouble, except from the dirt bikers, whose noisy machines frightened the cattle, and whose madcap racing around the hills injured the delicate prairie sod. Carl's roping skills had reputedly sent a message to the dirt bike community the previous year. According to Noah, his foreman had roped a couple of bikers as they blasted along the hillsides, and after a sudden jerk off their machines at one end of a lariat, an angry cowpoke and a twelve-hundred-pound horse at the other end, they'd changed their minds about using the Lazy SB as a racetrack. The word had spread, and the problem stopped.

No one ever came by to visit. Abby realized in the second week of June that no one was going to visit, either. People were busy. She was an outsider in a close-knit community. Not only had she committed the social crime of being an interloper who'd stolen one of the district's eligible bachelors from the potential pool of prospects for some local girl, she'd been visibly pregnant when she married him.

Small towns were small towns, and Glory obviously wasn't any different from Wicoigon in that respect. She was a new bride and a stranger, so it was up to her husband to introduce her to the community. But no one seemed to have less interest in socializing than Noah. They never went anywhere, except to town to shop for groceries. Still, she didn't want to complain.

Rain at the end of May meant that Noah had pushed the roundup and branding forward to the middle of June. He wasn't happy about that, as it had interfered with his spring planting. Abby didn't ask much about the ranch work. She was fascinated by it but decided she'd rather watch than settle for the brief answers her husband gave her over a late supper. Noah usually took a lunch with him when he left early in the morning and she rarely saw him during the day. He'd instructed her to call him on his cell phone if she ever needed him. So far, Abby had done just fine without him.

She wondered if Carl had realized how lonely she was. One day he came up to the house when Noah was away and asked if he could turn over a few flower beds for her. She'd been weeding in the overgrown patches by the house, pruning and pulling debris from under the rosebushes. It was satisfying work and a gorgeous day, sunny with blue skies and a cooling breeze from the mountains. The ranch was situated in a broad, shallow valley, with the river in the near distance, and the snowcapped Rocky Mountains in the far distance. There were no sounds beyond the chitter of crickets and the occasional cry of a bird. Magpies or swallows. She recognized many of the prairie birds as being the same ones she'd known in South Dakota.

"Can I give you a hand with that, missus?"

"Oh!" Abby sat back on her heels. Carl had approached silently and startled her. He was carrying a spade. She supposed that old Pat, snoozing under the lilac bush, was so used to the foreman that she didn't even bother to raise her head. Abby shaded her eyes with one grimy hand to look up. "That would be very nice, Carl. Do you have time this afternoon?"

Abby knew how busy both men were on the ranch these days.

"I can always spare time for a little beautification," he said. It was an odd comment. "I'm partial to flowers, myself, but the boss never seemed to care how the place looked. Cryin' shame, really. I guess it'll be different now that you're here, missus."

Abby reached out and took the hand that Carl extended and heaved to her feet. She was so awkward these days, but physically she felt great and she certainly wasn't going to sit in the house all day knitting tiny things. "Whew!" She pushed back the bandanna she'd been using to hold her hair off her face.

"I could just dig up around these peonies," Carl suggested. "Give 'em a boost. And I'll bring over the barrow and get rid of all this here chickweed and bindweed and pigweed you've been plucking. It'll only set seeds in the compost if you toss it in there." Carl stepped forward and carefully and steadily began to turn over the plot of dirt in front of the bay window.

He seemed to know something about gardening. Abby stood and watched him for a moment, easing her aching back.

"Can I bring you something to drink? Tea?" she asked, suddenly feeling much, much better.

"Tea? Yes. That would be real nice." Carl glanced briefly at her, and she caught the traces of a rare smile.

Abby hummed quietly as she fixed the tea. She had to admit she was getting used to the stuff since she'd been here. She usually put on a pot of coffee midmorning, for herself, and maybe for Noah if he came back to the house. Otherwise, it was tea in the morning and tea in the afternoon. She'd even stopped calling it "hot" tea.

Maybe one day she'd fit right in. People would think she was born and bred Canadian, only wonder if maybe she was from "back East" because of her slight accent.

And pigs would likely fly by then, too.

No, she had to keep her goals focused strictly on the birth of her babies. Then she'd consider what to do next. She'd had a letter from home that sounded somewhat conciliatory, but she certainly wasn't ready to go back to her parents' house. Not that they were inviting her. If Noah was agreeable to her staying for a while after the babies were born, she would. She needed time to get her feet under her and to make some plans. If he hadn't offered marriage when he had, she didn't know what she would have done.

"How's about a bit of a vegetable garden?" Carl had pushed his cap back and was scratching his chin thoughtfully. "Only a bit, 'nough for some lettuce. And radishes. Eh? Fresh radishes straight from the garden is always nice."

"Oh, gosh, Carl. I don't know." Abby laughed as she made her way toward him with the tray. There were a couple of lawn chairs on the grass, and a painted-steel patio table, round and somewhat rusted. She set the tray down heavily.

"I'd help you seed it, missus. Lady in your condition shouldn't be doing that kind of work, if you don't mind me mentioning it.'' Carl tipped his cap back into place and reached with one huge hand for a mug. ''Thankee, missus. This'll hit the spot, all right.''

Well, a garden *would* be welcome. Abby considered how much Carl didn't know about her situation. Would she even be here to harvest a garden? Mind you, lettuce took only a few weeks to harvest, and radishes, too. If the weather wasn't already a little hot for both crops. She had a craving for fresh beets. She could put in a short row of beets.

''I'd love one,'' she said suddenly, glad she had when she saw how his face brightened. She wondered if it was himself he was thinking of for the fresh radishes ''straight from the garden.''

''Over there by the back door?'' Carl pointed with his mug. There was a level sunny spot just beyond where the old clothesline had hung. There was no clothesline now, just the posts standing with pulleys still attached. She wanted Noah to string a line again. She liked clothes dried outside, and had already imagined a line hung with white diapers flapping in the west wind. And other little baby things. *Her man's jeans and shirts, her nightgowns.*

''Just a small one. Beyond the posts. What do you think?''

Carl nodded. ''A dandy place, missus. Right dandy. Plenty of sun. Not too far and not too close, if you know what I mean.''

Abby didn't, but she impulsively added, "I'll get the seeds in town tomorrow!"

"Uh-huh. And I'll barrow over some of that there horsesh—er, man-u-ure from last year's pile behind the barn. It'll be just the right condition to work into the ground, y'see." Carl went back to his slow, methodical spading.

What a good idea! Why hadn't she thought of a garden herself? It would be something to do. She supposed she'd been afraid to think of anything long-term. Even painting and wallpapering. But the Winslow homestead decor was so ghastly and out-of-date, she'd had to go ahead with that. And Noah would benefit, even if she left, whether he appreciated her efforts now or not. The paint had made a huge difference. She'd gotten rid of most of the afghans and taken down the venetian blinds and replaced them with fresh cotton curtains. She'd actually cleaned off the surface of the lovely old walnut dining-room table, which had probably been covered with folders and flyers and magazines and newspaper clippings for years. She'd polished the chairs and table with beeswax and lavender paste, and even Noah had been amazed at how nice they'd looked. He said his mother had brought them with her when she got married.

"And I'll help you put 'em in, the seeds, that is," Carl repeated, returning her attention to the garden. "I know the boss'll want me to give you a hand. He says you're doing too much already."

Abby glanced at him, surprised. "Did he ask you to help me today?"

"What's that, eh?" Carl pretended he hadn't heard her, so she didn't repeat her question. The foreman clamped his jaws together, as though he'd said more than he'd meant to, and went on with his spading.

Honestly, these men thought a pregnant woman was made of porcelain. She'd often reminded Noah that she wasn't sick, she was pregnant. She was strong, she was healthy. Women had babies every day. He didn't seem to hear a word she said.

But there was always the fear that what had happened before would happen again. She never mentioned that to Noah. Although it had been a dreadful accident of birth with her first baby—a pinched cord, a delay getting to the hospital, an inexperienced resident when she got there. It wasn't anything she'd done wrong during the pregnancy. She hadn't even had a glass of wine!

This time was different. She had every confidence in Kate Pleasance and the specialist she'd sent her to consult. The past was past. It had been an accident, that was all. She couldn't dwell on it.

Having Carl help her a little in the garden was one thing. But that evening, Noah dropped a bombshell.

"I've hired someone to help you out, Abby," he announced when he came in the door for dinner. These days he'd been showing up for dinner very regularly. Abby sometimes thought he made a point of being around so that he could keep an eye on her. The fact that he never actually admitted it irritated her.

"What do you mean—help me out?" She frowned.

"A helper. An assistant. Someone to give you a hand around here." He disappeared into the bathroom just down the hall and Abby heard water run as he washed his hands. She was in the middle of putting their supper on the table. She tried to absorb what he'd said.

He came back into the kitchen, looking a little defiant, she thought. "You need someone here to watch out for you."

"I do not!" Well, at least he'd finally said it.

"You do."

"That's ridiculous! Carl's here, you're here most of the time—"

"That's going to change, come Monday. We're taking a crew out on roundup and we'll probably be gone the better part of a week."

A vague suspicion she'd had now surged to the forefront of her mind. "You've put off roundup over this, haven't you? It wasn't just the rain we had at the end of May. You've been waiting until you got someone lined up to stay here, haven't you?"

Noah nodded reluctantly and sat down at the kitchen table. "Maybe."

"Well, damn you anyway, Noah Winslow!" She slammed the platter of pork chops she was carrying onto the table.

Noah looked up, surprised. "What the hell's this? I was just trying to help you, that's all. You need someone here."

"Help me? Maybe you could *ask* me if I needed help? Maybe you could mention that *you'd* feel better if I had someone here when you were gone? Huh? Maybe I could have a say in this. You're treating me like a child and an idiot, and I don't like it, Noah. I don't care what kind of ridiculous marriage we have, I don't deserve to be treated like a fool!" She plunked down the bowl of mashed potatoes she'd retrieved from the warming oven.

"Damn it," he said quietly. "Settle down. I know you're no fool."

Abby reminded herself to count slowly to ten. She went back to the counter for the salad she'd prepared, then returned to the table and took her seat across from Noah.

Noah calmly reached for a slice of bread and buttered it. He smiled at her, obviously trying to look chastened. "Hey, mashed potatoes—any gravy?"

"Yes, there's gravy," she said, feeling a smile creep onto her face. She had to admit, she found it hard to stay mad at Noah. It was annoying to be treated like an incompetent, but she saw his point. And, by his own admission, he had little experience getting along with women. He probably really believed he was doing her a big favor. He probably thought she'd have no objection, so there was no reason to ask her. He probably thought this was the kind of surprise women liked. She'd rather have roses.

"So, who've you hired to baby-sit me?" she asked, as she got up to pour the gravy from its dented saucepan into the china gravy boat.

"It's not that bad, Abby. Think of it. You alone out here while Carl and I are off for three or four days, maybe more? Miles from here?"

"You've got the cell phone," she said as she sat down again.

"Yeah, but you never know what can happen. Besides, even if you called, what could I do from out there? Out in some coulee?" His face was serious, even worried.

"I could call a cab from Glory," she muttered.

Noah didn't respond. He loaded some salad onto his plate. "I got Phoebe Longquist. She's a nice girl, seventeen or so. She's studying for her final exams and is taking the week off from school."

"Ben's sister?" Abby had met Ben Longquist when he came over to the ranch about noon one day and Noah invited him to stay for lunch. She'd realized then that she'd danced with him at the Dexters' anniversary celebration. He was finishing college in Edmonton and working for one of Noah's neighbors, Adam Garrick, for the summer.

"Yeah." Noah served himself from the platter of chops. "You'll like her."

"I'm sure I will," Abby murmured. She might as well look on the bright side. She had no choice, anyway. And at least it would be some female company. She took some salad herself and waited while Noah finished filling his plate with mashed potatoes and gravy. One thing she had to feel good about— he appreciated her cooking. She didn't think he really missed the sandwiches and frozen dinners he'd lived on before she arrived.

They ate in silence for a while, but it was a companionable silence, unlike the first week or so she'd lived there. Once she moved in, Noah had seemed to relinquish all interest in the house. Not, she thought wryly, that he'd ever had much. After he got over the fact that she intended to paint what had been his bedroom pink—what she called watermelon—with white woodwork and new curtains at the tall windows, he'd backed off. Altogether.

In a way, she wished he would involve himself more. It was his house. But then, she'd think sadly, having consultations and discussions about such things was what real married people did, not people who'd married the way they had—people who were almost strangers. Sometimes she felt he was treating her so *carefully* just to keep her at a distance. To make sure they didn't grow any closer. Was he that worried she wouldn't want to leave after the babies were born?

Abby felt tears prickle at the backs of her eyelids. She kept her gaze down, her hands folded across her stomach in what was becoming a habitual gesture, while Noah cleared the table, as he often did, and stacked the dishwasher. She noticed that he turned the radio on as he passed the refrigerator. Was that so he wouldn't have to talk to her?

To Abby's horror, the hot tears brimmed over and ran down her cheeks. She quickly rummaged in the pocket of her maternity blouse for a tissue. She felt huge and awkward and unwanted. She'd broken two fingernails gardening this afternoon. Her hair was a mess and her feet hurt. No wonder her husband didn't want to talk to her.

"Abby?" Noah put one hand under her chin and tipped it toward him. "Abby, honey—what's the matter?"

His concern turned on the faucet full blast. Abby felt her chin quiver, too. Her nose prickled. This was so embarrassing! Since her pregnancy, her moods had been up and down. This, she supposed, was part of that hormonal wash.

Noah squatted beside her, so that his face was only a foot or so away. "What's the matter? Why are you crying? Is it because of me getting Phoebe without asking you?"

Abby shook her head and tried to speak, but the words froze in her throat. She gulped, and Noah pulled her toward him. She leaned on him, taking comfort in his warmth, in his manly scent. She felt his arms go around her, his right hand awkwardly patting her shoulder.

"Okay," she heard him say soothingly. "It's okay, honey. If you don't want her, we can get somebody else."

She shook her head and raised her wet face. "I-it's not that, it's not that at all," she managed.

"What is it then?" Gently he drew her up, until she was standing with his arms around her. Her stomach seemed huge, pressed against him as it was. She felt like one of his Hereford cows out there on the hillside. Or a smallish elephant.

"It's just—just that I'm so alone out here." She tried to bite back the tears, but her teeth chattered. "I don't know anyone. I wish someone would come to visit me...." She knew she sounded like nothing more than a big whining baby and wished she could stop. But she *couldn't* stop, now that the dam had been breached.

"Visiting?" Noah frowned. "Is that what's bothering you?"

"No one ever c-comes here," she whispered. "I—I thought some of the women might come to see me, now that, you know, now that we're married. Your neighbors—"

Noah held her a little tighter. "Visitors? Is that all?"

"That *all!*" She pushed at his chest and raised her face to his. He wasn't smiling. "Maybe you don't care if anybody ever comes to see *you,* but you have no idea what it's like to be here by myself all day and never have anyone come to visit! I talk to the dog, to myself—"

"Donna came once," he reminded her.

"Yes, she did." Abby sniffed loudly. Donna had come two weeks after they were married and had spent the afternoon with her. "It was very nice of her to come that day. But she's the only one."

"Phoebe will be here—"

"When?" Abby raised her arm to wipe her tears from her cheeks. She saw Noah follow her gesture intently. His eyes were troubled.

"Tomorrow morning. We're heading out in the afternoon tomorrow. Probably be gone at least four days."

"Look, Noah—" She took a deep breath. "I'm sorry for getting carried away like this—"

"You're not carried away. You're just lonely. It's natural. I'm afraid I'm not much of a husband to you."

She stared at him for a few seconds, then felt the tears rush forward again. That was exactly it. She was lonely. She'd been lonely since Frank died, since she'd lost her job. Since she'd fallen into Jesse's arms, looking for comfort. Since her parents and her sister had proved so lacking in understanding and kindness. She was lonely here in a strange land, married to a man she barely knew although she'd lived under the same roof with him for almost two months.

"That's it, Noah," she whispered, uncaring of the tears. "It's not you, but I *am* so lonely—"

"Oh, Abby," Noah said hoarsely and pulled her close to him, against his chest so she couldn't see his face. "Would you rather go home again? Back to South Dakota?"

"No! No, I wouldn't—I want to stay here," she whispered. *With you.*

His arms tightened around her. "I wish you didn't feel so bad. Maybe when the babies come, it'll be different. I want you to be happy here—with me. I want you to be happy enough to stay."

Forever and ever. He hadn't said that but it was difficult to hear properly, with her head tucked under his chin, crushed against his shirtfront.

She could wish, though. It was what she'd always wanted to find—*forever and ever.* She hadn't found it with Frank, or with Jesse. Maybe forever and ever didn't exist, outside of paperback novels and movie screens. Maybe all you had was today. Maybe that was all you ever had.

CHAPTER ELEVEN

A SPRING ROUNDUP—although it was early summer now—was a thrilling time on a ranch, Abby discovered.

Noah and his foreman, some neighbors and a few hired hands took off for the hills, where they gathered all the cows and calves and gradually drove them down to the home ranch. This could take several days, depending on the ruggedness of the range, as each coulee had to be searched, as well as each gully and dry creek bed where a stubborn cow might be hiding out with her calf. Not all the cows were eager to be rounded up by the ki-yi-ing, rope-swinging cowboys. Many of the older cows must have remembered this little event from other years, and it undoubtedly was not a pleasant memory. Their calves had been taken from them by men on horses and they'd been driven into corrals and forced to listen to their bawling offspring as they were vaccinated, branded, castrated, dehorned and tagged. The calves were eventually returned to them, but not until after a lot of dust and noise and bovine bother.

Noah had told Abby that roundup was a special time in a cowboy's life. He said that neighbors helping neighbors was part of it, but so was the experience of being outside, under a big blue sky in the daytime and a trillion stars at night, ''cowboying'' as he called it. Campfire beans and boiled-up coffee tasted awful good, he said, after a long day in the saddle.

Abby envied him. She'd have liked nothing better than to go along, as some of the women did. Jeremiah Blake brought along a girlfriend who was almost as expert in the saddle as he was, and leathery old Amanda Dexter, a younger sister of the anniversary couple, who ran her own ranch in the foothills near Longview, never missed a roundup in the district. Carl swore she'd have to be tied up and left for dead before she'd stay home.

Abby liked Phoebe Longquist, who'd arrived the morning after her talk with Noah. Phoebe was a serious-looking girl in her final year of high school. She was tall, with long dark-auburn hair, which she generally wore in a neat French braid. She'd brought a small suitcase and a satchel of books and spent most of her time curled up in the armchair in the living room, reviewing her notes. She was a serious student, Noah had told Abby, and the Longquists expected her to get a scholarship to a good university that fall.

Abby was relieved that Phoebe was so quiet and undemanding. They talked in the evenings and watched television or listened to classical music on the radio. Abby cooked and Phoebe cleared up. Phoebe was curious about her pregnancy when Abby told her she was expecting twins, and Abby was happy to talk about it. It was a pleasant time. Abby felt so much better after a day or two with the young woman that when she recalled her fit of weeping with Noah, it was with embarrassment. Usually she prided herself on being strong, on being flexible and pragmatic—not a victim of her emotions like that. She had forgotten how moody a pregnant woman could be, probably because she'd been in the depths of grieving for Frank through most of her first pregnancy and hadn't noticed much of anything.

She hadn't realized how much she'd miss Noah. She'd grown accustomed to hearing his tread on the porch steps outside when he came in for supper. She'd come to know the note of his pickup's engine as he drove into the yard. She even missed the aroma of fresh-ground coffee first thing in the morning, wafting up from downstairs. Noah was always up before she awoke and he usually had coffee and juice and cereal, and sometimes bacon and eggs or pancakes, ready when she came down. He ate a big breakfast himself. If he left the house before she got up, there was always half a pot of coffee waiting for her. It was a little thing, a habit, but it was something she'd grown to treasure. Sometimes he'd leave a note for her, telling her where he was going for the day and when to expect him; often he didn't.

Phoebe tended to sleep later than she did, so Abby found herself downstairs first these days, making a cup of herbal tea for herself and preparing enough oatmeal porridge in case Phoebe wanted some. Abby had never had any of the fabled cravings such as peanut butter and pickles that pregnant women were supposed to have, but lately she couldn't get enough luscious steaming oatmeal with plenty of demerara sugar and milk.

Three days after the men had left, the doorbell rang, just as Abby was finishing her breakfast. It was about half past eight. Phoebe was still upstairs.

Now, who could that be? Abby made her way to the front door, swaddled in her dressing gown. No one ever came to the front door. Did that mean she finally had a visitor?

"Yes?"

"Ah, missus!" A slim Chinese man, middle-aged, bowed slightly and removed his hat. Standing behind him was a very old Chinese man with a white goatee. "Today's the day! Here we are."

"You are?" Abby shook her head, confused. "For what?"

"Boss didn't tell you? Ah!" The man who'd spoken gestured to the older man and said a few words in rapid Chinese. "This is my uncle, Ping Lee." He bowed again. "Georgie Ping at your service, missus. I'm the cook, he's the cook's helper."

"You're *cooks*!" Abby remembered her manners. "Please come in," she said, stepping back. "Did Noah send you?"

"Yes. Just a few days here. Mostly we cook for Mr. Blake's place." He leaned toward her confidentially. "My uncle doesn't speak English. Sorry."

"That's fine," Abby said, still woozy. Was she dreaming this, or had her husband hired some more help? Without telling her... "Come in, both of you."

"No. We have to check out the kitchen down at the cookshack. Open up and get everything ready. Your husband told me where the key is. Cheerio!" The two men made their way down the steps and only then did Abby notice an old station wagon, loaded to the gunwales, parked down the hill from the house. As she watched, they walked toward the vehicle, talking in Chinese all the while, then got in and slowly drove toward the bunkhouse, down past the barn and behind a small copse of cottonwoods. The older of the two was driving, the ancient one with the long white wisp of an old-fashioned goatee that looked like it had been tied with string.

Abby shook her head. *Should I look into this? Ask questions? Find out what's going on?* No, she decided firmly. Another bowl of oatmeal was in order.

ABBY THOUGHT the situation over as she finished her breakfast, then got dressed and walked down to the cookhouse, a rectangular wooden building next to the bunkhouse. She'd had no idea it was ever used. It was a very old building, with a sagging roof-line and several tin stovepipe chimneys. Outside, the younger man, Georgie, was wrestling a small propane cylinder into place, while the elder stood by with tools. Wrenches, pliers, a hammer. *A hammer?*

"Ah! Missus! No need to come out—"

"I just wondered what you were planning to do here at the ranch. I don't remember what my husband mentioned—" That was a lie; of *course* she remembered. Noah had said nothing whatsoever, but she didn't want to cause any distress to the two cooks. "I guess I've just forgotten, that's all."

"Ah, you are having a baby very soon, missus." Georgie looked at his uncle and said a few words in Chinese. The uncle bobbed his head and beamed. "Expecting women have plenty of excuses for everything!" Georgie laughed and his uncle smiled even more broadly.

I see, thought Abby. Two more men who think a pregnant woman is the next thing to a cracked egg. Incompetent at worst, fragile and delicate at best.

"So, what did Noah have in mind for the two of you?" She couldn't put it much plainer.

"I will get the gas hookup to the stove going, and then the fridge. It's gas, too. Then we'll bring in all the food and everything, and sweep out the place and start making lotsa chuck for the cowboys when they come in," Georgie said proudly.

Chuck or grub was what the cowboys called food, Abby had learned.

"Well, I can help with that. And Phoebe's here, Phoebe Longquist, she'll help out, too," Abby volunteered, making a sudden decision. It annoyed her that Noah had done it again—just assumed she wouldn't be able to handle things and gone ahead and hired someone else.

"No, no way. Mr. Winslow hired us to do the job. He said cooking for cowboys is way too much work for his wife, who is expecting a baby any day now—"

"Two more months. I'm not expecting until August."

"That's okay. No help. No way. Uh-uh. Definitely not." Georgie was adamant.

She was getting nowhere with the younger Mr. Ping. Curious, Abby peered in the cobwebby windows of the cookshack before she left. It looked as though it hadn't been used for a long time—not in years. The wooden floorboards were sagging; maybe the foundation had given out. There was a pile of dead flies under the window directly across from the one she was peering through. The ancient gas stove in the corner looked dreadful. She was glad she wasn't cooking on it. And the refrigerator was one of those oldies that had the rounded corners, the bread-loaf shape that had been popular in the early fifties.

Good luck, she thought, wiping her hands on her T-shirt. "Well, see you later!" she called to the Pings and walked back to the house.

"Phoebe?" she asked, when the girl came down for breakfast half an hour later, "have you ever been to a roundup?"

"Oh, sure. Plenty of times," the girl said, smiling. "They're fun."

"Uh-huh." Abby thought for a moment. "And what's the usual, you know, the usual sort of thing that happens when everybody gets back to the ranch with the cows and calves? What do people do?"

"Well, they usually do the branding in the morning. If they get back here today, they'll likely start early tomorrow while it's still cool. That's the way they've always done it in the roundups I've been on. Then they have a big meal and sometimes there's even dancing, if anybody plays an instrument, and then everybody goes home.'' Phoebe looked up from the toast she was spreading with jam. ''Why?''

''What sort of meal?''

''Oh, everyone piles into the kitchen, or dining room, depending on how many there are, and fills up. Adam Garrick always has big picnic tables set up outside under the trees if the weather's good—and it always is. I don't think they brand in the rain. Then he has a barbecue. And, of course, they always have prairie oysters, but I never eat them. I haven't been to a roundup at his place since he got married. Maybe his wife does it differently now. I don't know.''

''So the wife's in charge of things?''

''Uh-huh,'' Phoebe mumbled, swallowing her bite of toast. ''Or, on a really big place, the cow boss's wife or the foreman's wife is in charge. Usually the ladies bring stuff, salads or squares or something. There's always tons of food. Kids running around, that sort of thing. It's fun.''

''Is your family coming?''

Phoebe shrugged. ''Probably. My mom, anyway, because I think she's bringing my little brother over for the branding. Trev's a pretty good roper and Noah promised him he could rope some calves this year.''

Abby slowly digested this information. Roundup was a big deal, Noah had told her. Obviously it was a bigger deal than she'd realized. He'd hired Georgie and his uncle to prepare the roundup meal, assuming it would be too much for her. Abby tried to recall how many people had gone out with Noah and Carl. At least six others. That made eight, plus them. Ten. And if their families came...

Well, it *was* a lot of work. Imagine the potato salad that would disappear. And the rolls. And the meat. Cowboys were big eaters. Maybe Noah had been right—an experienced cook was needed. Or cooks. Still, she thought grumpily, he could have asked her.

But were they all going to eat in that horrible shack down there? Abby shuddered.

She wandered into the dining room. That big walnut table could seat ten. And they could get another eight around the kitchen table. And, if worse came to worst, they could haul the picnic table up onto the veranda and seat another six out there. Kids, maybe.

Abby cheered up. This was her chance to prove herself to the community. She knew farms and she knew farm women. Ranch women couldn't be that different.

Abby wasn't about to impress anyone with her bread-making skills, the way her mother would have been able to. But she could make darn good pastry. Once, when she was sixteen, she'd won first prize at the Wicoigon Fall Fair for her lemon meringue pie.

''Phoebe?'' she asked, when she came back into the kitchen. ''Want to go to town?''

"Sure. What for?" the girl asked, her eyes curious.

"Some supplies. I'm going to need a couple dozen lemons and some more eggs. Get the ones at the health-food store, they're free range. And pick up six pie plates for me, Pyrex ones, at the Co-op. And a couple gallons of ice cream, half vanilla, half chocolate. And some decent coffee, two pounds. Ground."

"You mean—drive myself?" Phoebe sounded surprised.

"You've got your license, haven't you?"

"Yes."

"Then you drive in and do the shopping for me. I've got a million things to do right here this afternoon."

"Like what?" Phoebe smiled.

"Like make some pies." Abby did a quick calculation in her head. Six pieces per pie. There were a lot of hungry cowboys and their families. "Eight, to be exact."

"Oh, Phoebe!" she called from behind the screen door as the girl went down the porch steps. Phoebe paused and looked back. "What are prairie oysters?"

Phoebe laughed. "Never mind, Ab. Trust me— you don't want to know."

BY THE TIME Phoebe got back, Abby had the pastry made. She'd never made it in such a big batch before, even though she did it in two lots. The oven only held four pie plates at once. She planned to produce the pies for the big roundup supper, which would probably be held the next evening, if Phoebe was right. She'd make the filling and meringue in the morning, and finish the pies then.

That meant she had to come up with some kind of dessert for this evening, if Noah and his crew got back with the herd today, as planned.

Strawberry shortcake. There was nothing to that—only the biscuits, strawberries and cream. She'd get strawberries somewhere and there was cream in the refrigerator. If they didn't have enough, they'd have ice cream with it. After all, there wouldn't be such a crowd this evening. Only the hands who'd been out on the actual roundup.

Abby sent Phoebe over to her mother's garden, several miles away, to beg or buy an ice-cream pail of strawberries from their garden while Abby made the shortcakes. Phoebe laughed and said she was sure her mother would donate the berries; she'd never sold them to a neighbor yet.

Another reason to have a proper farm garden, Abby thought, as she whipped up the rich biscuit dough from her grandmother's recipe. She rolled and cut individual rounds with a floured glass and popped them in the hot oven. She made two dozen, just to be sure. She was positive Ben Longquist could eat three, and Carl, for all his spare build, looked like a good eater to her.

When the biscuits came out of the oven and she'd piled them on a rack to cool, she walked down to the cookshack to see how the two cooks were getting on. They'd had trouble connecting the stove properly and Georgie was looking dejected.

"Man, oh man, Mr. Winslow's gonna be mad." He sighed. "You know where he might have a pipe wrench? We could use a pipe wrench."

Abby shook her head. "Listen. If you get the stove fixed, fine. Otherwise, there's been a change of plans," she said firmly. "I want everybody to eat up at the house tomorrow. This place is filthy and there's no way you two are going to be able to clean it up."

Georgie seemed relieved.

"I've made a bunch of pies for tomorrow and shortcakes for tonight," she went on, "and you two can do the meat and whatever else you've planned. But we're going to cook and serve it up at the house."

"You made pies?" Georgie sounded very impressed.

"I made pies," she repeated. "Lots. You're all coming up to the house for the roundup supper tomorrow."

"You sure, missus?" he asked worriedly. "Mr. Winslow's gonna be awful mad."

"He won't be. Leave him to me," she said, fingers crossed behind her back. She thought—hoped—Noah would be reasonable.

"Maybe we can put some stuff in the fridge down here, missus. It's working okay. Then we'll bring the rest up to the house. I can do the roast beef today. We'll have it cold for sandwiches tomorrow."

"Why not ham for sandwiches? I've got ham in the fridge."

"No way. Cowboys don't eat ham, just roast beef, missus. Roast beef and steaks. Beans, too!" He laughed and his uncle smiled.

"All right. So it's settled then. You're coming up to the house?"

"Settled."

"Great!" Abby smiled and the two men smiled back and bobbed their heads agreeably. Abby found herself bobbing back. She giggled. Phoebe was right: roundup could be a lot of fun.

ABOUT FOUR O'CLOCK, Abby left the kitchen to Georgie and his uncle—they had a huge roast in the oven and were peeling potatoes for a lunchtime salad next day—and went upstairs to lie down.

The twins were taking their toll on her energy, and she was grateful for the opportunity to rest. No matter how she wanted to represent herself to the men in the household, the truth was, she felt huge and awkward. Even rolling out the pie pastry had been exhausting.

Her back was killing her.

She dozed off and woke to the sound of Phoebe's voice on the porch downstairs, calling to the two men in the kitchen. "They're coming!"

The herd. Noah. Everyone. Abby lay there for a few moments longer, thinking. She couldn't believe the thrill of excitement that had shot through her veins when she'd heard Phoebe's announcement. At least, they were all right. If they were bringing the cows back, everything must have gone according to schedule.

Abby got up and swung her feet over the side of the bed. She stretched and pushed her hair away from her face, then got up and padded to the window.

There they were. It was a magnificent sight. Hundreds of cows on the other side of the river. They were coming around from a small gap in the river valley and being herded toward the wooden bridge.

Abby leaned on the windowsill. There was noise and dust and the bawling of cows and calves. Dogs barked. Cowboys on horseback rode back and forth along the herd, keeping them in formation. Which one was Noah? She couldn't tell from this distance, but she thought she recognized the tall, rangy form of Big Blue. Noah had said he planned to take the young gelding on his first roundup, see how much cow sense he had.

She raised the window and leaned out, breathing deeply of the heated afternoon air. She could smell the first pink roses on the climber that wound its way halfway up the house on two sides. It was an old rose, a survivor. The grass baked in the heat and the old cottonwood tree that stood at the corner of the drive waved gently in the breeze. It was another glorious day. For a few moments, Abby forgot she was a stranger here. She was one with the scene, a ranch woman waiting for her man to come home.

If only, she thought, sighing. She called down to Phoebe, "The Pings need any help?"

"I don't think so," Phoebe replied, shading her

eyes with her hand as she looked up at Abby on the
second floor. "They're sitting down and having a
cup of tea just now. Can you smell the meat in the
oven?"

"Yes." Abby gazed out at the herd again. The
first cows were cautiously approaching the wooden
timbers of the bridge. A cowboy rode up—or maybe
it was old Amanda Dexter—and flicked a rope at
the lead cow. She lunged onto the bridge, her calf
at her side, and the others followed. The herd strung
out onto the bridge, and the valley thundered with
the sound of their hooves. Old Pat got up from her
spot on the porch and barked and barked. She
whined and danced, excited as the humans. No
doubt she wanted to be out there with the rest of the
dogs, nipping at heels and dodging hooves.

Abby combed her hair and washed her face. Then
she smoothed her hands over the enormous bulge
that preceded her these days, talking softly to her
babies, and made her way slowly downstairs.

The Pings offered her a cup of tea, which she
accepted. It was green tea, Chinese tea, which tasted
good to her. She stood at the open kitchen door with
her mug in her hand. Two cowboys had come across
the river before the cows and were now busy keeping the first arrivals bunched together. A few cows
made a dash for it when they got to this side of the
river, but a burst of speed from a cow pony and a
yell from a cowboy quickly put them back with the
others. Gradually, the whole herd crossed the Horsethief River.

"What will they do with them now?" Abby asked

Phoebe, who was sitting on the porch balustrade, watching.

"They'll put them into corrals and let them settle down. Water them. Make sure they've got feed."

"Mmm." Abby watched a little longer, then thought of everything there was still to do. She'd make a huge pot of coffee with the buffet machine she'd found in the pantry. And they'd prepare some sandwiches for the hungriest of the crew. Cheese. Egg salad. Did cowboys eat egg salad? Supper wouldn't be for another hour or so.

Abby was busy spreading butter onto sliced bread when she heard the door open. She turned.

Noah. He hadn't shaved for four days and he looked wonderful. She wondered if her smile appeared as happy as she felt inside.

"Hello, boss!" Georgie said, wiping his hands together and bowling slightly. He looked very dapper and cooklike in a brilliant white chef's apron. His uncle wore one, too, over his dark cotton pants and jacket.

"Georgie! What're you doin' here?" Noah stepped inside. He'd glanced at Georgie, but his gaze returned almost instantly to hers. Abby felt excitement trickle up from her toes. She took a step toward him.

"I—I'm glad you're back," she said softly.

He smiled. "Is that all?" he asked. He came forward and wrapped his arms around her. "How's my bride?"

She looked up, startled. "What's—?"

"This," he said, before she'd finished her question. He kissed her. A tender, passionate, thorough kiss that had her blushing before he'd finished. He smiled again and she caught his quick glance toward the others. "Don't forget," he whispered, "we're practically honeymooners."

"I see," she said, still blushing. "Right." So that was all—a little exhibition for the Pings and Phoebe.

"And even if we weren't—" He kissed her again, and she felt his hand on her belly, caressing, soothing. She felt one of her babies—maybe both of them—kick.

Noah's arm was still around her. "How are my babies doing?" he asked, smiling down at her, his other hand casually on the shelf of her stomach.

My babies. Was it only show for the Pings? She didn't think so. She caught her breath. *My babies.*

"Fine. The babies are fine." *And so,* she thought, her heart hammering wildly, *is their mother.*

CHAPTER TWELVE

HE HADN'T HAD the feeling for years, maybe not since he was a boy. That feeling of anticipation rounding the last hill before the ranch came into sight, then the urge to spur your horse into a fast run and yell like a banshee. Home!

Of course, he couldn't do it. And even if he hadn't had five hundred cows and a crew with him, he was too old for that sort of behavior.

He'd been coming home to a dark, cold house for most of his years on the Lazy SB. The house wasn't cold and dark anymore. Hadn't been for more than a month. And there were home-cooked meals on the table. The counters were clean and the windows sparkled with sun he hadn't seen for years with those old venetian blinds down all the time.

The radio'd be playing that rock and roll station she liked, full-blast, and there'd be the scent of coffee or homemade soup on the stove. *Dessert.* Man, he was getting desserts these days! He'd put on a pound or two to show for it. Folks always said, looks like marriage is agreeing with you when they noticed you were gaining weight. Was it true? Was marriage agreeing with him? He was beginning to suspect it was.

Even old Pat seemed happier. The dog had had a few groomings and a bath since Abby'd married him, probably much to her surprise.

Noah had had a chance to think things over, spending three nights sleeping under the stars. He'd thought about his situation pretty carefully and kept coming to one conclusion: he wanted this to work. He wanted Abby to stay, Abby and her babies. They were going to be his kids, too, from now on. His family. He didn't know what would happen when and if Jesse came back. But his brother had missed his chance to play daddy. It was Noah's turn. And he wasn't giving it up.

That meant he'd have to smooth things with Abby. Ease into it. Get her used to the idea. Be a little more understanding. More tender. More thoughtful. He'd had no idea she'd get so bent out of shape over his hiring Phoebe. Frankly, he'd been shocked—he'd thought he was doing her a favor. Then there were the Pings. She was bound to be furious about that. But he was on firm ground there—no way was she cooking for a roundup crew. Not in her condition. No discussion on *that* topic. Besides, he was the rancher; he knew ranching. If she'd been from a ranch background, well, maybe. But she wasn't. She was a teacher, a farm girl. She wouldn't have a clue about cooking for a roundup and branding crew.

What a sight that was, coming into the broad river valley of the home ranch. All those healthy white-faces with their calves beside them. He was pleased with the condition of the cows. There were a few older dry cows that they'd missed separating out last fall; these would go into their own pastures now and eventually be shipped out. There were some heifers that hadn't calved; he'd have to keep an eye on them. One more chance and no calf, and he had to ship the heifer. You couldn't feed stock that had no payback or you'd go broke. He wasn't running a petting zoo.

And then the house, pretty as a picture up on that knoll. It definitely needed a coat of paint, which he'd see to this summer. Funny, he hadn't noticed it before. The roses Carl and Abby had pruned looked tidy and green, climbing up the house. The lawn was mowed. And there—right at the open window of his bedroom, leaning on her elbows—was his wife. Noah felt a rush of unfamiliar emotion but just then a crooked-horn cow broke away from the rest, bawling, her calf behind her, and Blue was off like a shot. Put Noah's mind right back on business.

Coming into the house, though, after the cows were safely corralled for the night, brought it all back again. Her hair was tied back loosely, pale tendrils here and there. Her T-shirt was huge, covering that big pregnant belly. She looked stunning to him. Beautiful. Her eyes were bright and blue, her face flushed. He hadn't planned on kissing her but he just did. After all, they were married, newlyweds despite the babies on the way, and if nothing else, the Pings and Phoebe would've expected it. Abby *hadn't* expected it, but she'd seemed pleased all the same. She'd been willing. Maybe even more than willing. Maybe there was something real for the two of them—the four of them—down the road. He could hope, couldn't he? So he kissed her again.

"Where's everybody?" she asked, her cheeks very red.

"They're coming in," Noah replied casually, tossing his hat onto the hat rack. He ran his hand over his stubble-roughened chin. "A shave and a shower's what I need."

"I like your beard," she said shyly, and he swore that if they hadn't had an audience, he'd have danced her around the kitchen. He definitely would have kissed her once more and taken his time about it, too.

"I'd better see who's staying and who's leaving," Noah said, glancing out the window. "Then I'll come back in and get cleaned up for supper." He nodded at the counter. "Looks like you've been busy, Georgie. Didn't the stove work down in the cookshack?"

"No, Mr. Winslow. The missus wanted us to come up here, use her kitchen. Everybody's gonna eat here tomorrow. I told her no way, she couldn't help." Georgie grinned and shrugged his thin shoulders. "But did she listen? No. She made strawberry shortcake. She made pies—"

"Pies!" Noah turned to Abby, smiling. "Is he *serious?*"

"I made eight pies," she said proudly. "Lemon meringue."

Noah's smile widened. Pies! What a woman. "Shortcake, too?"

"My grandmother's recipe. We're having that for

supper tonight. Phoebe brought over a bucket of strawberries from her parents' place."

"I see." Noah retrieved his hat and jammed it on his head. "Look, I'll go count noses, see how many will be here. Amanda, for sure, and Carl and my crew. Ben. Jeremiah and his girl might leave and come back tomorrow."

He had to get out of the house before he burst out laughing. To see Georgie Ping in a blindingly clean apron in the Winslow kitchen, Georgie's uncle with the wispy goatee tied up, as usual, with elastic bands—his wife giving the orders.

To the Pings? That was rich. He'd have to tell Cal Blake, where the Pings usually worked. Cal was always moaning about how ornery his cooks were. The Pings agreed with everything he said, Cal told him, smiling and bowing the whole time, then did exactly what they wanted.

Maybe he'd misjudged Abby. Eight pies! He'd always known she had grit; now he knew how tough and stubborn she could be, too.

A woman well worth keeping, in his opinion.

BEN LONGQUIST and Jeremiah Blake roped the calves in turn and brought them in one at a time to the center of the corral for the flankers, who grabbed the calf, front and behind, and threw it onto its side. The calves were vaccinated, earmarked and branded inside of a minute. Traditionally, the old-timers and ranchers handled the branding irons—in this case, Noah and Amanda Dexter. From long experience, Miz Amanda knew to within a degree just when the iron was hot enough to do the job and not to injure the animal. In Noah's father's time, they'd heated the irons at an old-fashioned wood fire, but these days they used butane heaters specially made for the job.

While one applied the brand, the Lazy SB, which was an *S* sloping to the left and a *B* sloping to the right, the other dehorned the calf with a special cone-shaped tool, which dug the growing nubs out of the calf's skull and applied an antibiotic paste to prevent infection. Dehorned cattle were easier to handle. At the same time, the knife man castrated the male calves, tossing the testicles into a bucket to be cooked up later as prairie oysters for the adventurous. They were dipped in buttermilk and cornmeal or flour and then deep-fried. Noah wasn't particularly fond of the traditional spring delicacy, but there were cowboys who looked forward to branding just for the menu. Give him a beefsteak, well done, any day. And not from the Lazy SB, either. Like many farmers and ranchers, he preferred beef obtained from his neighbors' ranches.

After branding, the calves were turned loose to mother up. There was always a lot of dust and bellowing from the worried cows and temporarily dazed calves running around bawling for their mothers. In the end all was well, and the cows that had been reunited with their calves would inspect their offspring, then move out onto the grass to graze while the rest milled anxiously near the branding area.

During a break, as they waited for Trevor Longquist to rope his calf, Noah noticed Abby sitting near the fence on a lawn chair, watching. He waved and she waved back, smiling.

Jeremiah Blake's lady friend hadn't returned for the branding, but other than her, the full crew was there, plus family members who'd been arriving since just before noon. Noah noticed that Nan Longquist—Ben and Trev and Phoebe's mother—stood near Abby, chatting. Amanda Dexter had remarked on the lightness and flavor of the shortcake last night, which augured well for Abby's acceptance into the community. If old Miz Amanda put in a favorable word, it carried plenty of weight. Nan Longquist would be a good friend, too, although she was probably twenty years older than his wife.

Noah was pleased. Things were progressing as well as could be expected, considering that three months before he hadn't even met Abby Steen. Or known about his brother's involvement with her.

That was the only dark shadow on an otherwise fairly sunny picture—Jesse.

He missed his brother. He'd never been on roundup without him. But he wasn't going to worry about Jesse now. They'd had a good gather this year. Only one cow missing, and she was an old one who'd been dry last year and probably hadn't had a calf this spring, either. He'd planned to ship her, anyway. This way she'd died somewhere on the range where she'd lived out her life—likely been dinner for a pack of wolves or a grizzly bear. He preferred that idea to shipping her to some packing plant where she'd end up in dog food and a glue bottle.

His calf crop was excellent, and the cows were in prime condition. This was the first year he'd used mainly offspring from his prize bull for breeding and the results were good. Big Blue had turned out to have a decent share of cow sense, which Noah had expected, considering that his granddaddy was one of Adam Garrick's top cutting stallions.

Yes. Life was good. And, from what he could see, it was only going to get better.

NOAH MADE A POINT of being more thoughtful and considerate with Abby. He left notes for her every morning, telling her where he'd be that day and when he expected to get back. He made sure she had his cell phone number, but she never called, except once when he was in Glory to remind him to pick up some milk.

He was glad to see that since the roundup, Abby had had some visitors. Nan Longquist came to see her several times, and even that tough old bird, Amanda Dexter, drove up one day in her pickup, an armful of rhubarb in the back for Abby. She'd taken a definite fancy to his wife, for which Noah was grateful.

Two weeks later, when he was driving her to town for her regular checkup with Kate Pleasance, he tried to figure out just how to broach the subject of maybe hiring Phoebe Longquist for the entire summer. The girl was free after her final exams that week, and Nan had told him privately that Phoebe would jump at the chance to stick around Glory and make some money for her first year of university. She had a boyfriend in town, working at the municipal hall, and the only other offer she'd had was for part-time at the town library, which barely paid enough to cover her gas.

He stopped at the mailbox at the end of his lane and shoved the handful of what looked to be bills and flyers into the glove compartment, then started the car again.

"You're going to be busy when the babies are born," he said, deciding he might as well jump right in. Man, that was an understatement—

"Yes," she agreed, glancing sideways at him. She was wearing some of the new maternity clothes she and Donna had bought on a recent trip to Calgary. A pale yellow dress, cut generously, with ties at the shoulder. Her figure was lush and full now; hardly resembled the thin girl he'd first met back in April. Her girth had expanded hugely and, according to Abby, Kate was now predicting the babies might come a little earlier than her mid-August due date. From now on, she'd be seeing the doctor once a week.

"I was thinking maybe you'd like someone to move in for the summer, help you out—"

"Move in?"

"Yes. What about Phoebe?" He risked a quick glance. She seemed interested, at least. "You got along pretty well with her, and her mother says she's looking for work after school's out this week."

"Move in with us? In the *house?*"

"Why not? She could come over on a daily basis, but it might be better if she lived in."

"But there's only three bedrooms upstairs."

Yes, and he was in one of them. Damn. Noah drove silently, digesting that fact.

"And we're going to need a room for the babies. I'd like to get that corner room fixed up for them. The one Phoebe slept in during roundup. Although I suppose I could have them in with me," she added.

"No way. You'd never get any rest." Damn, for a moment there he'd actually forgotten how different things were going to be once the babies arrived. "Uh, I guess we'll have to shop for furniture soon, huh? Cribs? Whatever they'll need?"

He looked at her and was surprised to see that she'd turned red and was avoiding his gaze. "I was wondering about that," she said finally. "Yes, I need to do some major shopping pretty soon, while I still feel up to it."

"How about we go to Riddley's when you finish with Kate today?" he suggested impulsively. The long-time Glory family department store carried just about everything. "We'll have lunch at Molly's or the Wild Goose, if you prefer, then we'll check out the baby department at Riddley's and the co-op."

She smiled and nodded, and Noah took that as not only acceptance of his plan to acquire the baby furniture but also his plan to hire Phoebe over the next couple of months.

He noticed that her color remained heightened, and she seemed thoughtful when he looked at her again, a few minutes later.

"Noah?"

"Uh-huh?" He swerved slightly to avoid a pot-hole.

"You could move in with me."

Noah damn near drove off the road. "With *you?*"

"I mean, just temporarily," she said hastily. "Phoebe could have your room then. You could—I don't know. You could sleep on a cot or some-thing. We could move in a temporary bed—"

"Or I could sleep with you," he said softly.

She turned a deeper shade of pink. "I—uh, I don't think that'd be a very good idea, but, you know—Phoebe would probably think it's weird that you're sleeping in another room."

"People do that. Especially when they're preg-nant."

"I suppose so." She chewed her lip. "Forget I mentioned it—"

"No. Hell, I think it's a good idea." He had no intention of losing this opportunity to make major gains with her—at her own suggestion, yet. "I'll move a bed in there. And we can fix up my room for Phoebe and the bedroom in the corner for the babies. You pick out some paint or paper, and I'll take care of the work. Right away. This weekend."

She smiled. It gladdened his heart to see that sim-ple, sincere smile. *Had she ever smiled at his brother like that?* "Thank you. I'll feel a lot better when we've got everything ready for the babies. I'll feel more—more ready myself, somehow."

The babies. The babies.

"Look, Abby." Noah took a deep breath.

Damned one way and damned the other. "I've been thinking. About after the babies come and all."

"Yes?" She sounded frightened.

He looked at her briefly. Her eyes were dark and wide. "I was wondering if, you know—if you'd consider staying on. For good."

"For good?" she whispered.

"Yeah. Staying here with me. Giving family life a chance—"

"You mean, stay married here at the ranch with you? Husband and wife?"

"And the babies. Yeah. That's what I mean." He dared to glance at her and was glad he had. Her eyes were bright and shiny and her smile was tremulous.

"Oh, I *would,* Noah! I really would like to try and give it a chance—"

"You would?" His reply sounded dazed to his own ears.

"Yes." After that, she gazed steadily out the window for a moment or two. Noah wasn't sure he could identify the swirl of emotions that he felt pumping through him. Relief, for sure. Anticipation. Wondering how their relationship would change. And hope. Plain, down-home hope that this could work. This crazy marriage they had.

"Abby?"

"Yes?"

He held out his hand and she gave him hers. "I know I said I wasn't cut out for marriage, but I'm starting to think maybe I was wrong. I like being married to you." He squeezed gently, savoring the feeling of her softness, her tenderness, her small hand fitting so perfectly into his. It was a good feeling.

"What do you think?" he asked. "Stay married? You and me?"

She nodded, smiling. "Yes."

He released her hand and she returned it primly to her lap—what was left of her lap.

So that was what it felt like to propose, really propose, to a woman.

Noah wanted to open the window of the car and yell to the magpies, the waving green crops on both sides of the highway, the crows up on the telephone wire. *I'm married! This is my wife!*

It was hot in town, and after Noah escorted Abby to the doctor's office, he left to do a few errands. So far, she hadn't asked him to stay with her during one of her checkups. He didn't know if Kate thought that was unusual or not. How many men accompanied their wives? He'd guess not many. Not in Glory. The waiting room was full, so he figured an hour at least before he'd have to come back for her. It was just about noon. She'd be hungry by the time they went over to the deli or to the hotel for a meal.

Noah couldn't wipe the smile off his face all the while he did his business. People waved and he waved back. People honked at him as he drove down Main Street and he honked back. He dropped in at his lawyer's, Lucas Yellowfly's, to pick up some documents Lucas had for him. Lucas asked what the hell he felt so good about and Noah replied, "Life." Then he went over to the municipal hall to double-check some water rights registered on his property. The rights dated way back, but he'd forgotten who owned them. After that, he stopped at the bank, just to say hello to the manager and remind him how good his calf crop looked this year.

Unlike a lot of farmers and ranchers, Noah was fairly solvent. He'd been a good manager. The Winslows had always been in the habit of putting every extra penny back into the operation. They weren't much for spending money on paint and paper for the house and new vehicles or fancy clothes for themselves or holidays down south. A tractor, now that was different. Or a good bull.

Noah had noticed the seeds coming up in the garden Carl had planted for Abby. He'd noticed how much better the flower beds looked, now that Carl and Abby had dug them out and weeded them. And Carl was keeping the lawn cut, too, at Abby's request. That reminded him—paint!

He went up the hardware and got the manager to contact a crew to come out and paint the place next week. Top-line Benjamin Moore, in a buff color, with white trim. Might as well have everything spiffed up before the babies came. Maybe they'd even have a party, a christening barbecue—was there such a thing? He'd have to ask his wife.

His wife! Man, he liked the sound of that.

Abby was beaming when he picked her up. Kate had said everything was going well, the babies were exactly on track, she was gaining the right amount of weight, her blood pressure was good—it was just a waiting game now.

Noah was happy to hear it. He took Abby to

Molly McClung's deli for lunch and afterward they spent two hours shopping for baby furniture. If it had been up to Noah, he'd have finished the transactions inside of fifteen minutes, but Abby wanted to look at everything, touch everything, look at blue linens, look at yellow linens, go to the toy department. He humored her. In the end, they ordered two cribs, both white, to be delivered the next day. He also ordered a fold-up cot, which he intended to install in her room. Not, he thought to himself, that he intended to sleep very long on that contraption. He figured he'd be in her bed before the end of the month. With any luck.

Noah carried out the packages of baby clothing, sleepers, diapers, pins and other supplies, plus sheets and cotton blankets, to the car. He was feeling more like a family man all the time. It was a good feeling. A great feeling.

On the way home, Abby opened the glove compartment and leafed casually through the mail he'd collected that morning. She'd told him she expected a letter from her sister, Meg, any day.

She paused, opened an envelope and he noticed that something fell out—another envelope, soiled-looking, with plenty of postmarks on it.

He heard her gasp.

"What is it, Abby—what's the matter?"

"This letter—" She held it up to him, her eyes anguished. She held the unopened envelope in her other hand. "It's from Mom."

"So?" He frowned. She'd been hearing from her parents since their marriage.

"She sent on this letter, from Jesse—"

"*Jesse!*"

"Yes. She wants to know what's going on. She thought I went to Canada to marry him—*oh, Noah!*"

CHAPTER THIRTEEN

ABBY WAS HORRIFIED. She'd never dreamed anything like this would happen. She hadn't bothered to inform her parents that she'd married her babies' uncle, not their biological father. She had thought it would only be needlessly confusing; she'd assumed her parents' main concern would be the fact that she was married. She hadn't thought one Winslow or another would matter to them. She hadn't thought they'd even remember Jesse's first name.

But her mother had. And now she was wondering what was going on, as they'd received a letter postmarked British Columbia, Canada, from the man they believed she'd married.

"What's in it—the letter? Open it." Noah ordered.

With fumbling fingers, Abby obeyed. A bank draft fell out, for one thousand and fifty dollars. Made out to her. Shocked, Abby held it up in one hand, between thumb and forefinger and stared helplessly at Noah.

"Well, what's he got to say for himself?" Noah demanded. He sounded angry.

Until then, Abby hadn't noticed the short handwritten letter that accompanied the money. She picked it up now and read it slowly out loud. "Dear Abby, I hope you've forgiven me for the way I ran out on you—" She heard Noah snort and ignored it. "I never meant to hurt you. I just couldn't face marriage right away like that. I needed some time to get used to the idea. Well, I've thought it over and—"

Noah swore loudly and Abby gazed at him. "Go on!" he muttered.

"—I realized it's definitely not for me. Maybe not ever. I have sent some money for you and the baby. I'll send more from time to time, when I have it. I hope you'll forgive me someday." She stopped and closed her mouth tightly.

"And? Anything else?"

"He just signed it, 'Yours, Jesse.'"

"*Yours!*" Noah swore again. "What a pile of—" he hunted for the appropriate word "—*garbage!* I'd say something more accurate, but not in front of a lady."

"Are you being fair about this, Noah?" Now that she'd recovered from the initial shock, she found Noah's response bewildering, not to mention rather inappropriate. "He's doing his best. He's sent money because he thinks I'll need it and—"

"Well, you can send it right back! You're my wife and my responsibility. So are those babies. From the moment we signed that marriage contract, they were *my* children. *I* pay."

"I don't suppose he knows we're married," she said slowly.

Noah paused, and seemed to consider that for a

while. Finally he sighed heavily. "No, I suppose he doesn't." He drove in silence for another mile or so. "Where's he sending it from? Is there an address?"

Abby turned the letter over. There was nothing on it to indicate his address. She looked at the envelope, which had two postmarks. They were smudged and hard to read. "One of the postmarks seems to be some place like Q-U-I-L-C-H—"

"Quilchena. Probably the store or hotel at the Quilchena Ranch."

"Looks like Merritt on the other—"

"He's in the Nicola Valley in B.C.," Noah said. "There's a lot of big ranches there. He likely found some work on one of them. Roundup, branding, whatever." He frowned and kept his eyes straight ahead.

"I guess he doesn't expect me to write back," she said lightly, turning the letter over again. "With no address like that—"

"Bastard doesn't *want* you writing back. He doesn't want to be found, that's what. He doesn't want anyone catching up to him and rubbing his nose in his responsibility, that's what!"

Abby remained silent. There was no point in her saying anything in Jesse's defense. Noah wasn't being fair, in her view, but he was Jesse's brother. He had to know him better than she did; he'd already proved that.

"W-what do you think I should do with this?" She held up the bank draft. "I can hardly send it back with no return address and it's already money spent. It's not like a check. I can hardly rip it up, can I?''

"No." Noah looked at her, and she thought she sensed the pain in his expression. "Put it in the bank for the kids, if you want. It's their money. Blood money from their biological father. Guilt money. Or give it to a charity of your choice, for all I care. Or put it on the bank in his account, the one where I put the money I got for his bungalow. It's there if he ever wants it.''

"Well…'' Abby folded the bank draft after a moment's hesitation and slipped it in the side pocket of her handbag. She didn't know what to think about this new development.

"I said it once and I'm going to say it again, Abby. You're my wife, and as far as anybody knows, those are my children you're carrying. I'm responsible for all of you. Everything and everybody! You're my family. Jesse can keep his damn money.''

She was silent the rest of the way home, as was Noah. She could only guess why he was so furious about Jesse's letter. Surely he wasn't still white-hot mad at his brother for running out on her. Everything had changed since then, for both of them. And hadn't he just asked her on the way to town today if they couldn't work it out for a lot longer than the birth of the babies? Maybe even forever? And hadn't she agreed? You'd think he'd be happy to hear that Jesse was okay, that he was working somewhere. That he wasn't coming back to claim parental rights.

Forever was a pretty big word. She wasn't promising anything right now, except to give it her best, and neither should he. It was one thing to try to make their marriage work. It was quite another to pretend they were madly in love with each other. To pretend that they were in this "till death do us part." Maybe they were, and maybe they weren't. At this point, there was no way of knowing.

The next day Abby and Noah spent the morning in what she was beginning to think of as the nursery. Or the babies' room. It was the upstairs bedroom at the other corner of the house, across from the room Noah was currently using. Phoebe had slept in it the three nights she'd stayed earlier in June. It had an iron bedstead with sagging coils and an old tufted mattress. Abby made Noah throw it all out. Fortunately, the ancient dusty carpet wasn't tacked down and she got Noah to roll that up and dispose of it, too. The hardwood floors, protected from damage under the carpet for all those years, were in perfect condition. There was a cherrywood vanity with a big round mirror; it had possibilities, but not for the babies' room. Abby had Noah and Carl move it into the attic bedroom, a room that looked as though it had been the repository for every unwanted item on the ranch since the house was built. One day, when she was slim again and feeling fit, she planned to go through that room. Who knew what she'd find in there.

Then, the following day, the day the furniture was supposed to arrive from Riddley's, Noah spent the afternoon painting the bedroom, after Abby helped him patch the old, cracked plaster. He wouldn't let her sand it, swearing it had to be bad for her health. Nor would he let her anywhere nearby while he painted, swearing the fumes had to be dangerous to a woman in her condition.

It was frustrating. She knew Noah was probably right, but she resented his high-handed manner. He had a lot to learn about getting along with someone on a day-to-day basis. Abby had to content herself with readying the babies' clothing, prewashing all the diapers and little cotton shirts and sleepers. She organized supplies for a new shelf, which would go on the wall when the paint had dried. Carl had sanded and oiled an old chest of drawers, which she was using in the nursery. For the walls, she'd chosen a sunny pale yellow, a straw color that went very well with the south exposure of the nursery and with the warm wood tones of the oak floors.

She felt a lot better by late afternoon when they'd finished. She puttered about, setting up the shelf of supplies—the cotton swabs, the alcohol, the diaper pins, the ointments and lotions, the tiny hooded towels and baby washcloths. She lined the drawers of the chest with white paper, then filled it with the freshly washed baby clothes. The curtainless windows were wide open to let in the breeze and banish the last of the paint fumes.

Noah put the cribs together and installed the plastic-covered mattresses, then left her to finish up.

He disappeared for a half hour—she had no idea where he'd gone—then reappeared, carrying things from his current room to what she'd come to think of as her bedroom. Abby's heart stopped in her throat. Of course. Hadn't he said he'd move into her room? Hadn't she invited him?

When she heard him go downstairs, she went down the hall. There was the roll-away cot set up, with sheets on it already, against the far wall of the bedroom. They'd be sleeping less than two yards apart. He'd hung his shirts and pants and various other things back in the closet that had once been his, next to the few clothes she'd brought with her and the maternity dresses she'd bought since. His dress hats were now on the top shelf, his belts hanging from the hook at the side of the closet.

Abby silently left the room before Noah could return. She could use a cup of something hot. Herbal tea? Hot milk? She'd reduced her caffeine intake, partly because it seemed to make the babies rambunctious and partly because she wasn't enjoying it as much as she used to.

She met Noah on the stairs. He smiled and put his arms around her, his eyes nearly on a level with hers as he stood one step lower.

"You really don't mind?" he asked.

"Mind?"

"What we talked about. Me moving in with you."

She felt her cheeks warm. "Of course not. When's Phoebe coming over?"

"Tomorrow morning. You're sure, huh?"

"Don't be silly. It makes sense. Don't you think?"

"Oh, I do," he murmured, his face very close to hers. "I do. But probably not the way you think."

He kissed her gently and she bent her head and rested her too-warm forehead against his shirt for a few seconds. She was so hot. She put her hands against his chest as she swayed slightly.

"Hey! I don't think this is the best place for getting to know each other better, do you?" He laughed and released her and backed down the stairs. She followed him, their eyes not breaking contact the entire way.

"I'm making some herbal tea," she said at the bottom of the stairs, willing her cheeks to cool. "Would you like some?"

"Regular tea. And make extra. Carl's outside." Whistling, Noah raced up the stairs again.

THAT NIGHT, Abby waited for Noah to come into her bedroom. Their bedroom, she corrected herself more than once. She hadn't decided what she thought about the change in their relationship—if there was one—but she couldn't get over her feeling of apprehension and, oddly, excitement. With her being eight months pregnant! She lay awake until nearly midnight, then fell into a restless sleep. He never showed up.

In the morning she discovered he'd spent the night in his own bedroom down the hall. He stripped the sheets and tossed them in the washer, then, after breakfast, headed off to the Gallant farm to pick up Phoebe, who lived with her parents on Joe Gallant's place. Joe and her mother, Nan, were brother and sister, and her father, Harry, worked for Joe.

Abby gathered a bouquet of the last of the peonies

and set the vase, an old cut-glass one, on the dresser. She made the bed and dusted the furniture. The room didn't look as though it had been lived in much. Perhaps Phoebe would make it a little more personal, put up some pictures, bring a favorite pillow. Noah hadn't done much except sleep there.

They were back in time for lunch. Phoebe was all smiles, delighted that she'd found a local job for the summer. Abby felt a bit guilty that she'd balked at the suggestion. She hadn't wanted Noah managing things for her, but the truth was, she needed help. She was feeling enormous and wondering how she'd get through another four weeks of this. The weather was clear and dry and hot. Perfect haying weather, but not much fun when you were twice your normal size, or seemed so. Taking a bath was becoming a major undertaking.

The fact that the babies were growing well and were strong and healthy kept her focused and doing her best to be positive. After all, what was another few weeks?

Phoebe was ecstatic over the transformation of the extra bedroom to the nursery. She oohed and aahed over all the little blankets and sleepers and produced her own surprise contribution, a hand-crocheted baby blanket.

"It's lovely!" Abby smoothed the folds of the brightly colored square. "Did you do this yourself, Phoebe?"

The girl laughed. "No way. Mom did. She's always crocheting or knitting something. She said she couldn't wait until the babies were born—she had

to get started on something right away. She'll probably have a second one ready when the time
comes.''

Abby folded the blanket and laid it carefully over
the end of one of the cribs. She was touched. This
gift, a handmade item from a neighbor, made her
feel well and truly accepted, in a way that nothing
else could have done.

Noah had disappeared as soon as he'd delivered
Phoebe. *Maybe he's relieved,* Abby thought, *now
that he doesn't have the full-time responsibility of
keeping an eye on me.* But then she reconsidered.
Noah had never, by so much as a gesture, seemed
to resent her presence. If anything, he couldn't say
enough about her cooking and the way she'd redone
the place. And he was always full of compliments.
He never, ever let on that she must appear an awe-
some lump to him now, much more like a hot air
balloon than a woman.

''And this is your room while you're here,'' she
said, opening the door at the end of the hall, opposite the nursery. She stood back to let Phoebe enter.

''It's super!'' Phoebe glanced around, then threw
her suitcase onto the bed. First out of the battered
case was a worn-looking teddy bear, which Phoebe
propped on the pillow. ''That's Norbert. He goes
everywhere with me.'' She didn't seem the least bit
chagrined that at eighteen, nearly ready to go off to
college, she still depended on her teddy bear for
comfort. Abby thought it was sweet.

''I knew you'd want to fix up the room yourself,
make it a little homier,'' Abby said. ''Anything you

want, just ask. There are more blankets, but I kept them off the bed as it's so hot these days.''

''Great! I'll just unpack and then I'll be down to see what you'd like me to do,'' Phoebe said cheerfully. She set a framed photo of her family on top of the dresser. And another one, of a handsome, dark-haired young man leaning against a tree. Already the room looked more inviting and personal.

''Your boyfriend?'' Abby asked.

''Hmm?'' Phoebe reddened slightly. ''No. That's just someone who works for my uncle sometimes. Sort of a friend.''

Abby gave her a curious glance. More than a friend, she'd guess. She moved to the door and paused to look back for a few seconds. Phoebe had thrown a skirt and blouse over the desk chair. She'd dropped an open case of cosmetics on the desktop and a gold-colored lipstick tube had fallen out.

Was it only women who had this knack of turning a house so quickly into a home? Imprinting their personalities so precisely on a space? Then Abby remembered the pussy willows Noah had set on her windowsill to welcome her when she'd first moved into his house. The pussy willows had mysteriously become two branches of lilac in late May, then a handful of Alberta hedgerow roses in June.

No. A man—some men—had the knack, too. It was just different.

THAT FIRST NIGHT, he sneaked into the bedroom long after Abby had gone up to bed, certain she was asleep. He paused in the doorway, which had been left partway open—an invitation?—to listen to the sound of her breathing.

No question, she was asleep.

Noah stripped off the old terry-cloth bathrobe he'd managed to track down at the back of his closet and got into bed, trying not to make any noise. He'd acknowledged her presence and her sensibilities by wearing a pair of boxers to bed; normally he slept nude.

He stretched out, lay back and rested his head on his clasped hands, then stared up at the ceiling and took a deep breath. He turned to face the window. There was a full moon and he could make out the ghostly outlines of the furniture and, as his eyes adjusted, the outline of Abby asleep on the bed—his bed—covered with a sheet. She'd obviously kicked off her blankets. He couldn't blame her. The bedroom was like an oven, even though the sun had gone down hours ago.

He'd planned to move in with her last night, before Phoebe came, but at the last moment, he chickened out. There was something about sleeping in the same room with this woman, with no one else in the house, that had seemed vaguely wrong. He was her husband, and yet he wasn't her husband. He was determined to regard those babies she was carrying as his, and yet they were not his. They were his brother's.

And was he going to try and make love to her? Soon? Make her his wife in fact as well as in law? In her current condition? No way. Yet to be in the same room and to be tempted to hold her, to stroke her smooth, smooth skin, to kiss her sweet, sweet lips...it was too much. The tension would kill him. He'd slept one last night in the other bedroom. There was no more going to Rachel for relief, either; he was a married man.

Noah turned slightly, onto his side, to observe Abby more closely. This cot was narrow and uncomfortable. The mattress had to be all of three inches thick. He stopped shifting around and let his gaze rest on her. He saw the pale glimmer of her hair on the pillow, the gentle rise of her breathing. He caught the half shape of her forearm, the upper arm lost in shadow. Her wrist was slender, her hands curled in sleep. Relaxed, tender. The huge swell of her belly. *Women were too frail to have babies. Too small. It was so hard, so much work.*

So many things could go wrong. He'd seen it with his own stock. Some cows had their calves with no more than a hiccup, it seemed, while others struggled for hours. And then, sometimes, the calf would be born dead and the cow would stand over it, bawling softly, urging her calf to stand, to suckle. *To live.* No one could tell him that animals didn't grieve.

Noah felt an enormous surge of emotion rise in his chest. He actually felt the prickle of moisture in his eyes, something he couldn't remember feeling, ever. Although he knew he'd cried himself to sleep when Casey had died, when his mother had died. He didn't think he'd cried at all when Jake left them. Sure, he'd been a little older then, but only a few months. They'd been a hard few months. His father's black rages, his endless quest for solace in the bottom of a bottle, his harangues. Both he and Jesse were too old and too quick for their father to beat anymore; if Jake had managed to lay a hand on Jesse, the younger, he knew he'd have Noah at his throat.

Jesse was all he had left. He'd protected his brother all his life. He'd stood up for him.

It was a hard thing—to hate your father so. And yet to love him, too, and to grieve that he'd left you behind like that. Just walked out one day and never came back. Never wrote. Never sent word to say he was all right. Never sent money to make sure the two boys and the old man had food on the table.

He just never gave a damn.

Noah took a deep breath and pushed his fingertips into his eye sockets. *And then Jesse'd left, too.* As if on cue, he heard the howl of Jesse's stray somewhere up the river valley. There was no lonelier sound.

Noah sighed and turned back to stare at the ceiling. The years had marched on. Everything was different now. He'd built this ranch into something worthwhile, just him and the old man and Jesse. And Carl, of course. He had a wife now, and a family on the way. He hadn't chosen the wife or the family; in a sense, they'd chosen him. But they were his now. *That's how it is.* No one was ever going to come between him and Abby or the twins when they were born. Not if he could help it.

Not Jesse. Not anyone. Not ever.

CHAPTER FOURTEEN

ABBY WAS SEEING the doctor once a week during this last month. Noah insisted on driving her, even though Phoebe could have done it. He wanted to be with Abby all the time, now that her due date was approaching. He didn't know how to explain it; it was just a feeling he had. That he had to be there for her. That she was facing an enormous challenge and needed him.

She never talked about her first baby, what had gone wrong. Sometimes, now, he wished she would.

"You want me to come in with you?" Noah asked, as they pulled into the parking lot by the medical clinic.

Abby looked at him in surprise. "You want to?"

"Well, sure," he said, as the car came to a halt. "I guess other husbands take an interest, don't they?"

"A few," she admitted. "I think more of them go to the prenatal classes than the doctor's office."

"We didn't do that." Noah stared out the window for a moment. He suddenly realized that all his experience was with expectant cows. "Do you wish you had?"

"No," Abby said softly. "Not really. I've been through it before. I know what to expect."

Maybe going to prenatal classes again would have been too painful, brought back too many memories. "Well? I could go in with you or run a few errands while you're seeing Kate."

She hesitated. "Maybe you should run your errands, Noah. I'll be fine."

There was no more discussion. But the next time they went to town, a week later, Abby asked him to come in with her.

"Hello, Noah," Kate Pleasance said when she called Abby in. "Here with your wife today? Good!" She stood with the manila file in her hand, smiling.

"I'll, er, wait until Abby's ready," he said, feeling terribly uncomfortable. The waiting room was full of pregnant women and small kids playing in the toy corner and bigger kids with runny noses and old people with coughs and tremors.

"Sure. I'll let you know when we want you. Come on in, Abby." Abby followed the doctor into the examining room. He watched her go, realizing how ungainly she was beginning to look. In among these other women, most in much less advanced stages of pregnancy, she looked very large. The twins were part of it, he realized. If she was carrying one baby, she'd look different.

Ten minutes later, Kate appeared and beckoned him into the examining room. His heart seemed to stop. What a stupid idea, coming in here. He hadn't really thought it through. What if she wasn't wearing anything? Noah's heart hammered in double time. Fear. Sheer fear.

Abby had on a white cotton gown, which tied at the back, and a white paper sheet covered her to the waist. She looked as uncomfortable as he felt.

"Sit down here, Dad," Kate said gaily.

Dad? Noah stared at her. Then he realized this must be her little joke, what doctors called the husband.

"Now, I suppose you'd like to hear the babies' heartbeats? They're good and strong. Very healthy babies you're having—right, Mom?"

Abby blushed and nodded.

Thank God the doctor just put her stethoscope on Abby's white-clad belly. He listened dutifully, once she'd located the heartbeat and handed the ear pieces to him. The instrument amplified everything. It sounded like a landslide mixed up with a bullfight in there, with maybe a car wreck tossed in.

"Is it always that loud?" he asked, frowning, and handed back the earpieces. Maybe something was wrong.

"Oh, sure. That's all the other stuff going on. Digestion, breathing, Abby's heartbeat, blood flow, the babies' heartbeats—here. Maybe I didn't get it right—listen here." She gave him the ear pieces again. "That's the other one."

Noah listened. He heard the distinct and rapid tat-tat-tat of a heartbeat going a mile a minute. He felt awestruck. This really was something. This was a real baby in there. Two of them. And they were going to be born soon. *His family.*

He returned the instrument to Dr. Pleasance and cleared his throat. "Sounds okay," he said gruffly. "Do they always go so fast, the heartbeats?"

"Yes. In utero, babies at this age have heart rates around one-twenty, one-forty. It's completely normal."

Noah nodded. He'd barely made eye contact with his wife. It was too damn personal, listening to her abdomen like that.

"Are you two still making love?"

Shocked, Noah gazed full at Abby. Her cheeks were bright red and she looked down at the sheet covering her.

"Er, *what?*" he croaked.

"Having sex. It's perfectly all right, you know," Dr. Pleasance went on, putting away her stethoscope. "Abby's healthy and fit, the babies are fine, and if you find a position that's comfortable for both of you and won't put pressure on the babies, it's not a problem. Some couples make love right up until delivery. Keeps everybody nice and relaxed." The doctor smiled brightly.

"Oh," Noah said lamely. At least she hadn't pursued her original question.

"I just thought I'd mention it because lots of couples are too shy to bring it up," she said cheerfully, with a smile for each of them. "I'll just go now and you can help Abby get dressed, Noah. I'll see you both next week, okay?"

Help her get dressed? Next week—both of them again?

Noah nodded, not knowing exactly what he was

agreeing to. "Look, maybe I'd better step out, too. It's kind of cramped in here."

"You decide." And with that, Dr. Pleasance exited and shut the door behind her.

Noah gazed at his wife. What the hell—? To his relief, she giggled.

"What's so funny?"

"You."

"Me?" Noah was astonished. He'd figured she'd be as embarrassed as he was.

"Yes, you. Anyone would think you'd never seen a pregnant woman before. Or that you'd never seen a woman without her clothes on before."

"Well, hell. That's different." Noah gathered every shred of courage he had. "Okay. I'll help you get dressed. What do you want me to do?"

"Never mind. You just turn your back and look out that window and I'll get dressed. If I need your help, I'll let you know."

Noah did just that. He stood at the window and tried to keep his mind on the scene outside. Except there wasn't much to see. Just a couple of magpies teasing a crow on the telephone pole, and a big cottonwood drooping in the heat on the other side of the parking lot. The grass was turning brown, the parched look of high summer. He had a hay crop lying on the ground right now, almost ready to be picked up....

And all the time, the rustle of womanly sounds behind him. Silk, lace... Noah shut his eyes, but that was worse. He opened them again.

"Okay. You can turn around."

Abby was flushed but fully dressed. Her hair was awry. He moved toward her to smooth it, but the expression on her face stopped him. "Abby?"

"You don't have to pretend with me, Noah Winslow," she said firmly, brushing ineffectually at her hair with the palms of her hands. "I know you can't stand to touch me. I know what I look like—one of your pregnant *cows!*"

"Abby..." Noah glanced at the closed door.

"You've made it perfectly clear. You never come to bed before I'm asleep, or you think I'm asleep. You can't stand to touch me anymore—"

"What!" He didn't touch her because he didn't think he could stop there.

"You just about die when the doctor makes a perfectly sensible and obvious suggestion for a married couple, that you help me get dressed when I'm—" she spread her hands to circumscribe her girth "—out to *here!*"

"Look, honey..." Noah stepped forward and she stepped back, glaring up at him. "I don't think this is a good place for a fight—"

"This *isn't* a fight. I'm just stating a few facts," she whispered back forcefully. "I'm quite aware I look awful. I'm quite aware I resemble a beached whale, but there's no need to be quite so obvious about it."

"If I knew you wanted me to touch you, damn it, I'd touch you. I thought it was better this way, that I leave you alone. You know, not start anything. Until the babies are born and—"

"I'm not made out of—of glass! And how would

you know if I wanted you to touch me when you never asked? You never tried. I thought we were supposed to be trying to work things out. I thought you wanted this marriage to last. But you've been avoiding me like the plague ever since you've moved into my room, so what am I *supposed* to think?''

He knew it wasn't a question she wanted answered. He stepped forward and put his arms around her, gently at first, then tighter when she struggled.

"Leave me alone. There's no point in touching me now!"

"Yes, there is. I want you to listen to me—"

"I am listening—"

"No, you're not. Now, *listen.* The reason I haven't touched you since I moved into your room—*our* room—" He glanced at the door again. He was trying to be very quiet. Last thing he wanted was the receptionist or doctor bursting in here wondering what all the ruckus was about. "The reason is that I didn't trust myself."

"*Trust* yourself! Oh-ho! That's a load of you-know-what."

"No, it isn't. It's true. I'm attracted to you, damn it, and I can hardly trust myself around you. It's the truth. I think you're the most beautiful, gorgeous, sexy woman I've ever seen, pregnant or not. I still can't believe how I lucked out when you said you'd marry me. If I touch you or kiss you or put my arms around you I—I just want to do more!'' He stared down at her. Her eyes, still stormy, had begun to soften. "I can't help it, you're driving me crazy!"

"I—I am?"

"Yes, damn it!"

"You mean, if you put your arms around me—like this?"

Following her glance, Noah looked down. His arms were around her, all right. Barely. He shifted slightly, so he was positioned a little more to one side of her, then tightened his arms again. "Yeah," he said hoarsely, "like this."

He lowered his mouth to hers and kissed her. She kissed him back. He felt her arms creep up until she'd encircled his neck and was pulling him toward her. He kissed her like a man who'd been waiting all his life for just this moment. Just this occasion. Just this opportunity.

In a doctor's examining room. With a roomful of wheezers and geezers out there. Was it possible to make love with a pregnant woman on a four-foot-long examining table?

"Damn it, Abby," he said rawly, coming up for air. "We can't do this—"

"We can!" she returned, pulling him toward her again and offering up her lips. "Kiss me, Noah—*kiss me!*"

He did. He kissed her deeply, thoroughly, and when he finally lifted his head he was breathing like a marathon runner. His heart was pounding. His blood was bursting in his veins. His pants were too tight. Various areas of his body were fit to explode. This was crazy, this was sheer, incredible craziness—

There was a light rap at the door. "Finished in there?"

Noah swallowed. "Yes," he managed to call back. Then he looked at Abby. "Are we?"

She giggled. His heart soared. When she giggled like that, she was just like an innocent girl. His wife. The woman he'd married. He could imagine her years ago on her father's dairy farm. A farm girl. Playing tag in the hay. Her eyes sparkled. Her cheeks were a gorgeous shade of pink. Her hair was still a mess. She looked absolutely beautiful.

"I guess so," she said softly.

He stepped back and smoothed her hair awkwardly. "Come on," he said, taking her by the hand. "Let's go home."

ABBY'S CHEEKS were on fire all the way back to the ranch. *Home,* he'd said.

If only.

If what had happened in the doctor's office meant anything, maybe *home* was a real possibility. She couldn't believe how he'd kissed her. As though he really, really cared. He'd wanted her, in all her mountainous pregnant glory. Just thinking of that made her feel like giggling again.

And she'd wanted him. Abby had to face the sobering fact that she wanted Noah Winslow more than she'd ever wanted a man before. Even more than Frank. That wasn't an insult to the dead. She and Frank had been practically children when they'd met and married. Certainly inexperienced. She'd been a virgin. She'd had a lot to learn about lovemaking and living with a man. She'd learned all that with Frank.

But Noah had touched some emotion inside her, some feeling she hadn't even known was there when she'd been married to Frank. Maybe life and all her sorrows had changed her. Maybe now she'd realized that she had something here with Noah Winslow, really *had* something, and whatever it was, it was worth keeping. Worth hanging on to.

Hormones had to play a part in it, both hers and his. She couldn't remember feeling particularly sexy when she'd been pregnant before, but then she hadn't had a husband around, either. Noah was a normal man; he had a normal, healthy appetite for the physical side of life. Being married and being unable to make love with his wife must be difficult for him. If she could believe that he really thought she was…*gorgeous, beautiful*. What else had he called her? *Sexy.* She looked down at her lap, what was left of it. Now *that* was hard to believe.

That night, Noah came into her bedroom twenty minutes after she'd gone upstairs. He had on an old tatty bathrobe, which he took off as she watched him. Thank heavens he had something on underneath, boxers. She'd only seen him without a shirt once, the day Jesse had left and she'd run over to Noah's place and banged on his door. His body was lean and well muscled. Fit. Very attractive. Very, very male.

She didn't think she was ready for this.

"I'm sleeping with you tonight," he announced. "Do you have a problem with that?"

"Uh, no. I g-guess not," she stammered, sheet pulled up to her throat.

"Okay." He walked around to the window side of the room, lifted the sheet and blanket and got in.

The mattress sagged, and she felt her weight tilt slightly toward him. He shifted a little and stretched, then turned to look at her. He was smiling. "I like this. It's a lot more comfortable."

"Is that why you're in here with me—so you don't have to sleep on that cot anymore?"

He drew her into his arms. "That's one of the reasons. And this is another...." He kissed her nose and her forehead and her lips. "But we're not going to make love, no matter what the doctor says. I just want to hold you and wake up beside you. Be with you."

"Mmm." She snuggled up beside him, wondering where she was going to put her enormous belly. Her most comfortable position these days was lying on her side with one leg drawn up and resting on a pillow.

"Comfortable?"

"Not really," she admitted. "I can't get used to having this cargo in front of me. I can't sleep on my back anymore because the babies kick too much when I do. I need to be on my side and—"

"Getting tired of it?"

"A little," she admitted. And her back ached, and her legs cramped and her feet killed her half the time. "I'm definitely ready to have these babies. The sooner the better."

"Here." Noah sat up and wedged a pillow under her abdomen. "Is that more comfortable?"

"Yes. Thanks."

They gazed at each other across the space that separated them. It was fitting, in a way, that it was the babies who came between them. This was about as close as they could get. Just as well, really... Abby didn't know what she could've done if Noah *had* wanted to make love. It was too weird, making love with your husband for the first time when you were nearly nine months pregnant. *With his brother's babies.*

Abby took a deep breath and let it out slowly. *Jesse.* Always, at the back of her happiness was the shadow of his brother, whether he was hundreds of miles away or not.

"You okay?"

"Fine." She smiled and he smiled back. He had a marvelous smile. She loved his smile. She saw it so rarely, although more often, these days, than she had before.

"I'm going to turn the light off," he said, reaching for the bedside lamp. "All right?"

"Fine," she murmured sleepily. Everything *was* all right now. Her husband wanted her. Maybe not tonight, but later. He didn't think she looked like a beached whale. Or, if he did, he didn't care. He thought she was *gorgeous.*

"Good night, Abby. Sweet dreams." He leaned over and kissed her nose and she smiled in the darkness.

"Good night, Noah. I think I will."

WHEN HE WOKE UP, he was tangled in the bedsheet and Abby was turned away from him, still sleeping. He was close behind her, and she had her head on his left arm and pillow, her hair tickling his nose. He gently raised his head to look at her.

He felt his loins stir as he had so many times already that night. How was he going to do this? Lie beside her every night, yet not be able to touch her, to bring her pleasure, to release his own incredible tension. It was crazy, just asking for trouble, this decision to move into her bed. They still had weeks to go.

How could he go back on it now? She'd only react in that ridiculous way again, figuring he was repelled by her. He didn't think she really understood how difficult it was for him.

He settled back down, content for a few more minutes just to breathe in the delicate scent of her skin, to glory in the softness of her hair. His right arm went around her. He felt the resilient softness of her right breast under his hand. Under her thin cotton nightgown. But he didn't dare press his hand over the swell of her breast, as he longed to.

A man could only take so much.

Instead, he moved his hand to her belly, rested his palm on the surprisingly hard surface of her abdomen. As if on cue, he felt the soft, swimming motion of one of the babies. A knee, or a heel, or maybe an elbow.

Noah took a deep, shuddering breath. He was so lucky. This was such a precious time to share with her, no matter who had fathered these babies. As the weeks wore on, he thought less and less about Jesse and more and more about himself as their father. He intended to be a real father to these twins. He didn't know how they'd work it out. Once they were older, he supposed, the truth would have to be told. They'd have to deal with the when and the how of it when the time came. He just hoped Jesse stayed out of the picture.

For now, all he wanted was to have this woman safe and happy in his arms. The protective feelings she aroused in him were astonishing. It must be instinct, he thought, to feel this way about a woman about to give birth. Maybe any woman.

Was it love? Maybe it was. Maybe he was already in love with Abby. He couldn't imagine life without her anymore.

Whatever it was, he liked the feeling. He hoped she'd return it eventually. If all went well. If he managed to restrain his natural bossy streak.

Then he grinned as he carefully removed his arm from her belly and pulled his left arm gently from beneath her head. She made a soft, sleepy sound and burrowed into the pillow.

Abby had a pretty fair bossy streak herself. He thought of the way she'd managed the Pings. The way she'd gone ahead with rearranging the house. They were well matched, the two of them. Him and her. Maybe things were meant to be, after all.

CHAPTER FIFTEEN

"HAVEN'T YOU HAD that baby *yet?*" demanded the scratchy voice at the other end of the phone line.

"*Babies,*" Abby replied patiently. "I'm having twins, Amanda. You know that."

Abby sighed. She was so tired of that question. She was two days past her due date, but you'd think she was a month late. The whole community kept phoning to see if the big event had taken place yet—or so it seemed. "Believe me, I'm more than ready."

"I suppose you are. Ma had my oldest brother in August and she swore that was the worst month ever. Too hot. Mind you, in them days we didn't have the air-conditioning and refrigerators for cold drinks and such like. It was just water from the well and drag it home yourself. Women had to work a whole lot harder than they do today!"

Abby laughed. She was very fond of the district's elderly female rancher. "Not harder than you, Amanda," she teased.

"Oh, I'd say so. Listen," the older woman said, "I've got more corn in my garden here than I'll ever use. I hate to see it go to waste. You want me to bring up a bushel or two? You could put it in the freezer.''

"Freeze it?" Abby said doubtfully. She wasn't as up on canning and preserving techniques as most of her neighbors seemed to be. "I could give it a try. Do you have to blanch it?"

"Throw it in some boiling water, just for a few minutes. Then you can freeze it right on the cob, or scrape the kernels off and put them in empty margarine containers. Nothing to it. I'll bring over my corn-cobber thingie, works like a charm. How about that?"

Abby really didn't feel like taking on yet another task. Her idea of getting through the day was to heave herself out of bed—thank heavens Noah had installed an air conditioner in the bedroom window—pull on a giant-sized T-shirt and maternity shorts, or a loose dress, push her swollen feet into flip-flops and waddle downstairs. The most she seemed up to these days was sitting under the linden tree in the shade, drinking lemonade and reading a novel.

"Well, okay. I'll give it a try. When will you be over?" Abby hoped it wouldn't be until the next day. She had another doctor's appointment this afternoon at three o'clock.

"About noon. I've got a fellow picking the corn right now. The fresher, the better.'' Amanda ended the call abruptly.

Abby stood there for a few seconds, gaping at the receiver, then hung it up.

She felt vaguely restless today. She'd already

cleaned the bathroom upstairs and had been thinking
of cleaning out the refrigerator. This corn business
would give her an excuse to put that off. Mind you,
having the fridge door open would at least provide
a little temporary chill. Amanda was right; the worst
of her pregnancy now was simply dealing with the
heat.

She picked up the dog's water dish, which was a
major effort, and refilled it at the kitchen sink. The
old dog gazed mournfully at her, as though she em-
pathized. Had old Pat ever had pups? Abby made a
mental note to ask Noah.

She looked in the refrigerator. Everything was
getting low. It was time to send Noah or Carl into
town with a grocery list. She didn't even feel like
shopping anymore, or going to Glory unless it was
to see the doctor. Who wanted to shop when you
could barely stretch your arms out far enough to
push a grocery cart?

She'd make a potato salad and put it in the fridge.
If Amanda stayed for lunch, they'd have that and a
tin of salmon. If not, she and Noah could have it for
supper. She shuffled to the pantry to get some potatoes and held her breath as she bent awkwardly to
fill her pan with potatoes from the bin. Honestly,
she could weep at how ungainly she was these days.
She'd be so glad when it was all over and she was
home and happy with her babies.

Amanda rapped on the kitchen screen door just
before noon. She insisted she couldn't stay for
lunch, as she had an appointment at Vulcan in an
hour. She carried in not one but two large wicker

baskets of corn, which she dumped in the middle of the kitchen floor, saying she'd like to take the baskets back with her.

"You'll be done shucking that corn in no time, Abby. Now remember, just blanch 'em a couple minutes, then toss 'em in some cold water and straight to the freezer. Easy as pie."

With those brief instructions, the old rancher headed out, slapping her worn straw hat on her skinny thighs, her white hair flying loose from the braid she kept it in.

Abby stared at the mountain of corn in dismay. Pat was sitting politely to one side, looking anxiously from the corn to Abby, then back again. If only Phoebe was here, but she'd gone to her mother's this morning and wouldn't be back until tomorrow.

She might as well get started. Abby drew a chair closer to the pile of corn and began shucking. She pulled the pale outer green leaves from the corn, then the inner silk and, not knowing what to do with it, dropped it into a separate pile on the floor beside her. She'd clean everything up after she was finished. The shucked cobs she stacked on the table. One fell off the pyramid she'd built, onto the floor, and Pat was on it in a second. The old dog retreated to the corner and began delicately removing the raw corn kernels with her front teeth. Abby started to laugh. Then she started to cry.

When Noah came in fifteen minutes later, she was wailing.

"WHAT THE HELL—" Noah couldn't believe his eyes. His very pregnant wife in a kitchen chair, corn spread out in front of her, corn shucked and piled on the table and corn husks and debris all over the kitchen.

And she was bawling her eyes out.

"What's the matter, honey? You ready to—you know, have the babies?" There was always that possibility. Noah had never been through this before. He knew cows and horses and dogs, but he didn't know women.

"No…" Fresh tears flooded down Abby's face and she reached for him, both arms. She looked pitiful. He knelt beside her and put his arms around her. She clutched his shirtfront and rubbed her eyes on his shirt like a child.

"I—I just can't stand this anymore!" she wailed. "I can't. It's too hot and I just want t-to die and I didn't know dogs ate corn and Amanda was here and she wouldn't stay for lunch and I haven't got anything organized for supper and I need to clean out the fridge and—"

"Shh." Noah took in the scene again, noting that Pat was guiltily gnawing on what looked to be her second cob of corn under the table. That dog was going to have indigestion, big-time.

"What's all this corn doing here?" Might as well ask the obvious question first.

"Amanda brought it over. She said she had too much—"

Noah stood up. "Well, it's going out—now. You're in no condition to deal with Amanda's extra corn crop.'' He wedged a chair against the screen door to keep it open and started picking up armloads of corn and flinging the cobs into the yard.

Abby stared at him in shock. After a few seconds, she said, ''What in the world are you *doing?*''

''I'm getting rid of this damn corn,'' he said, firing three at once over the porch railing and into the middle of the lawn. Half a dozen crows materialized out of nowhere to haggle over the unexpected snack.

''B-but Amanda didn't want it to go to waste....'' She seemed bewildered.

''It won't go to waste. It'll make compost. And bird feed. Pat'll eat a couple more.'' Noah grabbed up another armful and threw it out. Abby began to giggle through her tears. This was dangerous. The woman was on the verge of hysterics. They had a doctor's appointment this afternoon, in two hours.

''I—I don't think that's what she meant,'' Abby said, wiping her eyes with the edge of her T-shirt.

Noah fired the last of the corn out the door, then came over to Abby and gave her his hand. She stood, trembling. ''Look, you go upstairs and have a rest. It's air-conditioned in there and we've got to leave to see Kate in an hour and a half. Just take a nap or something. Pull yourself together.''

''You think I lost it?'' she asked, gazing tearfully up at him.

He shrugged. ''Maybe not. But you came close.''

Abby sighed. ''Frankly, I'm glad you got rid of that corn. I didn't want to hurt Amanda's feelings and turn her down but, well…'' Abby looked around the kitchen.

"I'll clean up this mess. You just go upstairs."

She looked at him for another long moment and he resisted the temptation he had to kiss her. She was already in hormone-overload and the last thing she needed was a sexually overcharged husband. He'd been having nightmares trying to lie quietly in bed beside her every night and not do anything more than hold her and kiss her occasionally, on the cheek or the forehead or, very briefly, on the lips. He was in a perpetual state of semi-erection these days, and it was no picnic.

"You want some help?"

"No, I'll be fine." Abby moved toward the hall door. She stopped and turned. "Thanks, Noah. I needed that."

"That's what husbands are for, right?" He smiled as she left, then gritted his teeth. *That and a few other things that are a whole lot more fun,* he thought, as he bent to start clearing up the husks.

Twenty minutes later, he went upstairs to check on her. She had stripped and was lying under a sheet on the bed. Her back was toward him, showing bare and smooth between the edge of the sheet and the mattress. The air conditioner was on full-blast and the air was cool. She wasn't asleep, and seemed a little embarrassed that he'd caught her in the altogether.

"How about I rub your back, huh?" Noah picked up the rosewater-and-glycerine bottle on the dresser and sat down beside her. He adjusted the sheet, then drizzled some of the clear fluid onto her back and watched as it raised goose bumps.

"Ohh, that's cold," she said. She sounded breathless.

He began to smooth the lotion over her back, trying to be as businesslike and impersonal as possible. But it *wasn't* possible. He ran his hand along the center of her back, caressing each knob of her spine. Then he ran his fingers lightly down the swelling of muscle on each side of her spine. She shivered again.

"Still cold?" He couldn't resist, nor could he help noticing how husky his voice had become.

"N-not really," she murmured. "It feels good, Noah."

"Soothing?"

"Mmm, yes. Soothing." She didn't sound one-hundred percent certain. For his part, he wasn't finding it at all soothing.

Noah kept stroking and kneading her back, working his way slowly down from her shoulders to the small of her back. And then a little further, to the soft swell of her buttocks beneath the sheet. Abby shifted and murmured.

Noah turned his attentions to her upper arms, spreading more lotion on his palms. This was torture, this was pain, this was incredible foolishness. But it had to feel good for her. She'd complained many times that her back ached constantly these days.

Man, how was he going to hold out until the babies were born, and even longer, until she'd recovered fully from labor and birth?

"How's that?" he asked, pulling the sheet up to cover her bare skin.

"Nice." She seemed very relaxed.

Noah put the top on the lotion bottle and got up to retrieve her hairbrush from the dresser. He began to gently brush her hair across the pillow. It was soft and gleaming and so fine. He worked out some of the matted parts along her neckline, damp from her perspiration. From her corn panic. Then he smoothed her hair, shocked to find what a sensual experience that was. Was there nothing he could do for his wife without setting himself on fire?

It didn't seem so.

"Okay," he whispered. "You try and sleep for half an hour and I'll wake you up in time to go to the doc's."

"Mmm." She opened her hand, which had lain loosely on the outside of the sheet. He put his hand in hers and she squeezed his fingers. "Thanks," she whispered.

Noah left the room with one long backward look. He hauled in a huge breath as he stepped into the hall and closed the door to keep the cool air inside.

He loved her. He could no longer pretend he didn't.

They'd make this marriage work; they *had* to make it work. There was no way he'd accept anything else.

THERE WEREN'T many people waiting in the doctor's office that afternoon. The receptionist ushered Abby in immediately. Noah still preferred to stay put until the main part of the examination was over before joining them. The weighing, the measuring, the blood pressure, the internal examination, he could do without all of that.

Today, the doctor had good news.

"You're ready to pop anytime, Abby," she announced—rather cavalierly, Noah thought. "One of the babies has dropped nicely into your pelvis, they're both in a good position, the cervix has thinned considerably. It's just a question of them deciding it's time to come out, that's all."

Noah was curious. "What do you mean, Kate—'them' deciding it's time?"

"When the babies are ready, they release a hormone that triggers labor. Crazy, but true. Mind you, if it takes too long we can start the process without waiting for a signal from the babies. Since Abby's already had one normal labor, she'd likely be easy to get started."

"How would you do that?" Abby asked, her eyes wide.

"Prostaglandins. We try that first, because it's gentle and natural. We have other substances we can use—other oxytocins, if necessary, but we like to start with the most natural and gentle if we can."

"Prostaglandins?" Abby frowned.

"They're hormones that are present throughout the body all the time. Seminal fluid, for example, is loaded with prostaglandins. Labor is often triggered by couples making love. I always recommend it in my practice." The doctor smiled. "Safe, gentle, fun. Makes sense, doesn't it?"

Abby was a fiery red. "Makes sense?" she croaked.

Dr. Pleasance laughed and patted Abby's tummy. "Love gets the babies started in there and, guess what? Love helps them come into the world, too. Makes sense to me, anyway!"

Noah wasn't touching that one with a ten-foot pole. "Well, I guess they'll be born when they're good and ready," he said gruffly. "No need to rush things."

"Easy for you to say," Abby retorted, sitting straight up and swinging her legs over the side of the examining table. "Done here, Kate?"

"All done. You know about the early signs, Abby, right? And you certainly know what labor pains are. Even if you think it's false labor, give me a call."

"Don't worry, Kate," Abby said. "The minute anything happens, I'll call."

On the way home, Noah stopped at the Co-op grocery store and picked up some salads, buns and barbecued chicken, plus orange cheesecake for dessert. Abby said she had something she wanted to get in the ladies' clothing store next door while he was in the Co-op.

"Supper," he said as he got in and reached into the back seat to deposit the bags. He thought Abby looked rather drawn since the visit to the doctor. She hadn't said much. Maybe he'd underestimated how much this pregnancy was tiring her.

They ate outside, under the linden tree. Noah pulled over the old wooden picnic table, so it was in the shade, and Abby produced a red-and-white-checked tablecloth from somewhere, which he spread out.

They had iced lemonade and ate directly out of the cartons. The chicken was delicious and they finished it right down to the bones. Abby's appetite hadn't suffered, at least.

Noah had noticed when he got back that most of the corn he'd chucked out of the house had been neatly piled up by the garden under the clothesline. Carl must have been busy. His foreman must be wondering what the heck was going on up at the house, Noah thought with amusement. Not that he'd ever ask.

Abby insisted on washing their few dishes and then, as she'd mentioned earlier, cleaned out the refrigerator. He didn't know why she was so stubborn about taking on so much, but he didn't dare question it, knowing he'd get an argument. Afterward, she sat at the kitchen table and wrote out a long grocery list. She brought the list into the living room, where he sat reading the paper, and asked if he or Carl would fill it the next day.

"You sound like you're getting ready to go away on a long trip," he teased.

"I'll be going into the hospital soon, and after I get back with the babies I know I won't feel like going shopping right away," she replied seriously. "We need all these things."

"Don't worry," he said, shaking his paper a little. "Carl or I will take care of it. Anything else?" he added as she stood there looking at him.

"No," she said. "I just thought I'd take a bath and go to bed early." She paused. "That's all."

Their eyes met and held for a few seconds too long, and Noah had a sudden flash of what might be in her mind. Surely not. Surely she wouldn't initiate lovemaking with him just to speed up the birth process, as Kate Pleasance had hinted that afternoon. After what he'd been through the past few weeks? Lying beside her, not daring to touch her beyond the occasional pat or hug? She'd *use* him like that? Some little voice deep inside, which he quickly stifled, yelled *go ahead—use me, use me.*

He had to be wrong. She wouldn't do a thing like that.

Noah continued reading the paper. The dry season was having an effect on the hay crops throughout Alberta, which meant that if he didn't take enough off his own hay fields this month he'd be buying at a premium in the fall. Cattle prices were good, though—knock on wood. They'd been down the past few years as consumers bought less red meat, and a lot of producers had gotten out of the business. Now, with a concerted ad campaign by the Cattlemen's Association, extolling the virtues of the new leaner beef, consumption was up and so were the prices, due to lower supply.

Up, down. A fellow could go broke if he zigged when he should be zagging. Noah kept a careful eye on prices all over North America and he rarely got caught out. But it could happen any time. Feed prices, beef prices, other animal commodity prices. If pork got too cheap, people ate less beef.

He leafed through the classified section, aware that he'd heard the water stop running upstairs. She'd be sitting in the tub now in all her pregnant glory. He'd never seen her completely naked, without any clothes on. She always went to bed before he did and always wore a nightgown. The closest he'd come was this afternoon when she'd gone up for a nap. Even at the doctor's he always turned around while she got dressed. She was modest to an extreme.

Noah noted that there was an upcoming auction in Red Deer. Some of those round balers were on the list of items for sale, and he could use another one. Maybe he'd go and have a look.

Then he ran his eye down the livestock column, just to see if there were any cows or bulls on offer that would be an asset to his herd. Nothing there.

It had been quiet upstairs for a long time. Was she all right? It must be tough getting in and out of that tub by herself. Why didn't she take a shower the way he did? She seemed to prefer the bath. Maybe it was more relaxing.

He'd better go up and check.

Noah climbed the stairs, his heart thumping. He knocked lightly on the bathroom door. "You okay in there, Abby?"

"Why wouldn't I be?" came the response through the door. He grinned. Yup, she was okay.

"Just checking to see if you needed a hand out. You know—just trying to be helpful."

He heard the swish of bathwater as the plug was pulled. "I'm coming out now."

Good. At least she hadn't gotten stuck in there or anything.

He heard the rattle of the doorknob and then she stood before him, just as he'd imagined, in all her full, feminine glory.

Wearing nothing but a hot-pink feather boa draped around her shoulders.

Noah gulped.

"Ever been seduced by a pregnant woman before?"

CHAPTER SIXTEEN

NOAH STOOD STILL for at least five shocked seconds. Then he found his voice. "No. Can't say as I have."

"Don't you think it's about time?" Her eyes twinkled naughtily, but he could see the fear there, too. As if he might reject her. As if he might be repelled by her.

He let his gaze wander over her hungrily, from the full white breasts, tipped with pink, the vast girth, looking hard as a drum. Her shoulders and breasts and thighs looked soft and luscious. He'd said she was gorgeous to him, and she was.

He stepped forward and drew the ends of the boa together so he could pull her toward him with one hand. He held the other behind her neck and paused, just before he kissed her. "Does this mean what I think it means?"

"Yes," she said breathlessly, "it does. Doctor's orders."

"I thought so," he said, nibbling at her lower lip. Then he captured her mouth in a long greedy kiss while he allowed his other hand to release the boa and travel all over her, everywhere he could touch, everywhere he could reach. He took her left breast into his hand and felt something melt deep inside him. He was so hot for her. This could be dangerous.

He heard her soft whimpers—of desire? Of relief that he'd gone along with her little game? Of anticipation?

"Oh, honey," he murmured as he transferred his attention to her throat, her ear, the curve of her jaw. "I thought you'd never ask."

"I didn't think you'd want me," she whispered. She'd put her arms around his neck and he could feel her abdomen pressing hard against him; he could feel the softness of her ripe breasts.

"Abby, I adore you!" He kissed her hungrily again, finally wrenching his mouth away. "I've wanted you for a long, long time."

"Y-you didn't even like me at first. Remember?"

"That's true, but I do now."

She smiled and shivered.

"You're freezing. Let's go to bed." He led her into their bedroom and watched as she climbed onto the bed, still wearing nothing but the boa. He went to the window and turned the air-conditioning down. Then he came back to her, a silly grin on his face, and started stripping his clothes off.

If she thought he didn't want her...she had only to use her eyes.

He climbed in beside her, as naked as she was, and this time didn't hesitate to take her in his arms. He kissed her mouth, her neck, her breasts until she cried out, breathless. Then he kissed her drum of a belly, exulting that he was going to be the father of these babies. Soon, as soon as they were born. He wouldn't be the kind of father who walked away, like Jake. Like Jesse. He'd be a real father, the way his mother's brother, his Uncle Brandis, had been to him. He would be there for them. Always.

"How'll we manage this?" she whispered, looking worried and excited at the same time.

"I don't know yet," he said, kissing her again, thrilling to the taste of her mouth, the scent of her skin, the softness of her everywhere. "But we'll figure it out."

Later, when he'd brought her as much pleasure as he could with his hands, his mouth, his lips, he helped her into a comfortable position on her side, wedging a pillow under her belly. She drew her leg up and sighed and he held her tightly, kissing her ear, her throat, as she pressed his left hand to her breast.

"Abby. I want you to know this," he said, as he began to enter her, ever so carefully, ever so gently. She drew in a quick breath and arched her back, inviting him to join with her. "I want you to know this, Abby, honey. *I love you.*" He pushed until he was fully inside her. He nuzzled her hair and found the shell of her ear with his lips, then whispered roughly, "I love you, baby. I do."

She gasped. He moved slowly, ever mindful not to hurt her in any way, or to put any pressure on her abdomen. He held her tightly with both arms, his brain and blood exploding with the pleasure, until finally his body answered him and he made the ultimate connection with her and with his unborn children. The connection he'd longed to make.

He held her, trembling, in his arms, waiting for her breathing to subside, as his did. Finally, he raised his head to look at her. She turned toward him, to look into his eyes. "You okay, Abby?"

"Better than okay," she whispered. "A million times better than okay."

"Doctor's orders, huh?"

"Yes. But it feels more like love, Noah," she murmured sleepily, still with the cat-that-got-the-cream smile on her face. "Feels absolutely perfect."

"That's exactly what it is—love. I love you. I've loved you for a long time. This is real. I'll always love you, Abby. I know I will."

In ten minutes, his wife was asleep beside him. Noah couldn't relax. His blood still hammered in his veins. He couldn't process everything that had happened since he'd come home at noon to find her sitting in front of a mountain of corncobs.

Now this.

Now this almost cosmic binding he'd felt with the children she carried in her womb. If the doctor was right, he—Noah—would have something to do with their birth. Maybe they'd been started accidentally, by his own brother, but now that they were close to being born, they were his. Completely and totally his. Nothing could have made him happier. Nothing could have made his world more complete.

ABBY WOKE UP to the sun streaming through the window. For a few minutes she felt disoriented, wondering why she was entirely naked and her legs were tangled with Noah's. He was awake, leaning on one elbow, studying her.

"How are you this morning?" he asked with a smile.

Then she remembered everything.

"Fine." She sat up a little, covering her breasts with the sheet, feeling rather shy now, and ran one hand through her tousled hair. "The same."

"The same?"

"Well, not the same." She smiled. "But the same as far as the babies go." She noticed the bedraggled feather boa draped over the headboard. She'd felt so silly buying it in Madge's Unique Boutique the day before, while Noah was in the co-op, but she was glad she did. It was the very goofiness of it that had worked. She could never have come straight out and asked him to make love with her, not in her condition. No matter how helpful he was trying to be. Not considering the circumstance of their marriage. And now—she felt herself flush with pleasure—everything was different. Now he said he *loved* her.

"Oh." He sounded a little disappointed. Surely he didn't think they'd make love, then have labor start right away. When would they know if it *had* worked? She had no idea. Maybe they'd have to repeat the experiment. She definitely wouldn't object.

"Let's just wait and see," she said, leaning back against the pillows and yawning widely. "I'm still not awake." She patted her hand against the sheet covering her abdomen. "What do you have planned for today?"

"I'm not going far. I'll give that grocery list to Carl. He can get the stuff at the co-op. Maybe he can take all that corn to Rachel first, for her pigs—"

"Rachel?"

"Rachel Melnyk. Er, she's a friend, a divorcée, who runs a pig farm not too far away. She's sentimental about her favorite old-timers and keeps them in a pasture and gives them treats like corn and apples. Kind of a seniors' home for swine."

"That's nice."

"Yeah. She's different. Likes her pigs, all right. Sells breeding stock so she can tell herself they aren't going into chops and sausages, the way hogs generally do."

She nodded. "Send Carl over there with the corn, with my compliments. I'm glad to see the end of it. And please, Noah—don't worry about me today. I can call you if anything happens. Babies aren't born in an hour, you know."

Famous last words. By midmorning, she was feeling some odd twinges, not really cramps but tightenings across her abdomen. Then, an hour later, she suddenly realized that maybe these were labor pains and decided to time them. To her shock, they were coming regularly—six minutes apart!

Fumbling, she dialed Noah's cell phone number. He answered on the second ring, sounding as rattled as she was becoming. "Abby! You started?"

"Yes," she said quietly. *One of us has to take this calmly,* she told herself and it obviously wasn't going to be her husband. "I think so."

"Damn! I'll be right there, honey. Sit down, take

it easy. Is your bag packed? Never mind, I'll do it when I get there!'' He slammed down the receiver, and ten minutes later, pulled up to the house in a cloud of dust.

He leaped out of his pickup and Pat barked crazily on the porch. She'd probably never seen her master in such a mad hurry.

''Abby!'' He burst into the house. She had to giggle. He looked pale and his hair was standing on end. What had happened to his hat? She didn't want to ask.

''I'm ready.'' She stood, indicating the small suitcase beside her. He strode over and grabbed it.

''Let's get going. Are you all right, honey? Why'd you pack this? I could have done it for you. Did you carry this downstairs by yourself? Damn it, Abby—''

''Hush.'' Abby waddled toward the door, with Noah hanging on to her elbow, trying to help. ''Let's just go.''

''In the pickup?''

''Why not? It's got gas and two seats, hasn't it?''

''Okay, okay.'' Noah helped hoist her up onto the passenger seat. The truck was quite a bit higher than the car.

Noah got in. He still looked completely rattled. He gripped the steering wheel tightly and took a deep breath. ''Holy cow, holy *cow*,'' she heard him murmur.

She put her hand on his arm as he went to start the ignition. ''Noah?''

''Yes?'' He glanced at her. He looked so strong

and handsome to her. So absolutely right. The man she'd grown accustomed to, the man she'd grown to love in her heart—could she trust the feeling? Could she allow herself to love this man, her husband, who'd be the true and real father to her babies? But she couldn't think about that now. She had to get through the next few hours, maybe longer.

"Just relax," she said softly. "Please. There's no hurry, believe me. And one more thing before we go—"

"What's that? We forget something?" he asked, his voice anxious.

"Kiss me."

His frown broke into a big smile. "Hey, I can do that," he said.

And he did.

LIAM CASEY WINSLOW, seven pounds twelve ounces, was born at five minutes past three in the afternoon. They'd discussed names during her labor. Daisy Amanda Winslow—as Noah said, they could hardly call her "Corncob"—was born twenty minutes later. She was a lot smaller, at five pounds four ounces, and her birth was far more traumatic. She was breech presentation, and Kate and the visiting specialist had quite a job to turn her and help her into the world.

Noah was at Abby's side. When his son was born, he sent up a quick prayer of thanks to the Almighty, although he'd never thought of himself as a religious man. *His son.*

Liam Casey Winslow, named for his brother at

Abby's insistence, was born squalling and wrinkled and red, with arms and legs milling like propellers. He was the most gorgeous thing Noah had ever seen. Kate laid him on Abby's breast, wrapped in a warm flannel sheet, while she dealt with the rest of the birth, and Noah just gazed at the newborn in awe.

"Isn't he beautiful?" Abby said, raising her head to look down at her son. "Isn't he just the most wonderful baby you ever saw?" His son was turning his head to nuzzle at Abby's breast already. He knew what he wanted. He was rooting for a teat just like a little whiteface calf. Noah wanted to laugh and cry at the same time.

Noah squeezed Abby's hand, unable to answer.

Then Kate asked him to step outside for a few minutes while they turned the other baby. She said it wasn't something a new father would want to see. Noah died a thousand deaths out there, pacing back and forth, running his hands through his hair, sending up promise after promise, if this would only come out right for the baby. For Abby. He'd never look at another woman with lust in his heart, he'd never speed on the highway again, he'd invite homeless people for dinner every Sunday....

Then a nurse beckoned and he raced back into the delivery room. Abby looked worn and tired. She was pushing with all her might with the doctor's encouragement. What a trouper.

Then, suddenly, he had a daughter. A tiny, perfect creature that cried a little, then stopped and stared up at him, unblinking. In wonder. He swore he saw the centre of the universe in that midnight-blue gaze. He had a *daughter!*

They both wanted to call her Daisy and Abby wanted Amanda for her second name. Old Amanda Dexter had never married and had no children, and Abby felt this would be a tribute to her. Noah agreed. Besides, who'd brought all those damn corn-cobs? Who was to say that excess corncobs didn't trigger labor?

Daisy was whisked off to the special nursery for extra attention, because of her more difficult birth. Liam went straight into the newborn nursery and, after accompanying Abby back to her room and waiting until she dozed off, Noah stood for at least an hour, watching through the window in the visitors' area while his son alternately slept and screamed his head off. His lungs were in wonderful condition.

Then he went out and bought three dozen long-stemmed red roses, one dozen for each baby and a dozen for their mother. One of the nurses helped Noah arrange them in water at Abby's bedside while she slept.

Abby wept when she saw them. Then she blew her nose and said she was starving and wanted to see her babies. Noah sat beside her while she had tea and toast. Two nurses wheeled in two bassinets, one with a blue blanket and one with pink.

Abby looked at Noah. Tears ran down her cheeks again. "Noah, can you believe it? They're healthy and beautiful and—and *alive!*" He wrapped his arms around her while she sobbed and sobbed.

Only then did he realize how much she'd dreaded this experience, how deeply she'd worried that the terrible accident of birth that had befallen her first daughter might happen again.

"Shh, baby," he said, patting her back and kissing her hair. "Everything's fine. The twins are fine. I love you, Abby, *I love you!*"

Abby pulled back and turned her wet face to his. "Oh, thank you, Noah!" she whispered. "Thank you for being there for me. I needed you so much. I still do. Thank you for *everything!*"

IT WASN'T QUITE a declaration of love. But it was the next best thing. Noah left the hospital about eight o'clock. He'd never been happier. He felt on top of the world and kept slamming his hands against the steering wheel, overcome from time to time by all that had happened in the past twenty-four hours.

She was healthy. The babies were healthy.

Nothing, absolutely nothing, could be better.

His brain began to click in as he got nearer to the Lazy SB. He'd have to make sure Carl had gotten the groceries....

He'd have to tell Carl about the babies. He couldn't wait. Damn, he should've bought some cigars in Glory. He didn't smoke, but wasn't that what you were supposed to do? Hand out cigars?

Noah stopped at the rural mailbox at the junction of his ranch lane and the highway. There was the usual clutter of junk mail, bills, maybe a few letters—including one from Abby's parents. He'd have to remember to take that to her tomorrow, when he went to visit her at the hospital. When could she come home? He'd have to ask Kate.

Noah noticed another letter in the pile when he got to the house and tossed it on the table.

Jesse. Addressed to him.

Swearing under his breath, Noah ripped open the envelope.

Noah, Guess you're surprised to hear from me—

You got that right, Noah muttered.

I've been working on the Quilchena and the Willow Springs this past couple months. I sure hope you got over me taking off the way I did. I figure Abby's better off without me.

I wrote to tell you I'd heard news about Dad. I talked to an old wrangler one night at the Coldwater Hotel tavern who said Dad worked at the Willow Springs for a few seasons, back about the time he walked out on us. The old guy didn't know where he'd gone from there. I'll ask around and let you know if I find out anything else. Don't write, since I'll be moving on shortly. Your brother, Jesse.

Noah walked to the window and looked out. He noted absently that Carl's old Dodge pickup wasn't down by the bunkhouse where he usually parked it.

Your brother, Jesse. Noah took a deep breath.

Abby certainly was better off without him. Noah didn't think Jesse would ever change. There was a lot more of their father in him than Noah had realized. Not that Jake had ever been easygoing and generous the way Jesse was, but the lack of regard for responsibility—it all added up.

And yet Jesse had finally heard news of Jake. Working the Willow Springs Ranch out in the Nicola Valley—what would that be now, twenty years ago? Eighteen? He'd walked out when Noah was sixteen.

Sometimes Noah had a dream about Jake coming back. In the dream, Jake would be coming up the dusty road, walking, walking, getting closer but no closer. And he'd always wave to Noah. And even though he was so far away, Noah would hear him say, "I'm sorry, Noah. Please forgive me, son. I love you. I've always loved you."

But he'd never get any closer and he'd never come home and then he'd just disappear again.

It wasn't going to happen—ever. Jake was never coming back, no matter what Noah dreamed. Most likely, he was dead. And, even if he was alive, Noah knew, deep in his heart, that he didn't want his father back. Jake would be a stranger now, even more of a stranger than he was before. What would Noah possibly have to say to him now? *I didn't need you, Jake. Look at this place, look at my herd—I did it all myself, me and Jesse. We didn't need you.*

Still, Jake was his father. Had he felt the way Noah felt today, when his children were born? He must have, yet somehow Noah couldn't imagine it.

He folded up the letter again and stuck it in his shirt pocket, then bent to fondle Pat's ears. The old dog had been nosing his knee for attention.

"What do you think, old girl—babies coming to live here with us, huh?" he said, as he picked up the dog's dish to refill with kibble. "Yep, couple of babies to liven up the old place. Pull your tail. Poke your nose. Squeeze your ears, huh?"

Just then he heard the sound of a pickup's engine outside. He glanced at the kitchen clock. Twenty minutes to nine.

Carl?

Carl Divine stood by the kitchen screen door, his hat in his hand, a sheepish, somewhat disoriented look on his face.

"What's the problem, Carl?"

"Nuthin', Boss. Got these here groceries for the missus. Uh, I got a little behind, meant to bring 'em along earlier—"

Noah peered at his foreman, suspicion dawning. "You been at Rachel's all this time?"

Carl reddened. "Not all the time, Boss. Her kids was away and we, uh, we got to talkin' 'n' stuff. Afternoon just kinda slipped by."

'N' stuff? Noah grinned. "Talking, huh? Listen, I'll give you a hand with those bags."

Well, well. Who'd have thought? he mused as he followed Carl onto the porch to help carry in the groceries. In Noah's experience, Rachel wasn't all that much for talking. She was an action kind of woman.

Looked like maybe his reticent foreman was, too.

CHAPTER SEVENTEEN

ABBY CAME HOME from the hospital four days later. When they arrived back at the Lazy SB, Carl was waiting for them, sitting on the top step of the porch with an assortment of ranch dogs around him, including Pat.

He presented Abby with a small box, carefully wrapped and liberally taped. "For the young Winslows," he said, with an awkward semiformal bow.

Abby's eyes filled with tears. "Oh, Carl. Do come right in and see the babies. I can hardly wait to show them to you."

Carl reddened and hemmed and hawed, but in the end he accompanied them into the kitchen.

Noah carried Daisy. Abby couldn't be sure, but she felt somehow that he favored the girl. She had no doubt he would be evenhanded with the twins as they grew up—she couldn't believe she was actually daring to think in those terms these days—but something about the tiny girl had captured her husband's heart. Maybe fathers were partial to daughters, anyway. She'd never been able to test the theory; her own father had produced two daughters and no son.

Liam was a lusty, strong baby, who already seemed to know exactly what he wanted and when—usually right now. And Abby was only too happy to oblige. That meant she was spending a good part of each day nursing the twins in turn, with a few extra rounds for Liam. They slept well, fortunately, but she'd really had no idea how much of the day a baby took up—in this case, double time.

The ranch house was sparkling clean; Phoebe had outdone herself. And there, taped to the wall of the kitchen, was a computer printout banner reading: *Welcome home, Abby and twins!* Phoebe stood underneath it, grinning. She must have done the banner at her home, where they had a fairly sophisticated computer for the Longquist children.

"What a welcome!" Abby handed Liam to the anxiously waiting Phoebe.

"Oh, what a beautiful baby, Abby!" Phoebe jiggled Liam lightly in her arms.

"*I* think so," Abby said proudly. She turned to Noah. He was showing Daisy off to old Carl, who was peering worriedly into the folds of the cotton blanket. Daisy was sound asleep, her tiny face relaxed.

"Ah, she's a beauty, all right, Boss. A beauty, God bless her," Carl said, stepping back, as though afraid to breathe the same air as the infant. "And that's a fine boy you got there, missus. A fine boy. We'll have a couple new ropers in a few years, eh, Boss?" He winked at Noah.

"You bet, Carl," he answered, barely taking his eyes off the child in his arms. "Well, Abby? I guess we should deposit these two somewhere." He suddenly looked bewildered, as though he'd just realized they were now at home, where they all belonged, and there were two brand-new creatures in the house who weren't going anywhere soon.

"Not their cribs. Let's put them in the bassinets in the living room for now. I need to get organized."

He smiled at her and she felt herself blush. He was so attentive these days, so tender, so loving. She couldn't believe this was the stern, grim-faced man she'd met only months ago. He truly seemed to be happy with her, with the babies. It was an answer to all her prayers. She wanted their marriage to work with all her heart, and there was no reason now that it wouldn't.

Even her parents had finally seemed to come around, now that the babies were born. When she'd called her mother the morning after the birth, her mother had wept softly on the other end of the line. That had surprised Abby.

"Mom? For heaven's sake, aren't you happy for me? Don't cry—"

"Oh, I'm *so* happy. I'm so glad it's come out all right, dear. It's just that—that after the way you left here and after the way we were so hard on you— Abby, I feel terrible. After losing your first one like that 'n' all," her mother said. "We were too hard on you."

"Never mind, Mom. That's all over now. I've got two beautiful healthy babies, grandchildren for you and Dad, a wonderful husband who loves us all—I can't wait until you meet them."

"Your father and I were thinking we might make the trip up there at Christmas, if that's okay with you and, er, Noah?'' her mother continued gruffly. ''We'd like to see the dear little babes, you know. And you.''

Not Noah? Still, Abby was glad her parents were being more sensible. Maybe with her no longer on the scene—and no explanations necessary to their Wicoigon neighbors—they'd come to see how narrow-minded and foolish they were being. She'd had regular letters, too, from her sister, Meg. Maybe eventually, the whole family would accept everything that had happened to Abby in the past year. Maybe eventually, everything would come out right.

Except for Jesse. Noah never mentioned his brother. Neither did Abby. After receiving the bank draft, which she'd deposited in the account Noah had opened for him, she'd tried hard to forget about Jesse. He was a big unknown. Surely someday Noah would want to be in touch with his brother—his only remaining relative. Other than, perhaps, a father. But Noah didn't know whether he was alive or dead. Nothing anyone could do about that, since according to Noah, he'd been gone for nearly twenty years. Jesse was different.

The next day, Phoebe's mother, Nan, came to visit. She brought another crocheted blanket and two pairs of knitted booties. Carl's gift had turned out to be two silver spoons, which surprised Abby. She was touched that he felt her babies had been born so lucky.

The day after that, Abby had three visitors. Amanda Dexter came, bearing a child-sized pair of chaps and a lariat ''for the boy'' and a child-sized western saddle "for the girl." She said she wasn't much good on baby stuff, but they'd find these handy when they got a little older. She was very pleased they'd named Daisy after her, and laughed when Abby told her the theory about the corncobs hastening labor. Old Amanda clearly expected her to raise a couple of ropers and riders, too.

The stream of visitors seemed endless. As tiring as it was, Abby welcomed everyone. It was a mark, she believed, of her acceptance in the community. Many of the faces she recognized from the Dexters' wedding anniversary celebration. Donna Beaton came, of course, with plans to have a proper welcoming party for the babies at the end of the month, when Abby was feeling stronger. Perhaps a christening celebration. She insisted she and her daughter and Phoebe would do all the organizing.

Cal Blake and his wife, Nina, came with their little girl, who was entranced with the babies. Joe, Phoebe's uncle, came to visit, bringing little Alexander and Ellie along and making apologies for his wife's absence, as she was out of town. Phoebe explained to Abby that Joe and Honor Gallant were raising his sister's two orphans. Even Glory's postmistress came, Myrna Schultz, who said she'd decided she'd have to leave her wicket if she was *ever* going to get a look at the new bride, not to mention the twins.

Throughout it all, Abby felt herself growing stronger and stronger. The trauma of the birth was fairly short-lived. She felt great now that she no longer had to waddle around. She wasn't her old self quite yet, but every day made a difference.

Thank heavens for Phoebe, who did the laundry, prepared many of the meals, kept the furniture dusted and the rugs vacuumed. Abby didn't know what she'd do when Phoebe went off to college at the end of the month.

Ten days after they'd come home, Noah surprised Abby by following her upstairs when she went to put the babies to bed. It was only about nine o'clock. He watched her as she tucked them in, each on a separate washable lambskin that had been gifts from Donna. The babies seemed to feel very comfortable on the soft wool fleece and generally dozed right off.

Then, when she'd finished, she looked at him across Liam's crib and smiled. The tenderness in his eyes as he smiled back was wonderful to see.

"I saw Kate in town today," he said quietly, one eyebrow raised. "At the co-op."

"Oh?" She gathered up the soiled T-shirts and sleepers and deposited them in the twins' laundry bucket.

"I, uh, asked her—you know, how long before we could make love—"

Abby met his gaze. "I'm surprised she didn't bring it up herself, aren't you? She seems obsessed by the subject."

Noah laughed. "A little. Anyway, she gave me a big lecture about birth control and then said whenever you feel comfortable with it. So…" He took a step toward her and pulled her into his arms. It was so wonderful to be able to hug and kiss close to each other like this, without a huge belly coming between them.

"So?" she teased, feeling a new excitement. Hugging and kissing was all very well, but she was desperate to make love—to *really* make love—with Noah. "I thought we were supposed to wait, I don't know, six weeks or something."

"Nope. Kate said that was outdated advice. As you'd probably guess, all *her* advice is right up-to-the-minute. The latest stuff."

Abby giggled softly.

"So, uh, I was wondering—*are* you feeling comfortable about it?" He started to kiss her gently, but Abby clung to him and the kiss grew hotter. He raised his head, eyes gleaming. "I don't want to force the issue, you understand. I want to consult you fully on this."

"You're not forcing the issue. I'm ready whenever you are."

Noah swept her up in his arms, to her immense surprise. "Man alive, I've been ready for so long I've lost count of the weeks. We've been bride and groom, now we're parents, but damn it, we've never really been lovers. We've haven't even made love properly yet."

"What are we waiting for?"

"If we get lucky, those two will stay asleep for at least an hour."

"Well, then, let's not waste time."

They didn't. They were in bed within a few minutes. Noah was a wonderful lover, she already knew that, but now she could join him completely in their lovemaking. She was able to welcome him and participate and show him exactly how eager she was for him. He brought her satisfaction beyond her wildest dreams, and they were lucky enough that the twins didn't wake up for nearly two hours, long enough to explore each other's bodies thoroughly and to make love until they were both finally and fully satiated. Then, after Abby nursed the twins when Noah brought them and he took them back to their cribs, changed their diapers and put them down to sleep again, the lovers themselves fell asleep, happy in each other's arms. As far as Abby was concerned, it was the best day—and night—since their wedding. Maybe the best of her entire life.

Two weeks later, the twins were baptized in the old church up on the prairie where Noah's mother had been laid to rest nearly twenty years ago. The sun was hot, even in the morning during the service, and the grainfields all around were thick with the scent of ripening barley and wheat, gently rippling in the breeze. The end of August was a busy time for all the farmers around—more for the farmers than the ranchers—but the church was filled to over-flowing when Daisy Amanda Winslow and Liam Casey Winslow were baptized and received into the community of Glory. Afterward, Noah took his family for a walk out into the churchyard and showed them where the twins' grandmother, Macy Mc-Affrey Winslow, was buried. And beside her, their Uncle Casey, who'd died at the age of twelve. And their great-uncle, Brandis McAffrey. Next to Macy was an empty spot, reserved for Jake Winslow, at his mother's request in her will.

Abby placed the flowers she'd brought for the service on his mother's grave. Noah took a deep breath, feeling gratitude for all his mother had done in her life, hard as that life was. For the love he'd always carried in his heart for his brother, Casey, companion of his youth.

Noah felt he'd finally stepped into the place Macy had helped to make for him here. For him and his family. He was a good rancher. Now he'd be a good father and husband. He was continuing the long pioneer tradition of the McAffreys.

Donna Beaton and Phoebe had planned a big afternoon barbecue and party after the christening, so they'd stayed back at the Lazy SB, along with Donna's daughter, Jennifer, to carry out the last-minute preparations. Most members of the congregation were returning to the ranch after church to take part in the celebration.

There were tables set out under the trees, rented pavilions pegged out on the lawn to provide shade, washtubs full of ice and beer and lemonade, bowls and bowls of salads. Carl presided over the half-barrel barbecues. A bright white apron had been found for him somewhere, and he wore it and the chef's hat Donna had brought from town with pride.

Noah wasn't completely surprised to see Rachel there, along with her two youngest children. She hadn't been at the church for the christening. It seemed she'd been at the ranch, helping to get everything ready. She'd agreed to assist Carl with the barbecue as long as she received guarantees that no pork would be served. It was a beef crowd, mainly ranchers and farmers, so there was no danger of that. Rachel winked once at Noah across the heads of the crowd and he smiled back. He was pleased to see how attentive she was to his foreman. In fact, she looked besotted. Carl Divine was a dark horse, a man of many talents, apparently.

The lanky foreman had sat in on the first Winslow Sunday dinner at home, after the babies were born— Carl could qualify as homeless, Noah figured. He was definitely pleased by this development with Rachel. Carl could use a good friend. And a good woman friend was all the better, in Noah's view.

Appropriately, Amanda Dexter had brought corn, and plenty of it. The younger children sat around shucking the cobs while their elders got big pots of water boiling on the propane burners that had been set up. There were cakes on one of the long tables— butter and ice and cream cakes and layer cakes. Bean salad and potato salad and lettuce salad. Every kind of Kool-Aid. Plenty of iced tea and beer. Pickles and fresh rolls and deviled eggs. Vats of cabbage rolls. Ice cream tubs, frosty and melting on the tables. Hot dogs and hamburgers for the kids and mustard and ketchup and relish. Mothers chasing children with tubes of sunscreen in their hands; dogs barking and scrambling after sticks.

Noah stood to one side, watching over the proceedings. He was proud that his children's christening had led to such a big, boisterous community celebration. He noticed one of his babies—Daisy, he could tell—being passed from knee to knee among the elderly folks under the shade of the linden. His eye roamed until he saw Abby, nursing Liam discreetly, sitting with a circle of women in lawn chairs. She was laughing, and he felt his heart warm and swell with pleasure and pride.

Thank heaven for the day she'd come into his life so unexpectedly. *Thank heaven? Thank Jesse.* He banished the thought.

Abby was an eager and passionate partner, a warm and loving mother, an excellent cook, a beautiful woman in every way. He couldn't imagine life anymore without her or the twins. Luckily, he didn't have to. She was staying the course with him. No question. Their marriage was real, solid, something to believe in.

And the twins. If anyone had told him a year ago that he could spend upward of an hour watching a baby play with its own hands or drool or just sleep in the shade, he would have called that person crazy. But he'd been sure the other day that Daisy had smiled at him; when he pointed it out to Donna, who'd been visiting, and she'd said it was likely gas, he'd been outraged. Gas? Of course it wasn't gas— she was smiling at her daddy.

He'd turned out to be just as goofy a new father as any other new father.

If anyone had ever told him that there was no sight on earth more beautiful than a mother nursing her child, gazing at the trusting little face with love and tenderness, making cooing little motherly noises—he'd have called that person crazy, too. Yet he'd often put down his paper or turned from the television just to watch Abby nurse the twins. They'd gotten into a kind of routine. He'd hand her one, she'd nurse while he changed the other, then he'd take the first one and change his or her diaper. They'd reduced their changing and nursing times by about fifty percent, in his judgment, from those early days when they'd brought the babies home. At first, he'd found diapering an awkward procedure and was worried about hurting the tiny flailing limbs. It had taken him at least ten minutes; now he could change a baby in three minutes flat.

But he had to get over this. He was neglecting his business. Now that the end of August was just around the corner, with Phoebe going off to university the day after tomorrow, with Carl telling him they urgently needed parts for one of the new balers, with a crew to hire for fall roundup and end-of-season fencing, with orders coming in from his regular customers for replacement bulls and feeder steers—it was high time to start paying attention to ranch matters. Time to stop playing brand-new daddy.

He'd relax and enjoy this Sunday afternoon with his neighbors and then, come Monday, tomorrow morning, it was back to business.

It was past six o'clock by the time the last of the neighbors left. Even though Noah said he'd take care of cleanup, Donna and her crew stayed for another hour to collect the rented propane burners and barbecues and tables and chairs and stow them in the back of her company van.

Finally, at around nine o'clock—the sun was just dipping below the horizon—Noah climbed the porch steps for the last time. Everything was shipshape. Except for a fresh pile of cornsilk and husks on the compost pile and chunks dug out of the lawn where some of the tables had been, you could hardly tell that he'd had more than sixty people to a lawn party that afternoon.

It had been a long day. As soon as he'd helped Abby deal with the twins and watched the news, he was hitting the sack. He was pretty sure Abby felt just as exhausted. She'd been excited and happy today, but endless nights of interrupted sleep had to catch up with a person. He hoped their lives together would fall into a nice, easy routine and they could both get back to basics. Just him and her and the twins. And Carl Divine.

He stood for a moment at the top of the steps and looked out over the silent corrals and equipment sheds and barns, and farther, across the river. The river was low, since it was dry season. His cattle were getting enough water, thanks to the wells he'd had the foresight to drill on his range a few years back. As old Brandis liked to say, a ranch was just water and grass—take care of it and it'll take care of you.

Some ranchers weren't so lucky in this kind of weather. Some were even reduced to hauling water to their stock.

He was proud of the Lazy SB and what he'd made of it. With Jesse's help, of course. And now, with a son and a daughter, he was even prouder. He had a thriving ranch, a legacy to pass on to them someday. It meant something to a man, something important.

He went inside. All was quiet. He supposed Abby was upstairs with the children. He refilled Pat's water dish and then climbed the stairs himself.

"How's it going, Abby?" He'd noticed during the afternoon that she'd spent a lot of time rocking Daisy and nursing her. The baby was having a hard time settling.

Abby was looking a little harassed. Liam was fussing in his crib, turning his face from side to side and waving his fists angrily.

"Why don't you take Daisy downstairs and walk her for a bit," she suggested. "I don't know what the problem is. A little tummy upset, I guess." She handed him his daughter, all dressed in a clean sleeper and with a thin flannel wrap around her. "Maybe it's something I ate." He'd heard that before—the refrain of the nursing mother.

"Sure. I'll put her down in the bassinet when she goes to sleep. That way I won't disturb you and Liam coming back up here."

"Good idea."

As he left the room, Abby picked up Liam and settled resignedly into the nursing rocker in the corner of the room, fumbling at her bra strap.

That's all you wanted, wasn't it? he crooned to Daisy, who was almost asleep in his arms by the time he reached the bottom of the stairs. *Just wanted your daddy to hold you for a while, didn't you, little girl?*

For good measure, he walked with the baby, up

and down the hall. Then, as she continued fast asleep, he stood in front of the window for a while as it got darker outside and talked to her. He described everything he could see, telling her how much fun she was going to have growing up on a ranch.

The long mournful howl of his brother's stray penetrated the darkness, and Noah felt a deep sadness for a few minutes. Too bad no one could get near that creature. He'd tried; Carl had done his best. It was a shame, the stray foraging out on those hills, never leaving the ranch for long, but too frightened to come in and get his share of feed with the other dogs. Noah supposed he caught rabbits and mice and the occasional bird to keep himself. Maybe even crept into the odd ranch house in the dead of night to steal from the ranch dogs' bowls. Probably not much different from the life he'd had before Jesse came upon him, twisted and broken and left for dead at the side of the road. Against all odds, the animal had recovered. Physically, anyway.

Noah turned on the television; it was the middle of the news. He carefully laid the sleeping baby in her bassinet, and stood for a few minutes, admiring her. Then he went back to the television to catch the end of the broadcast. When it was over, he channel-hopped for a few minutes, wondering how Abby was managing with Liam.

Then Pat barked, twice, in the kitchen.

Damn. Noah hurried into the kitchen to speak to the dog. He was afraid she'd wake the baby. And besides, what was she barking for? She'd been fed and watered, and enough boys had thrown sticks for her that day to last her a week.

His flesh prickled. That bark—

A vehicle drove into his driveway. Noah couldn't identify it, saw only the sweep of lights. Probably somebody coming back for something forgotten at the party. Sunglasses or a lawn chair—

The rap at the door sounded familiar and then, before he could answer, the door opened.

Jesse stood there on the porch, with a six-pack of beer in his hand and a big grin on his face. His little terrier–blue heeler cross whined at his feet. "Hey, man, how you doin'? I'm back."

CHAPTER EIGHTEEN

NOAH'S THROAT went tight. "What—what are you doing here?" It was the only thing he could think of to say.

"That any way to greet a long-lost brother?" Jesse grinned and walked into the kitchen and plunked the beer down on the table. "Man, you sure changed things in here!" He glanced around the clean, tidy kitchen, shaking his head. Then he whirled. "And, hey! Where the hell's my house?" He laughed, as though a house disappearing off the face of the earth was a tremendous joke.

Noah had recovered. Slightly. He took a step into the kitchen and folded his arms across his chest. "I thought you'd left, Jesse. For good. I sold your house. Amos Petersen moved it down to his place—"

"Sold it!"

"I put the money in an account at the credit union for you. Money, too, from stuff of yours I sold to Art's, furniture and such. I hadn't got around to selling your horses yet. Don't worry, the money's all there."

Jesse stared at him for a moment, then gave a low whistle and wrestled a can of beer out of its plastic

collar. He popped the tab and handed it to Noah.
Noah hesitated, then took a step forward and accepted the beer from his brother. A beer was the last
thing he felt like. He had to get rid of Jesse. Now.
What if Abby came down?

"I see Brandis's trailer is gone, too."

"Yeah. I moved it over by the bunkhouse." Noah
drank a long draft of the beer. It was an American
brand, not to his taste. "Carl's living in it now.
Saves heating the bunkhouse."

"That's my brother, all right!" Jesse laughed.
"Saving a nickel wherever he can."

"It all helps," Noah said agreeably. "What
brings you back here, Jesse?"

"Man, I don't *get* you!" Jesse popped the tab on
his own beer and took a deep swallow and wiped
his mustache with the back of his hand. "This is
home. I missed the old place, believe it or not. I
couldn't wait to get back. I needed some space there
for a while this summer, get my head straight after
that business of, well, you know—that woman and
all."

Noah saw red. He forced himself to remain cool.
He had something to tell Jesse. But maybe he was
jumping to conclusions. Maybe his brother wasn't
interested in Abby anymore.

"So, I guess you got plans to pick up some work
around here, eh, Jess?" he began hopefully. "I
know Cal Blake's looking—"

His brother placed one hand, palm down, on the
kitchen table. "I could've stayed at the Willow

Springs, they were begging me not to quit. But I decided this is where I belong. Right here.''

Noah cleared his throat. ''Jesse, I hate to break the news to you like this, but everything's changed since you left. Everything's different. There's no way you're coming back here. Not to the Lazy SB. We can talk about it, figure out something else.''

Jesse stared at him, astonished. ''What you mean, man—not coming back here? This is my home!''

''Not anymore. I'm happy to work something out with you, divvy things up fair and square. I'll pay you rent for your quarter interest in the ranch, if that's the way you want it. You're my only brother, after all, and there's family feeling—''

''What the *hell* you talking about, Noah?'' Jesse's voice rose at the end and his little dog whined. Pat barked sharply.

There was a thin cry from the living room, the sound that Noah had dreaded. Stella put her ears up and barked madly.

''*Quiet!*'' Jesse ordered his dog. She immediately sat down on her haunches, ears pricked but silent. ''What the hell's that, Noah? You got company? Why didn't you say something?''

''Wait here a minute.''

Noah went into the living room. Daisy's lower lip was trembling like crazy and her eyes were filled with tears. ''Hey, baby,'' he murmured softly and picked her up, reveling in her sweet, soft baby scent. ''Come on and meet some of the family.'' He took a deep breath. There was no escaping it. It had to happen sooner or later, and it looked like it was going to be sooner.

He walked back into the kitchen and Jesse's jaw dropped. "A *baby!* What the hell—"

"This is my daughter, Jesse," he said, looking his brother straight in the eye. "She's just about three weeks old now."

Jesse had gone white under his tan. "Jeez, Noah, I didn't know you had something like this on the go." His voice was hoarse. "I didn't know anything about it, I swear—"

Noah heard Abby coming down the stairs, and he set his shoulders tightly. Jesse obviously had no idea what had happened since he left. He'd had no news from Glory at all in the months he'd been gone.

"What's going on, Noah? I thought I heard voices—*ohmigod!*" Abby stopped, shocked, and met Jesse's equally shocked gaze. She was wearing her nightgown and dressing gown and slippers, a pretty embroidered silk outfit Noah had bought her when she was in the hospital. She carried the sleeping Liam in her arms.

"This is my wife, Jesse. Abby and I've been married since shortly after you left."

"Abby!" Jesse looked from him to Abby and back again. He could barely speak. "But this is my—*my*—"

"Not anymore," Noah said firmly. "Abby's my wife and these two babies are my son and daughter. This is Daisy Amanda and that's Liam Casey, the one Abby's holding. I guess that makes you their Uncle Jess." He emphasized the word uncle.

Jesse had sunk into one of the kitchen chairs. His face looked terrible, and Noah felt cruel. He cursed himself for the way he'd had to tell his brother. But there'd been no choice. He had to make clear right from the start that there was no going back. That this was *his* wife and these were *his* children.

Noah felt Abby tug at his sleeve. He moved, so that he was closer to her and put his free arm around her shoulders. They must present an ironically happy family tableau to Jesse. He was sorry about that, but it couldn't be helped.

"Jesse!" Abby burst out. "This is a...a surprise."

Noah dreaded what she might say. Her cheeks were very red. She'd actually never said she loved him, even though he believed in his heart that she did. She never talked about Jesse, except to defend him. She'd never talked about her first husband, Frank. Noah had often wondered if she didn't still harbor feelings for her dead husband, too deep to confide to him, the man she'd married so unexpectedly. He'd often wondered if she harbored feelings for his brother, too, although she'd never let on or said anything that might make him think so. Just that she seemed to sympathize with him so much...

"Jesse," she went on gently, "I'm sorry for the way things worked out. But—"

"Twins," Jesse broke in, dazed. "So you had twins, after all."

"Yes." Abby clutched at Noah's arm under his sleeve. He sensed the tension in her. Liam stirred and made a small mewling sound. Stella's ears pricked again.

"It's my fault," Jesse said brokenly. "I never should've run out on you like that. I should've stayed and faced the music. Noah's right, I'm a damn coward."

Noah felt bad for him. He'd pulled Jesse out of so many scrapes over the years. He'd stood up for him against their father's fists. He'd defended him against schoolyard bullies who'd taunted the Winslow boys for having a drunken father. There was nothing he could do for his brother now. The truth was, Jesse needed to grow up. It was long past time. He was nearly thirty.

And hadn't Noah bailed him out yet again, by marrying the woman he'd gotten pregnant?

Noah no longer thought of it that way. He could only think how lucky he was that Jesse had brought Abby into his life. He had Jesse to thank for that.

Jesse seemed to pull himself together. He let out a laugh that held no humor, only bitterness. "I suppose you married her that very Friday. No sense wasting the appointment—"

"That's right," Noah said quietly. "I did. You left her high and dry with nothing and nowhere to go. I stepped in and asked her to marry me instead, and she agreed."

"So I guess she decided she was in love with you, huh!" Jesse threw out bitterly. "Not me! Or did it matter?" He half got to his feet and for a few seconds, Noah thought Jesse might want to have it out with him. But he wouldn't, not with Noah holding a baby in his arms.

"She never was in love with you, Jesse," Noah said evenly, praying he was right. "You know that. It was circumstances all the way." His brother slumped back down at the table and dropped his head in his hands.

"Yeah, I know that—"

"Jesse," Abby interrupted hesitantly.

Noah wanted to shush her. He wanted her to stay out of it. This was between him and Jesse. There was nothing between his wife and Jesse, not anymore. He couldn't bear it if there was.

"Jesse, listen—" she tried again.

Jesse didn't indicate he'd heard her. But when she repeated his name, he glanced up. His eyes were bloodshot and too bright. He looked as if he was on the verge of tears.

"Jesse, I know how this must seem to you. You had no way of knowing about Noah and me. But this is the very best thing that could have happened. For me, for the babies. You—you walked out, just like Noah said. I still have the note you left. There wasn't anything I could do. And when Noah asked me to marry him, I jumped at the chance to stay here. I had nothing to go back to—"

"You had your folks. You could've gone back to them. I sent money to you there—I'm not *that* bad, you know," he said, his voice rising.

"I know. You're not a bad man. Not a bad man at all," Abby said. "I know you were just overcome with everything that went on. It all happened so fast. I—I felt the same way sometimes."

"You did?"

Noah wished she'd go back upstairs. He didn't like this. He felt as though he was caught between these two, in a lovers' quarrel. He didn't want to be reminded that his brother had made love to this woman before he had, that these two babies were, in fact, his brother's children, not his.

"Yes," Abby replied. "I felt something was wrong when I got here. You didn't want to touch me. I felt you'd had a change of heart about asking me to marry you. But you wouldn't come right out and say it."

"Yeah, and supposing I did," Jesse said with a harsh laugh. "Then what? You'd still have married me?"

"I don't know," Abby admitted, twisting a tag on Liam's blanket. "I don't know what I would have done. But I do know this is for the best. I'm glad I married Noah. He loves me and I—I love him. I love Noah more than I ever dreamed I could ever love someone again. After losing Frank and—" she paused and took a deep breath "—after my first baby and all. I have to thank you for that, Jesse. For bringing Noah and me together."

Noah looked at her. He couldn't believe what he'd just heard. She'd not only said she loved him, but she'd committed herself to him, in front of his brother, this man who'd accidentally fathered these two beautiful children he was determined to call his own, one lonely winter weekend in Minnesota. *She loved him.*

Liam stirred again and Abby turned to Noah, bewildered. This had taken a lot out of her, and it had been a long, exhausting day.

"Let's take these two upstairs and put them in their beds," Noah said quietly. He indicated Jesse still sitting slumped at the kitchen table and gestured that they should leave him alone for a few minutes. Abby nodded.

Just then Stella went to the door and whined. Noah was sure he heard another sound, a sort of scratching.

"Can you get that, Jess? Looks like she wants out."

Jesse got up and went to the kitchen door. He stumbled once, then opened it and Noah heard him swear softly. He pushed open the screen door and the little terrier-heeler shot out. *"Noah,"* he heard his brother call out, his voice strangled with emotion. "It's *Champ*—"

The spring-loaded door slammed behind him. Noah went over to it, still carrying Daisy. He looked through the screen out into the darkness.

There on the back porch, looking ghostly under the naked porch light, was his brother, down on his knees, arms around the skinny stray, Champ. Noah felt emotion lodge in his throat. Jesse's broad shoulders shook. The stray was licking his face, seeming unaware of Noah's presence, his scrawny tail thumping on the boards of the step.

Noah turned away and shut the door gently. He didn't close the inner door all the way.

"It's the dog," he said quietly in answer to Abby's look of inquiry. "The stray. Must have recognized the truck's engine or something."

They went upstairs, each carrying a sleeping baby. Noah placed Daisy in her crib and the infant barely stirred. Abby did the same with Liam.

"Oh, honey," Noah said when they'd stepped out into the hall. "I love you so much—so much!" His voice was rough with emotion. He held her tightly and savored the warm, sturdy feel of her in his arms. *His wife!*

"I love you, too, Noah," she said, her voice shaky. "I didn't really know how much until today, until tonight. I'd never told you but I wanted to, so many times. It just…just felt right, saying it now, downstairs. I loved my first husband, too, I loved Frank—but this is different. I love you in a way I never thought I would."

He bent his head toward hers, overcome for a moment. Then he felt her tense.

"Listen, Noah—" She pushed back and he released her slightly so he could look down into her face. "Jesse can stay here tonight. It's only decent. He's family. He can sleep in Phoebe's room. I want things to work out, for all of us—"

"He's not living back here on the ranch," Noah said. His mind was made up on that subject.

"No. I understand how you feel," she said. They were practically whispering. "But I think it would be wonderful if you could become friends again.

The way you were before. He loves you and you love him, any fool can see that. He's your only brother—"

Noah kissed her. "Listen, you let me take care of that. You go to bed now. I'll go down and see how he is. He seemed pretty shaken up to see that mutt show up on the back step. They're old buddies again."

"Thank heaven! Oh, thank heaven for that," Abby said. She kissed him briefly and he watched her walk down the hall to their bedroom.

"I'll be up shortly," he called in a quiet voice.

She smiled and went inside, closing the door behind her.

WHEN NOAH GOT BACK downstairs, Jesse seemed to have recovered somewhat. He was in the kitchen, rummaging through Noah's cupboards. "Where you keep your dog food?" he asked. "I'm gonna feed that goofy dog. He looks like he half starved while I was away. Didn't Carl look out for him?"

"He tried," Noah said, casually opening the broom closet where he kept the dog kibble. "He wouldn't let anyone near him. He's your dog, Jess. He's always been your dog."

"Yeah," Jesse said, smiling. His eyes looked haunted. "That's the truth, ain't it? I missed that mangy son of a gun, you know that? I think old Stella missed him, too."

Almost cheerfully, he took the pan of dog kibble out onto the back porch. Noah was hugely relieved. If Jesse was acting normal again, it meant he intended to get things back on track between them as soon as possible. Noah put the kettle on.

Ten minutes later, Jesse came back in, and Stella trotted in with him. "Damn old dog won't come into the kitchen. I tossed him in the back of the pickup on an old tarp I've got there. Guess he's used to living outside. That's okay. I don't think he's going to go far." Jesse shut the door. "What's that? Tea?"

"Yeah. Want a mug when it's ready?"

"Just like Ma, eh?" Jesse had an odd look on his face. "Remember how she used to fix tea for us when we were sick, even when we were little kids? Lots of milk and honey?"

Noah nodded. He hadn't thought of that in a long, long time. "Sit down, Jesse. You got a place to stay tonight?" No matter what Abby said about patching things up with Jesse, he wanted to make it clear that this was just temporary.

Jesse grinned up at him. "I was figuring on staying here." He shook his head. "I didn't know my house would be missing. I guess I could bunk down at the bunkhouse, or with Carl. I wouldn't mind seein' that old buzzard again."

"He's got a lady friend—"

"*No!*" Jesse laughed as he took the thick ceramic mug from Noah.

Noah grinned. "Yep. Rachel's got her eye on him. She was here today at the barbecue, keeping watch, making sure none of the other single women got any ideas."

"Rachel Melnyk? Man, oh man! Good for Carlos." Jesse laughed. It was the big, healthy laugh of a man who lived most of his life outdoors. Noah's heart felt good just to hear it. Abby was first in his life, but Jesse had shared the most with him. They'd grown up together and spent their adult lives working together. Noah took his mug and went to the window to look out onto the dark yard, the barn and corrals beyond. The river beyond.

Finally he turned. "I'm glad you're home, Jesse. Real glad." It had been hard to say, but it was the truth and now that he'd said it, he felt relieved. Lighter, somehow.

"Thanks, Noah." Jesse paused. "I—I'm glad to be back. No matter what. But I gotta tell you, man, I'll be heading over to the Willow Springs again, just as soon as I see a few people around here and get caught up. This isn't the place for me I thought it was. I don't hold nothin' against you. That's just how it is. I'll take the mutt with me this time. Be company for Stella."

Noah stared at his brother for a long time. He saw Casey's easy smile, his mother's eyes, the broad shoulders and powerful musculature of his father. He saw Brandis's way with a joke, and other things, from other Winslows and Millers and LaSalles way, way back. He'd see those in his children, too. In Jesse's children. In children they'd both have in the future. Cousins. Friends growing up together, on the land. The way he and Jesse and Casey had.

"You never heard nothing more about Pa, huh?"

Jesse glanced at him. "Nope. Just that wrangler who said he'd been through that way years ago."

"Did you ever wonder, Jesse, if Pa'd come back?"

His brother considered. He took a sip of the hot tea. "I don't know, Noah. I never thought too much about it. In a way, Brandis was more a pa to me. I felt worse when he died than I did when Pa walked out."

"I know what you mean." Noah came and sat down at the table with his brother. He felt a huge load slip off his shoulders.

Jake Winslow wasn't coming back. They'd never see him again. Most likely, he'd died in a gutter somewhere. All they could wish for was that he'd died drunk and didn't feel the pain. Or the loneliness. He wasn't going to turn up on the Lazy SB one day and say, "I'm sorry, son. I'm sorry for the way I treated your ma and I'm sorry for what happened to Casey. It was my fault. And I'm sorry for being such a bullheaded son of a bitch and such a man of anger and pride that I hurt damn near everybody I ever loved and ever loved me. Forgive me, son, and we'll start all over again. We'll make it come out right this time."

It wasn't going to happen. Ever. But he'd patched things up with Jesse. And the babies were born and healthy. And Abby...he'd never dreamed he'd love such a woman and have her love him back the way she did.

"Hey, you hungry?" Some host he was. Maybe Jesse'd driven all the way from B.C. tonight. "Abby does the cooking around here, mostly, but I can still put together a pretty good sandwich. She's never quite got the hang of that.''

"No." His brother shook his head. "I grabbed something on the way through town. Thanks." Then he looked at Noah for a moment or so. Noah wondered what was on his mind.

"Noah?" he said softly. "I'm glad you named the boy for Casey."

Noah nodded. It had been Abby's idea. "Yeah."

"And, uh, I think it's best this way, you know. I'm glad you and her got married. I—I'm not ever going to say anything about—well, you know. It's just between you and me and her. I swear to God you never need to worry about me coming between you and her or you and the kids. You understand?''

His brother was offering to step aside. Freely. Noah reached over and clasped his brother's hand in a thumbs-up handshake and clapped him on the back. "Hey, time to hit the sack. Abby's got a room fixed up for you, your old room. Tomorrow's another big day around here.''

"Big day?''

"Those two babies wake up awful early.''

Jesse smiled.

Noah followed him up the stairs after he'd locked the doors and turned out all the lights. Pat settled down in her basket in the kitchen and Stella followed her master upstairs. Noah was pretty sure the little dog intended to sleep at the end of Jesse's bed, just like always.

He said good-night to his brother at the door to his bedroom, then went back down the hall toward the room that he and Abby shared. He stopped in at the nursery. His son. His daughter. The most beautiful babies on earth. He was the father now. Jake wouldn't ever be back. Jesse was leaving again— and Jesse had relinquished his rights. It was up to him, Noah. He'd stepped up into the father's place.

And he was going to do things differently, now that it was his turn.

Abby welcomed him into her bed, into her arms, and Noah kissed her sleepy mouth and settled in, holding her tightly.

He heard a night curlew call from the big linden tree outside. Yes, everything was going to be just fine.